"Pace exhibits a keen eye for characters, both human and canine."
—*The Newark Star-Ledger*

"A whimsical, fanciful story . . . Pace writes with wit, confidence, a delightful and gentle voice, and a keen eye that misses nothing."
—Lee Harrington, bestselling author of *Rex and the City*

"I read the first page and I was hooked. I loved Alison Pace's voice."
—SheKnows.com

Through Thick and Thin

"[A] sensitive and knowing exploration of the trickiness—and value—of meaningful relationships."
—*Kirkus Reviews*

"Endearing . . . craftily portraying the balancing act between work and play, family (be it four-legged or two) and friends, and food and fasting."
—*Publishers Weekly*

"A tale of two sisters that charmed me, and even better, introduced me to the wry and artful writing of Alison Pace."
—Elizabeth McKenzie, author of *MacGregor Tells the World*

"Pace's revealing tale about the bond between two sisters reflects the very real and complex nature of relationships . . . Simultaneously heartwarming and emotionally charged."
—*RT Book Reviews*

continued . . .

Pug Hill

"I adored *Pug Hill* . . . a great example of a single-girl-in-the-city narrator who's not sparkly or ditzy, but neurotic and a little sad . . . You hope for good things to happen to her, and cheer when they do."
—Jennifer Weiner

"Pace is enjoyable and clever, throwing in sly commentary on our current social scene, à la Jane Austen." —*The Miami Herald*

"Smart and witty." —*Library Journal*

"Alison Pace's dry and breezy wit makes this a delightful, funny read for pugs and humans alike."
—Wilson the Pug with Nancy Levine, authors of *The Ugly Pugling*

"All at once touching, witty, and so very smart. I love this nervous and self-deprecating narrator who makes low self-esteem not only funny and endearing but enviable. There's a terrific comedic eye at work here and a tender heart—a most satisfying combination." —Elinor Lipman, author of *The Family Man*

"Playful, funny . . . the story of a woman confronting her fears and the adorable pooches that can help her do it." —*Pages*

"Pitch-perfect and deftly written . . . a funny, charming, and touching novel."
—Robin Epstein and Renée Kaplan, coauthors of *Shaking Her Assets*

"Alison Pace isn't afraid to tackle serious subjects, even as she delivers a wry and witty portrait of a woman growing up and growing into herself at long last."
—Joshilyn Jackson, author of *Backseat Saints*

If Andy Warhol Had a Girlfriend

"*If Andy Warhol Had a Girlfriend* is pure, guilt-free pleasure. When you're not laughing your head off, you're in the middle of a remarkably honest and heartfelt story about a woman who has to find love inside herself before she can find it outside."

—Joseph Weisberg, author of *An Ordinary Spy*

"Laugh-out-loud funny." —*Booklist*

"A funny, feel-good fairy tale set improbably in the high-powered international art world. *If Andy Warhol Had a Girlfriend* will give hope to the most relationship-weary heart."

—Pam Houston, author of *Sight Hound*

"A poignant and very funny look at the dating life of a fictional New York gal." —*The Washington Post*

"This book is GENIUS! I stayed up all night laughing hyena-style." —Jill Kargman, author of *Arm Candy*

"Art lovers, dog lovers—even EX-lovers—will love this fun, funny book." —Beth Kendrick, author of *Second Time Around*

"A laugh-out-loud look at art fairs, true love, and overindulged miniature schnauzers. A great read!"

—Kristen Buckley, author of *Tramps Like Us*

"A funny, snappy, beauty of a read—I loved it."

—Sarah Mlynowski, author of *Me vs. Me*

a pug's tale

alison pace

BERKLEY BOOKS, NEW YORK

THE BERKLEY PUBLISHING GROUP
Published by the Penguin Group
Penguin Group (USA) Inc.
375 Hudson Street, New York, New York 10014, USA
Penguin Group (Canada), 90 Eglinton Avenue East, Suite 700, Toronto, Ontario M4P 2Y3, Canada
(a division of Pearson Penguin Canada Inc.)
Penguin Books Ltd., 80 Strand, London WC2R 0RL, England
Penguin Group Ireland, 25 St. Stephen's Green, Dublin 2, Ireland (a division of Penguin Books Ltd.)
Penguin Group (Australia), 250 Camberwell Road, Camberwell, Victoria 3124, Australia
(a division of Pearson Australia Group Pty. Ltd.)
Penguin Books India Pvt. Ltd., 11 Community Centre, Panchsheel Park, New Delhi—110 017, India
Penguin Group (NZ), 67 Apollo Drive, Rosedale, Auckland 0632, New Zealand
(a division of Pearson New Zealand Ltd.)
Penguin Books (South Africa) (Pty.) Ltd., 24 Sturdee Avenue, Rosebank, Johannesburg 2196,
South Africa

Penguin Books Ltd., Registered Offices: 80 Strand, London WC2R 0RL, England

This book is an original publication of The Berkley Publishing Group.

This is a work of fiction. Names, characters, places, and incidents either are the product of the author's imagination or are used fictitiously, and any resemblance to actual persons, living or dead, business establishments, events, or locales is entirely coincidental. The publisher does not have any control over and does not assume responsibility for author or third-party websites or their content.

PRINTING HISTORY
Berkley trade paperback edition / June 2011

Library of Congress Cataloging-in-Publication Data

Pace, Alison.
A pug's tale / Alison Pace. — Berkley trade pbk. ed.
    p.   cm.
    ISBN 978-0-425-24119-6
    1.   Museums—Employees—Fiction.   2. Pug—Fiction.   3. Dogs—Fiction.   4. Art thefts—
Investigation—Fiction.   5. Metropolitan Museum of Art (New York, N.Y.)—Fiction.   6. New York
(N.Y.)—Social life and customs—Fiction.   7. Chick lit.   I. Title.
PS3566.A24P95   2011   2010046225
813'.54—dc22

PRINTED IN THE UNITED STATES OF AMERICA

10   9   8   7   6   5   4   3   2   1

For Cindy and Jenn

acknowledgments

My thanks are many and they go in particular to Susan Allison, Leslie Gelbman, Danielle Stockley, Erin Galloway, Rita Frangie, Amy Schneider, and all the great people at Berkley; to Joe Veltre, Sarah Mlynowski, Joanna Schwartz, Robin Epstein, Elinor Lipman, Sarah Melinger, Stacey Joslin, Cooper Joslin, Lin Randolph, Lisa Fielack, Allison McCabe, Christine Ciampa, Anthony Roth Costanzo, Jane Pace, Michael Pace, Joey Pace Weber, Occo Weber, Remi Weber, and Carlie; and to pugs.

chapter one

Pug Night

It was a decision we would later look back on with regret. There were pugs running loose in the Metropolitan Museum of Art. Imagine a vast army of pugs attempting to summit the grand central staircase of the Met. Only, the pugs were not on the stairs. They were contained—if the word "contained" can even be used in the same sentence as "pugs"— in the Temple of Dendur Hall, a great expanse of rose-hued marble running the length of one side of the museum. True, this fact was only a small solace. But I've long been a believer in taking solace where you can get it.

At the center of the Temple of Dendur Hall, the namesake temple has been reconstructed and elevated so that people, and now pugs, can walk around it and within it. In front of the temple, there is a reflecting pool. An entire wall of the room is made of slanting windows that look out into Central Park. That night, an early evening in late April, the setting sun flooded in through the wall of windows and bathed the room, and the pugs that ran throughout it, in shades of orange, red, and purple. I remember that. I remember the light. Some of the pugs pounced on the rays of light. Others strode dangerously close to the aforementioned reflecting pool.

Classical music played in the background. A long buffet table covered with a thick white cloth held a stunning arrangement of flowers, rows of champagne flutes, and many plates of canapés. There was tuna tartare on tiny, perfect potato chips; mini quiches; slices of filet mignon on bite-sized pieces of fresh baguette. Two tuxedoed men stood behind the table, their backs to the grassy knoll of Central Park just outside the window, making sure that the champagne glasses were all filled to the same height, that their rows were perfectly spaced, that their numbers on the table remained exact. They were vigilant in making sure that none of the hors d'oeuvre trays ran out or ever looked skimpy. They were good at this. Waiters were weaving gracefully throughout the room, refilling champagne glasses, passing a selection of the hors d'oeuvres from the table, and, most likely a first for them, keeping an eye on close to fifty pugs.

The pugs were also vigilant. They ran wild through the room. They ran up the stairs that led to the temple, into it, around it, and through it. They were zealous as they forged a track, panting and gasping and struggling for air like so many marathoners. The floor was perfect for sliding, and the pugs slid. They returned, frequently and without fail, to the long and inviting buffet table, where they would sit waiting, hinting at their anticipation in the way that only a panting, bulging-eyed pug can. Their goal: a taste of the passing snacks.

The pugs were gathered that night to honor one of the museum's top donors, Daphne Markham, a famed New York philanthropist who had recently announced plans to donate a substantial sum to the museum. And I was there. And even better, my pug, Max, was there, too. Though I usually think of my job at the Metropolitan Museum of Art as one tremendous perk, this particular perk of being with Max at a party at the Met *for pugs* was, for me, the ultimate.

Gil Turner, of the Development Office of the museum, had planned this party in Daphne Markham's honor due to the fact that the aforementioned anticipated donation was "far beyond significant." His words, not mine. Gil Turner is a man who often says things like "far beyond significant." And he says those things in a tone of voice and with a method of delivery that can best be described as haughty.

This party, which had come to be called Pug Night, was

the museum's Gil Turner–engineered acknowledgment of Daphne's gift, its way of saying thank you in advance.

The reason for the pugs was simple. The pugs were there because Daphne Markham loves them. While Daphne was world famous for her philanthropic endeavors, she was almost as famous for her love of pugs: pugs in general and specifically her own pug, Madeline. Daphne Markham is a person who is often photographed arriving at parties, benefits, and dinners. She is always beautifully dressed. And she is always toting her butterball of a pug, Madeline. I'm the first person to know that dogs are not allowed everywhere, that one cannot tote her canine wherever she may please. But if one is Daphne Markham, one can. It was this—Daphne's love for pugs, her long history of generosity to the Met, and her most recent plans for a "far beyond significant" gift— combined with a just-about-to-open exhibition of nineteenth-century paintings from the museum's collection, that had gathered fifty pug-loving patrons here at the museum.

The night was not exactly a democratic or far-reaching or "all pugs are welcome here" type of night. Pug Night was more a gathering of the most glamorous pugs in New York City, of pugs belonging to socialites, philanthropists, and *les amateurs d'art* world. Pugs are very popular in New York; I'd long known that. But before that night at the museum, I'd never known how many extremely fancy New Yorkers had a pug to call their own.

It was as if the pages of *Town & Country* and the Sunday Styles section of the *New York Times* had come together that night in the Temple of Dendur Hall, in tandem with all those pugs off their leashes. I had heard that an event like this had happened once before, years earlier, when Sotheby's had a pug-friendly preview for the Duke and Duchess of Windsor auction. Apparently Wallis Simpson had been a great appreciator of not only the pug but also of a great deal of pug accoutrements. I wondered if Gil might have culled the concept and maybe even parts of the guest list from Sotheby's.

The beautiful people looked beautiful. The pugs, almost every single one of them, looked crazed with glee. I kept a careful eye on Max, stationed over by the buffet with so many others. A smaller pug in a pink rhinestone harness sat right next to him. I should admit that many pugs are smaller than Max. Max's weight has ballooned in recent months. But I'm on top of the situation. I've been working on an exercise regime for him. I do my best to walk him across the park twice a day, with bonus activity excursions on weekends. I gazed across the room at the wonderful, if perhaps a bit porcine, Max and thought about how much I loved him. I watched as this other, leaner pug looked up at him as if he were her leader. I got that. In the year that I've known Max, I've come to see that he is very wise, and patient, and thoughtful. I'm certain that in a situation like this he acts as a role model to other pugs. Surely the others see that in him.

"Yes, I think they're going to drop a snack any moment now," I imagined Max saying to his new friend. "I really do."

As Max and his new companion continued to sit with laserlike focus in front of the buffet table, I took a moment to look around the room. On the side of the room farthest from the sloping wall of windows stood Valentino with his cadre of seven pugs circling close around him. Valentino's pugs did not stray. They did not heed the siren call of the canapé. They did not run wild through the room as so many of the other pugs did. Pugs are nothing if not savvy. Valentino's pugs jet around the world on a private plane. Valentino's pugs live in a stunning palazzo in Rome, a chalet in Gstaad, *un château* just outside Paris, the largest private house in London, a house in Tuscany, another in Capri, and a New York apartment right by the Frick museum. Valentino's pugs, no fools they, didn't let Valentino out of their sight. My pug lives in a third-floor walk-up alcove studio on a kind of sketchy block, albeit very close to the park. Thoughtfulness aside, Max had better-dealed me for the hors d'oeuvre table the moment we'd arrived.

I hung back, watched the pugs, hoped the slightly girthy Max didn't get too much to eat. I didn't socialize very much. I'm not generally a cocktail-party-with-the-patrons-of-the-museum kind of person. I'm one-or-two-good-friends to someone else's entourage. I'm stay-in-with-a-good-book to someone else's night-on-the-town. I am more of what I'd call a background type.

Andy Warhol once said, "I'm the type who'd be happy not going anywhere as long as I could watch every party I was invited to on a monitor in my bedroom." I think that pretty succinctly sums it up for me. Except for this party; this party I wanted to be at. As soon as I'd heard about it, all I could think was: pugs. In the Metropolitan Museum of Art. It made me think, and I almost never think this: How could I miss it? The answer was simple: I couldn't. No, technically I had not been invited. But! I worked at the Met, and I had a pug. I'd decided faster than I decide most things that I would absolutely stop by. I'd never once thought of it as crashing.

For a moment, as I stood off to the side in the Temple of Dendur Hall, surrounded by pugs, I had that feeling that everything was right with the world. Usually I'm a firm believer that you should avoid such a feeling, because surely it's written somewhere that as soon as you feel something like that, everything in your life will go very wrong. But still, I felt it. I felt as if my only care that night, other than maybe my hope that Gil Turner didn't cotton to the fact that I wasn't on the guest list, was finding a photographer for a portrait of Max for my boyfriend, Ben.

Sometimes, just because it's easier, I call Max "my pug." Technically, he's not. Technically, Max is Ben's pug and I'm his caretaker ever since, eight months after we began dating, Ben took a job with Lawyers without Borders and left, full of hope and purpose, for a five-month stint in Kinshasa. Really. In case you're not familiar—I wasn't—Kinshasa is in the Democratic Republic of the Congo, in sub-Saharan

Africa. It is not ideal. But I love Ben and admire what he's doing. I love Max, and I'm grateful that even if I do not at this moment live in the same country as my boyfriend, I have his pug. It counts for something. It counts for a lot. Perhaps I had more on my mind than the portrait, but the portrait was up there.

Then, quite slowly at first and then faster, the whole system began to melt down. I watched as a fawn pug, a long-legged, remarkably slender pug, the Lara Flynn Boyle of pugs, skidded on the marble floor and slid across the entirety of the eastern side of the room, barking as she went. In a different corner, a rather large, almost perfectly round pug in an orange leather harness first showed tooth, and then lunged with a great deal of snarling at a much smaller pug who'd been outfitted for the occasion in a tartan sweater. A black pug who for a second I thought to be Max, but luckily wasn't, vomited in a corner. Another one skidded across the south end of the room, making a soft howling noise as he progressed.

I scanned the room quickly for Max. He was still fixated on the amuse-bouche. Assorted pugs were peeing on several different surfaces. One left what could be viewed as a calling card on the polished marble floor. Maintenance men appeared with rolls of paper towels and spray bottles. Party guests fell silent, hushes ensued, and then people began to talk again.

In the background, Daphne Markham could be heard

calling out "Ahoy!" over and over again as if a record were playing, one that no one had realized had skipped.

"Ahoy!" she said to everyone who passed her. Her voice crescendoed throughout the room, over the din of conversation, over the clink of champagne glasses, punctuating the occasional pug-mishap-related hushes that broke out. "Ahoy!"

I leaned back against the wall. From this vantage point, I saw Gil Turner enter the hall. As he entered, he paused for a moment and straightened his tie. He took an iPhone out of his pocket, glanced at it with a half sneer, and then looked out across the room. As he did, his half sneer turned into a smile. He shifted his shoulders back and strode into the room like a famous actor onto a stage. He glided across the floor, almost like a pug who had lost his footing, and headed over to Daphne and her famed, held-aloft pug, Madeline. He looked happy, confident, pleased with himself. He didn't yet know that his party, along with the pugs within it, was teetering very close to the precipice of out of control.

"Ahoy!" Gil called out to Daphne, and I smiled, I think because something about Gil calling that out to her didn't quite work and it fell flat. He sounded foolish. Not nice, I know, but Gil didn't always bring out the best qualities in me.

I looked again toward Max, still way over at the far end of the buffet table. Suddenly he perked up and stood very alert, at attention. Then, it was as if everything else in the room had gone dark and a single bright spotlight had been shone upon Max. I looked across the room at him standing so still and watchful. He reminded me of these two German shorthaired pointers we sometimes see in Central Park. Like pointers who'd just seen a gunned-down grouse, Max was frozen, rigid, determined, moments away from bursting into action. Right then, he was the absolute embodiment of the calm before the storm. The calm part I could see; the storm part I knew was coming. Keeping an eye on Max was no small task in the sea of serpentining pugs, but it was made at least a little easier by the fact that Max is a black pug, and also, by his waistline.

I believe that just as the animals in the tsunami knew to get the hell away from sea level, I somehow knew something not good was a-coming. I also somehow knew that that moment was as good a moment as any for a fortifying sip of champagne. I took a sip of my champagne. I took a step toward Max, still statuesque beyond yonder buffet table. And then he wasn't, neither statue still nor beyond yonder buffet table.

Max took off like a bullet in my direction. For one last delusional moment I allowed myself to believe he was running right toward me, that this was nothing more than a dramatic outburst of affection. But it was not so. Instead of bounding into my arms in a pug reenactment of the final moments of *Lassie Come Home*, Max stopped several yards away from me. He stopped right at Daphne Markham's heels and began barking up at her and her pug, ferociously. He barked more ferociously than I believe I have ever seen any pug bark.

Someone I recognized from photographs in magazines turned to another and said, "That's not okay."

"No," someone else who happened to be wearing a tiara agreed. "It's really not."

Daphne's pug, Madeline, safe in Daphne's arms but perhaps outraged at the assault, angled her face ceilingward and began to howl. And then (then!) she jumped down from Daphne's arms and began running, at full speed, in the direction away from Max. Completely unfortunately, that direction also happened to be on a collision course with the reflecting pool. I hastily put my champagne on the tray of a passing waiter and hurried through the crowd.

"My goodness!" I heard someone say as I passed.

"Oh, dear God!" someone else exclaimed as Madeline lost her footing and slid several feet before landing directly in the reflecting pool. It is to date the only time I have ever seen a pug aquatic. I will say she did a remarkably good job of swimming herself to safety.

By the time I arrived at the reflecting pool's edge, Daphne was there, too, collecting the soaking-wet Madeline in her arms. Max, who was now foaming at the mouth, had followed her. A crowd had gathered, a crowd that unfortunately included Gil.

"I'm so sorry," I said, as I swooped down on Max and

picked him up. Not that Max had ever had an outburst like that before, but picking him up had always had a remarkably soothing effect on him. This time it didn't. Max continued to bark, to foam a little at the mouth, too, and his new airborne status served only to set off the unsettling wheezing sound he sometimes makes.

Daphne Markham was calm, sanguine, wet. Someone asked if she'd like to go to the ladies' room to towel off there.

"Yes, yes, all right," I heard her say. She held Madeline close as several waiters offered rolls of paper towels. She looked over at me and smiled. Shamed, I looked away. And then, without another word, Daphne carried Madeline out of the hall. Several people followed her. Throughout the room, people began gathering up their pugs and heading toward assorted exits.

The weight of what I instinctively knew was Gil's stare bored into the back of my neck. I turned to see his eyes, usually so beady, bulging out at me in exaggerated exasperation. He jutted his nearly nonexistent chin in my direction and mouthed the words, "Out. Of. Here."

chapter two

What the Pug?

I fled the Temple of Dendur Hall and the Pug Night within it. I carried Max through the rooms of medieval arms, past rows and rows of knights in shining armor. As we walked, Max began to settle down. The noise he'd been making, a sound something like howling, once again became his familiar soft snuffling, punctuated by an occasional wheeze. At the grand central staircase of the museum, we turned left and right and right again, and through a door you'd most likely never notice if you were visiting the museum, into a world you'd never see. We walked together through the behind-the-scenes hallways and corridors, past secured doors beyond which were curatorial departments, the development office, public relations, education, exhibition coordination, and shipping, until we arrived at art conservation, my department.

At the door to the Conservation Studio, I opened up my bag to look for my ID card. Sliding said ID card through a slot by the door was the only way to unlock it. It took me a minute to find it. It usually does. I am a person who can often be found looking for something. I have in the past spent a fair amount of time looking for any number of things. Among them: self-confidence, poise, a modicum of inner peace, happiness, a pug, and a boyfriend. It took me a while to find everything, and my favorite part of the search was that I found pug and boyfriend at the same time. If only, I thought as I peered deeper into my bag, the boyfriend were actually in New York. Not that self-confidence, poise, a modicum of inner peace, to say nothing of happiness and a pug, were anything to sneeze at.

I found my ID card at last. I slung my bag back over my shoulder, balanced Max on my hip, slid the card through the slot, and listened for the click-click sound that designated entry to the studio. I opened the door and walked in. To my surprise, the studio was dark. I reached over to a panel of switches just to the right of the door and flipped them up, turning on one row of overhead lights and then another, illuminating the vast space. Though it was of course much less vast than the Temple of Dendur Hall we had just fled, the studio was still large and sweeping, organized, and clean. Throughout the room: priceless, breathtaking, beautiful—though at the moment in need of some consultation or repair—works of art. Paintings, sculptures, objects, placed with precision on easels, laid out with care on examination tables. I stopped for a moment, squirming pug still in hand, and took it all in. I almost always did this. It was rare for me to walk into this space that had been the center of my work life and my home away from home for the past eight years without thinking what an amazing place it was to be. Even then, in the aftermath of Max's seriously embarrassing outburst, I thought it.

I walked with Max over to my workstation, a nookish L-shaped area that held my desk, computer, and files on one side, and easels, canvases, tools, and brushes on the other. In the middle, I had a stool upon which I swiveled from the administrative tasks at my desk to the restoration tasks at my easel, occasionally gleefully. I've long thought a swiveling stool can bring out glee in even the most serious people. I placed Max down, just to the right of my desk.

"Stay," I told him, and looked down at him seriously for an extra moment to make sure he knew I meant business. He looked back up at me. I wanted to believe that the possibly contemplative expression he wore was meant to convey a renewed commitment to obedience. Crazed outburst aside, there wasn't a lot of reason to think otherwise. Usually Max stays quietly at the bottom of the stool, snoozing or just looking around, whenever I bring him with me into the studio. That's saying something, as I bring Max to work with me with a perhaps alarming degree of frequency ever since the discovery of Alan and Belle, two, as luck would have it, pug-loving security guards at the employee entrance on the north side of the museum. They both pretend they don't see Max when I arrive at their posts with Max stuffed in his Sherpa carrying bag. In order to make an at least passing attempt at canine concealment, I momentarily wrap him in a sweatshirt so he cannot be spied through the mesh of the bag. I think this tactic works well, or not, considering that Alan and Belle would let him in regardless. As an added bonus to the "Every Day Is Bring Your Dog to Work Day" that has become my life, both guards let me know in advance when they're not going to be on duty, and those days I leave Max home. I'll refrain at this juncture from getting into too much detail about what happens when one of them isn't there without warning. But it has, on one or two occasions, gotten extremely stressful.

And once we're past the museum entrance and inside the studio, it's fine. All is well here. Max is like the fourth conservation colleague. Everyone here loves him. Really, how could they not? I looked down at Max again. After his display of horrid behavior at Pug Night, I considered that I should zip him into his bag while I gathered my things, even though he hates the Sherpa bag with the power of a thousand suns. As I reached down to get his carrying case out from underneath my desk, my cell phone rang. I stopped midreach, stood back up, and retrieved my phone. As I did, I saw the international number flashing across the screen, and I thought, *Oh, good, Ben.*

"Hi, Ben," I said, putting the phone to my ear.

"Hey," Ben said. The instant I heard his voice I thought it again: *Oh, good, Ben.* I often thought that. I glanced quickly at my watch and counted six hours ahead so I knew what time it was for him.

"Hey," I answered back. "It's late for you there, everything okay?" I listened to the faint hum, the connection to Kinshasa that was always like a fan whirring in the background, and smiled, knowing that on the other side of that fan was Ben, who'd be home in two months. I remembered how right after the last election, I'd been nervous that Ben would get a job in Washington. But Ben did not get a job in Washington. Ben got a job in Kinshasa. Which just goes to show you something about worrying, only I'm not completely sure what that something is.

"Not so late," he said. "And I had to hear how it went." When last we'd spoken I'd told Ben of my plan to (real casual-like, so that no one would notice) slip into Pug Night.

"Not well," I answered. "Do you want the long version or the short version?" I asked.

"Umm," he said, sounding a little sheepish, "hate to say it, but . . . short version?" I could have guessed as much. When all of your phone calls with your beloved take place over such a vast expanse of miles, when there is very spotty reception in Kinshasa and often a great deal of concern over a generator, most conversations are the short version.

"Max attacked the guest of honor. And her pug." I explained, slightly amused by the mental picture I now had of the scene, but mostly mortified by it. "I'll fill you in on the grimmest of the details by e-mail, though," I added, thankful in a way to not have to retell that which I'd just lived through and wished I hadn't. "But it could have been worse," I summarized.

"Like so many things," Ben said back, and I could hear the smile in his voice.

"Exactly," I said, and smiled a little, too. We talked for the few minutes we had, a conversation composed mostly of "I miss you" and "I miss you, too" before someone in some background far away said something to Ben. I had no idea what it was about. For all I knew it was about a generator, and he had to go.

"You'll say hi to Max for me?" Ben asked, before signing off.

"Of course I will," I told him, lamenting the fact that he didn't have time to say hi himself. I always enjoyed listening to Ben greet Max over a transatlantic, trans-everything call. Ben missed Max. Max, I was sure of it, returned the sentiment. As of course did I. Lately however, I'd been taking a lot of my missing-Ben energy and putting it into the plans for getting the aforementioned portrait of Max done for

Ben. It was important to put that energy somewhere, because energy like that, if it's not put somewhere, will take you to the bad place. And Ben would love a portrait of Max. I had two months left to have it all done.

"All right, then," Ben said next. "Two months." This was how we usually signed off. Over the past months, as the number crept down to four, to three, and now two, and so on, Ben and I had begun a tradition of ending each of our brief conversations with an announcement of how long it would be until he was home.

"Excellent," I said. "I'll see you soon." I've learned that optimism, especially when the man you love lives in war-torn Africa, is a really important quality.

"I love you, Hope," he said, right before hanging up.

"I love you, too," I said back. I hung up and felt the way I always felt after talking to Ben, certain in the knowledge that I did really love him, that he loved me, but also a little blue, and mostly, more than anything else, wishing he lived here.

I started throwing stuff into my bag. Judging by the angle of the light streaming in through the basement windows of the Conservation Studio, I calculated that if I left right then I'd have enough time to walk home across the park before it got dark.

As I tossed my phone into my bag, it was as if the small sound it made as it banged against something else in there had been a starting gun. Max, who'd been completely quiet, obedient, docile even, for the duration of my phone call with Ben, twirled his head around like an owl and looked up at me with great urgency. His eyes were extra large, his gaze intense. His tongue lolled out the side of his mouth as he made a quick slurping noise. With a few grunting pants, he whipped his head toward the corner of the studio, hoisted himself up, and, like a bullet, took off, gasping, snorting, wheezing, across the room. I will admit that my first thought was not about the art. My first thought was that I was worried about Max's ability to breathe. Sometimes when Max gets very excited he starts wheezing so much, and he gets so phlegmy, that it becomes quite the legitimate worry. He persevered. He charged clear across the room and then came to a stop in the far corner, as if he'd been drawn there by some powerful pug siren song. He started barking at something there, and wheezing even more, then making a great variety of noises—some of them a bit unsettling.

"What the . . . ," I said, dropping my bag back down on my desk and hurrying across the studio.

Once there, I saw that the object of Max's ire (rage? obsession? truth be told I wasn't really sure) was a small painting. It was leaned up against the wall right next to the back door of the studio, a less-secure area, a place where no one in his or her right mind would ever leave a painting. I pulled Max away from the painting and bent down in front of it, both to use my body to block Max from getting any

20

closer and to get a better look. I held Max behind me and leaned in. It was a small, beautiful, important nineteenth-century still life—a picture of pansies by the French painter Henri Fantin-Latour. It was jewel-like, stunning enough that it could take your breath away, small enough that it could be carried around easily, or even overlooked if it were, say, resting nonchalantly against a wall.

This painting was part of the exhibition of nineteenth-century paintings from the museum's collection that was opening the next day. There was no earthly reason why this painting should be here in the studio, or at least none that I could think of. If it needed to be restored—which, at least to the naked eye, it didn't—there were channels to be taken, forms to fill out, protocols to follow. As a rule, I try not to get on an "I work at the Met" high horse too often, but at that moment, I kind of had to. In the Metropolitan Museum of Art, paintings did not simply get dropped off for conservation like a worn-down shoe dropped off at a cobbler. I had no idea what could be going on, but I knew right then, squatting in front of those unaccountable pansies, trying desperately to keep my crazed pug at bay, that something was wrong. Possibly very wrong.

I had to act quickly. I scooped Max up, thankful I'd made it across the room before he had lunged into the painting, horrified at even the thought of such a thing. Pug in hand, I hurried across the studio and put Max in his bag and zipped him in. I did my best not to be distracted by the gasping, the wheezing, the snorting, and then to make matters worse, the howling, which in the case of Max sounds like a long, not at all unsoulful "wooo."

"Max, honey, shh," I said in as soothing a voice as possible, and dashed back across the studio to make sure no harm had befallen the Fantin-Latour. I couldn't even let myself think how very bad it would be if any sort of harm at all were to befall it. I crouched back down in front of it, studied its surface, its frame, gently pulled it away from the wall and studied its back. Everything seemed to be in order. I breathed a sigh of relief. And then I wanted to unbreathe it. Sure, everything was in order, except for the fact that this painting, these beautiful delicate pansies, part of the exhibition that opened tomorrow, should not be here. It should be upstairs in the nineteenth-century paintings exhibition. It should be hanging on a wall, ready to be viewed by the thousands of visitors to the museum tomorrow and for many days after that.

I picked up the painting, one hand on the bottom corner and the other hand on the opposite top corner to be as safe as possible. When dealing with priceless, timeless, incredibly important works of art, safety is always of the utmost importance—so much, in fact, that it causes people who normally wouldn't use words like "utmost" to use them. I carried the painting with me to the examination table in the center of the room and turned on an additional overhead light. As I set the painting down, for one horrible split second I think my heart stopped. Something about the painting was off. Something in the corner didn't look quite right. It was nothing concrete, nothing you could look at and say, "Look, this is wrong," but it was a hunch, something a trained and practiced restorer might have.

And then I saw it: the tiniest bit of paint splatter, almost but not quite microscopic, in the corner of the frame. This was wrong. This painting was not right. This was definitely not right. I picked up a magnifying glass and examined the corner of the frame. I put the magnifying glass down. I took a deep breath. I needed to get a black light and shine it on the suspect corner. I stopped short of that which would confirm my fears. There was something else I needed to do first.

The only sound in the Conservation Studio was Max as he stopped howling and started to bark in the background. I headed back to my desk, turned on my computer, and pulled up our department log, the one that accounted for every painting to come in and out of the studio. As I suspected, there was no record of the Fantin-Latour being in the Conservation Studio. I picked up Max in his transport bag and slung the strap over my shoulder. I walked toward the door at the far end of the studio, the one by which Max had discovered the painting. I opened the door. In this order: I thought I saw a shadow rounding the corner at the far end of the hallway outside the studio, I blinked and the shadow was gone, I got a strange chill, and then I wondered if maybe my mind was playing tricks on me. I wondered if maybe I should have looked outside that door the moment Max ran over to it.

I walked quickly back to where I'd left the Fantin-Latour on the examination table. I carried it with care to the safe and locked it inside. I went back to my desk and placed the still-bagged but now-quiet Max in the bed I kept for him under my desk. I sat on my stool. It swiveled under my weight but yet brought with it no sense of joy. I had to look up his phone number, because in all the years we'd worked together, I had never once called him on the phone. I picked up the receiver and held it in my hand for a moment without dialing. I stared at the keypad, and as I did, from underneath my desk Max started to growl. It was a low, steady growl that gave me the same chill I'd felt when I looked into the hallway.

"Shh, shh," I said, trying as much to quiet my riled-up pug as my racing heart. I stared harder at the keypad until it started to get blurry. I was stalling. I was wasting time, time I didn't have to waste, and I knew that. I took a deep breath and I dialed. The phone rang once, twice, and then he picked up.

"Hello."

I took one more deep breath. "Hello, Elliot?"

* * *

For what felt like a hundred years, Elliot didn't say anything. To say that Elliot Death (it is a horrible last name, yes, but for what it's worth, it's pronounced "Deeth"), Head of Conservation at the Metropolitan Museum of Art, was the methodical, thinking-before-speaking type would be a tremendous understatement. I knew this well about Elliot, my former coworker and current boss ever since his promotion when our then boss, May, had suddenly decided to leave. I should get this out of the way. I've worked with Elliot for four years. I've worked *for* him for almost two of those. For a number of those years I was unrequitedly in love with him. I'm not anymore.

I looked straight ahead, over at the workstation where Elliot would be, were he actually here in the studio with me and not pausing, silent, on the other end of this phone call. I started to feel dizzy as I waited.

"So, what you're saying," Elliot finally said, "is that Henri Fantin-Latour's *Pansies* appeared in the studio and when you looked at it you didn't think it looked right?" He put an extra, labored emphasis on the word "Pansies" and I didn't know why. It distracted me, and for a moment I was the one not saying anything. I shook my head quickly in an effort to revive and focus. And then I returned to the phone call, to the pansies, to Elliot.

"Right," I said. "Or wrong." And then another long, interminable, excruciating pause.

"Did you black-light it?" he asked eventually, referring

to the method, embraced by art world professionals and actors on *CSI* alike, of shining a fluorescent light on a surface in order to see things not visible to the naked eye. I remembered, an instant too late, that I try to never think of the word "naked" in the same sentence as Elliot anymore.

"No," I said. "I didn't. I thought I should probably call you first."

"Right, right," he said. I lingered on that repeated word. I thought how both of us kept saying the word "right." "Right," he said again, as if to underscore my point. "It's good that you called me."

"Yes," I said. It was. It was good that I'd called and good that I hadn't black-lit on my own. If it turned out that everything was not at all right no matter how many times we bandied that word around, I didn't want any more of this to happen just on my watch. *At least,* I thought, *let it be on my and my boss's watch.*

"It was just there by the door?" Elliot asked.

"Yes," I said, preparing to wait forever while Elliot mulled my one-syllable answer.

"Okay." He spoke again almost immediately, throwing my whole worldview momentarily out of order. "I'm coming in. I'll be there soon, half hour tops."

"Okay, good," I said.

"Right. You'll stay put until I get there?" he asked.

"Of course," I said, and then, just as I was about to say good-bye, about to hang up the phone, Elliot said my name.

"Hope?"

"Yes?"

"Actually. In the meantime, I think it would be a good idea to go up to the exhibition and see what's there. Go to where the Fantin-Latour should be," he directed. "Maybe the real Fantin-Latour is just there on the wall where it should be and then this will all be much less of a problem than it might be."

"Right," I said. "Of course," as if I'd thought of taking exactly that logical measure. I hadn't. Maybe the real Fantin-Latour would be up there, where it should be; there was really no reason to think that it wouldn't be. Maybe there'd be nothing to worry about. Or at least less to worry about. But then, of course, maybe it wouldn't be there. Maybe when it came to things to worry about, there would be plenty.

"Elliot?"

"Uh-huh?"

"What if it's not there?" I asked, giving voice to that which would probably be so much better left unvoiced. There was again a pause.

"Then call security."

"Okay."

"Or, wait. Don't call security. Wait, just wait. I'll be there as fast as I can," he said. He said it all much more urgently than he ever said anything.

I hung up the phone and sat there for a moment with

Max in his bag at my feet and stared out into the space of the empty studio. I thought that it was strange that Elliot wasn't here. Elliot was always here. He was always in the Conservation Studio, always right there at his workstation across from me, hunched studiously over a painting. Elliot was extremely diligent, extremely work oriented. For as much time as I spent at the museum after hours, Elliot spent more. No matter how early I ever got to work, Elliot was always here. No matter how late at night I stayed, how many weekend afternoons I popped in for a few hours here and there, Elliot was here. Always. Always Elliot. It was weird, more than weird, that tonight, for the first time, no Elliot.

*   *   *

I took Max out of his bag, gave him a treat and then another one for good measure, and attached one end of his leash to a hook underneath my desk. I pulled out the curtain I'd rigged for the purpose of concealing him, though of course as I listened to the chompings and lip smackings coming from behind the curtain I wondered, not for the first time, if a pug could ever be truly concealed.

"Back soon," I whispered as I retrieved my ID card and cell phone from my bag and left the studio via the front door. I turned and made sure the door had locked behind me. I didn't head back to the public area of the museum, in order to make my way up to the second floor where the poised-to-open exhibition of nineteenth-century paintings from the Met's collection was to be on view, to the place where the Fantin-Latour should in fact be. Though I count the central staircase of the Metropolitan Museum of Art as one of my favorite places in the world, and though I will take every opportunity I can get to ascend it, I didn't then. I turned right at the end of the hallway, walked the few steps out to one of the interior staff elevators, and, for one of the first times in years, took it up to the second floor.

As I stepped off the elevator, I paused for just a moment, taking note of the quiet. The stillness of the museum after it has been closed to the public for the day is unlike any other quiet I have ever experienced. It's bigger, greater, more in-tense. I took a deep breath and turned in the direction of the exhibition.

The overhead lights were off. The floor lights were on and the glow of the exit signs above doorways created an effect that, even though it never had before, right then felt strangely sinister. I looked down at my cell phone, becoming aware of the hour for the first time since I'd discovered the pansies. It was eight fifteen. So much more time had passed than I had realized. Through my strong and only getting stronger sense of unease, something that was getting closer to dread, I made my way through the dimly lit hallways. I was familiar enough with the layout of the museum—where the corners were, which turns to take, which corridors went where—that I could have done it blindfolded.

All at once I rounded the corner to the entrance of the exhibition, looked up, and saw, about thirty feet in front of me: Gil Turner from the Development Office and the ill-fated Pug Night. What on earth was Gil doing there? He was standing, his long, lean, blue-pinstripe-suited frame statue still. He had one hand on his waist and the other at his mouth. Even from that distance I could see he was biting on his fingernail. It was the only movement he made. His blond head, led by his long pointed nose, angled down toward the ground.

In the next instant Gil's head snapped up and his eyes widened and everything changed. He came rushing toward me, the effect of which made it seem as if he'd been rushing out of the exhibition all along, as if he hadn't been standing there stock-still and deep in thought only a moment ago. I wondered in the instant before he reached me if Gil had been hurtling toward me from the start.

He stopped, much too close to me, mere inches away. "My God!" he said loudly. He looked down at me and, perhaps realizing only then how very close he was standing to me, he stepped back. The smooth and unlined skin on his face was splotched with red. I stared at Gil and Gil stared at me, and then he raised his chin. He is a man who is very weak of chin. I looked away from his face to the rest of him, his suit, his shoes. Gil was always beautifully dressed. He wore perfectly tailored suits, with shirts whose custom-made origins were touted by monograms sewn into sleeves; he had a seemingly never-ending rotation of Hermès ties, an ongoing parade of tiny, whimsical animals, bugles, beach balls, and balloons.

"What are you doing here?" he spat, his head whipping to the entrance of the exhibition and back to me again. I stared back at Gil without answering, a bit more deer-in-the-headlights than I really would have liked to be. I wanted to get into the exhibition, walk two rooms into it, and verify that the Fantin-Latour was hanging where it was supposed to be. I did not, however, want to tell Gil this. Also, why was Gil there?

"I need to check something in the exhibition," I said at last, purposely vague, standing up a bit straighter as I said it. I wondered if somewhere there was a giant metaphysical scoreboard, and if so, did I just get a point for at least trying to project self-confidence even when I felt little? I imagined that probably the metaphysical scoreboard of the universe was not so quick to give points away.

"What's that?" Gil demanded, the pitch of his voice ratcheting up, quickly approaching frantic.

"I need to verify something," I said, raising my own markedly less weak chin.

"What?" Gil again inquired, an eyebrow raised. His forehead began to glisten in the low light. We stood facing each other as if daring the other to blink, and in that moment of standoff, I thought for the first time that maybe I shouldn't have listened so blindly to Elliot, even if he was my boss. Maybe I should have called security right away, or even the police. Suddenly I wasn't in the darkened and rather eerie Metropolitan Museum of Art with Gil breathing heavily in front of me. For a moment, I was somewhere else, a world away, and it was Saturday morning and I was watching cartoons, retro cartoons. Woody Woodpecker was on and someone, I don't know who, my recall only gets me so far, was saying, "None of this would have happened if Woody had gone straight to the police."

"Hope," Gil said, looking quickly to his right and then his left. "Don't go in there."

I looked him straight in the eye; I felt another shiver down my spine. "I have to," I said.

"Hope, listen to me," he stage-whispered. He grabbed the sleeve of my jacket. I tried to pull away, but he held fast. "You cannot go in there. The Henri Fantin-Latour has gone missing." He said "gone missing" as if the pansies themselves had just popped out of their own accord. My heart skipped a beat, and not at all in the good way.

"I know," I whispered back to him.

"What?" He let go of my jacket as if it had just burst into flame. "What are you talking about?"

"The Henri Fantin-Latour," I said. "It's in the Conservation Studio. We don't know why." I used the "we" on purpose. I told myself I was just throwing in Elliot for good measure, not throwing him under my out-of-control bus. "I came up here to verify," I said. Gil's expression did a three-sixty. He looked briefly perplexed before circling back to haughty and landing once again on frantic.

"Then we have to get down there right away!" he snapped. "Quickly!" he added, in a way that made me wonder what came after frantic. He placed his hand on my elbow and started to turn me back toward the elevator. While my interior monologue went the perhaps not entirely mature way of, "Ew, Gil Turner is touching me," I managed to think that though Gil was many things and a great many of those things were unpleasant, he was not my boss. I did not take orders from him.

"I can't, Gil," I said as I wrestled my elbow away from his clutches. "I need to see for myself. And for Elliot."

I ran, full-out ran, into the exhibition, and went two rooms deep, with Gil following at my heels like a hysterical Pomeranian. And when I got there, I saw. I saw exactly what I'd been expecting, exactly what I'd been dreading. I saw it plain as day, or more appropriately, plain as night. In front of me, down low on the wall and close to the corner: a wall label for Henri Fantin-Latour's *Pansies* detailing the painting's provenance, measurements, date, and medium. It was placed just to the right of an empty space. Gil was right. The Fantin-Latour wasn't there. The Fantin-Latour had gone missing. And, just like that, everything was wrong.

I looked closer. There was a scrap of paper on the floor

right underneath where the painting, had it been there, would have been. I bent down to pick it up, and right as I saw what it was—the little slip of paper that was always in place when a painting was taken from its spot, usually for cleaning and restoration—Gil snatched it from my hand.

"What?" he said, looking down at it. I took it back from him to look at it again. This piece of paper should say who had signed out the painting, what for, and when it would be back. This piece of paper could maybe tell us something. I looked down: The paper said that the Fantin-Latour had been signed out by the Conservation Department. My department. Gil leaned over me and read the same words that I did.

"Did you sign it out?" he asked.

"Of course I didn't," I said, because, of course, I hadn't. I remembered the way Gil had looked at me when I'd first rounded the corner to the exhibition and found him standing deep in thought at the entrance. The way he had looked when he'd looked up at me—frantic, scared, so surprised to see me there—made me think he had to know I hadn't signed out the painting. Only, he wasn't looking at me that way anymore.

chapter three

Forward Ho!

I kept my arms crossed tightly in front of me as the elevator sliced down to the first floor. Gil stood beside me, tapping his foot. I was unsure whether the low wheezing sound I heard came from the elevator or from Gil. If I'd had to choose, I would have said Gil. When the doors at last opened, Gil and I both abandoned all sense of caution (to say nothing of composure or customary museum staff conduct) and sprinted in the direction of the Conservation Studio. Gil got there before me but had to wait because I had the card that would unlock the door. He did not wait patiently for me to catch up to him. He grabbed the locked door handle with both hands and tried in vain to twist it one way and then the other.

"*Gil,*" I said under my breath, and edged around him to slide my pass card in the slot. As soon as the lock clicked and unlocked, Gil pushed in front of me to charge through the door. I followed.

As we entered the room, I saw Elliot at the center workstation crouched over the Fantin-Latour. I couldn't remember telling Elliot I'd put the pansies in the safe, but I must have because obviously he'd found them in there. He was examining the painting in the same place that I'd had it half an hour before, back when all of this had been only possibly bad, instead of most likely catastrophic. Half an hour ago this still could have turned out to be nothing. Half an hour ago this could have been just a fake that had shown up in the studio while the real one hung in its rightful place, a breach of security certainly but not what it now seemed like—a calling card of sorts, the indicator of a stolen painting. I longed for that time as if it were a faraway place that I'd been to once, a lifetime ago, and to which I had always yearned to return.

Elliot's face was close to the surface of the painting, and he held a loupe to his eye. He looked up and saw us both standing there. He straightened, placing his magnifying glass to one side of the painting with one hand, brushing a stray curl off his forehead with the other. Elliot's light brown wavy hair was always a little disheveled; right then, it was even more so. From where I stood across the room from him, I thought his eyes looked rimmed with red. He looked right at me for a split second. Sometimes when Elliot looked right at me like that, I forgot everything else. It happened then. Elliot looked at me and I forgot everything that was happening, and then Elliot looked at Gil and I remembered.

It's hard to work with someone you used to be in love with.

"You should tell him," Gil said, bringing me, as much as I didn't want to be there, back to the present.

"There's nothing on the wall upstairs," I told Elliot, "and there's a sign-out slip saying our department has the painting."

"Yes," Gil piped in, leaning over my shoulder. "A sign-out slip from your department."

Elliot continued to stare over at both of us, his expression serious. And then he looked back down at the painting.

"What?" Gil said. Elliot looked back up.

I could tell by the look on Elliot's face that what he was going to say next wasn't going to be good. Even so, I held on tight to the hope that Elliot would say everything was okay. Right. Right would mean not fake. Right would mean the real Henri Fantin-Latour pansies were with us in this room and not at some unknown elsewhere. Right would mean not disaster. I stood there across the room from Elliot, waiting for what he would say next. I was a rock climber who had lost all of her rock-climbing gear. I was clinging to the cliff face, scrambling for purchase, hoping for the best, while all along dreading the worst.

Elliot leaned back on his heels, brought his hand up to his forehead again, and looked right at Gil, not at me, and then he said, "It's not right."

I looked at Gil. He was a deflated shell of the dramatic figure he'd been upstairs. I watched as he ran his hand over his forehead and down one side of his face. His pale eyes closed briefly, and he swallowed in a way so pronounced that I could see it and hear it. I heard Max, whom in the past half hour I'd come closer to forgetting about than I ever had before, as he began to rustle around behind the under-desk curtain. Gil opened his eyes and stared back at Elliot. Elliot walked forward a few steps until he was in front of the examination table and then leaned against it, the Henri Fantin-Latour *Pansies*—make that the officially fake Henri Fantin-Latour *Pansies*—now obscured from view.

"It's a fake," he said, and then he paused. "It's a really good fake, it's a fake that could probably get past a lot of people." He turned around to look at the painting behind him, stayed that way for a moment, and then turned back to us. He shook his head. "This could possibly even get past a curator. On an off day. Though maybe not. But still," he said, and paused once again. He shook his head, in disbelief, in something else, I couldn't tell. Elliot was as inscrutable as he'd ever been. "No matter how good it is, it's a fake."

And then Max started to bark. Gil startled and turned quickly around toward my desk.

"Oh God!" he exclaimed.

I turned and walked to get Max. And in that time, I will admit I did not say anything at all about how the very first thing we should do is call the police. In the small amount of time it took me to walk the distance back to my desk and free Max from the confines of his curtained area and return, Gil had become visibly more agitated. Gone was the slow gulping calmness that followed Elliot's announcement; here was a pacing Gil, a jumble of nervous energy Gil, and, once I was close enough again to see, a profusely sweating Gil.

"I hope that's *your* pug?" Gil gasped.

I nodded. "Yes," I said as I picked Max up.

"I mean, the party ended so abruptly," Gil continued, pausing to stare hard at me for a moment before ratcheting up the hysteria level in his tone. "Imagine if some of the creatures escaped? Imagine, right now, they could be lurking, everywhere, throughout the museum?" He craned his neck to get a better look at Max. He started to pace across the room.

"That didn't happen," I said. "This is my pug. Max." Gil stopped walking and closed his eyes. He brought his index finger up to the space between his eyebrows and began tapping it there over and over again. I heard him breathe in deeply and let it out in jagged bursts. He opened his eyes and looked at me and Max.

"So you don't think there are other pugs on the loose?"

"No," I said, stopping just short of both rolling my eyes and stating that we had far more pressing things to worry about than imaginary rogue pugs running loose throughout the Met. "Just Max," I said in lieu. In spite of my better judgment, I held Max out toward Gil, as if the mere sight of Max would defuse the tension and turmoil. In a perfect world it might have. This was not a perfect world. Gil visibly recoiled at the approaching Max.

His face awash with a new look of disgust, Gil turned away and began looking through the room again. As he walked, Elliot said, "We need to focus on the fake painting and the whereabouts of the real one." I think all of us, maybe even Max, winced in unison at the word "fake."

"I think what we've got to do is hang it back up," Gil said anxiously as he came up against a wall, turned, and headed back toward where Max and I were standing near Elliot, who had, perhaps symbolically, walked farther away from the Fantin-Latour. "We've got to hang it back up and not breathe a word, not say anything about this to anyone." He whipped his head around, looking from me to Elliot to Max and then to the examination table. I looked at Elliot. Elliot looked calm, cool, and collected. He appeared to be legitimately considering this idea. But then Elliot looked at everyone and everything this way. I once again had visions of Woody Woodpecker in my head, so I added in, "Maybe we need to go to the police?"

"Hope"—Gil turned to me—"no! Think about what

you're saying. A painting has been taken from the museum! If we call the police, it will turn into a public relations nightmare for the museum. And it could be very embarrassing for Daphne Markham, seeing as this happened at her party. Remember, her donation is a *planned* donation, not a donated donation. What if she takes it back under a cloud of scandal?" he asked, before lowering his voice. "The museum could lose out on a tremendous windfall. I could lose my job." He stared right at me for one long moment and then began to talk again. "Listen to me, please. For now we've got to hang it back up and take some time, a few days, weeks if we need them, and try to figure out what happened. No one will notice." Gil said the last part almost as an aside, and then he looked down and focused on the floor in front of his feet. I noticed the flexed muscles protruding from the side of his face as he clenched his jaws. "I never, ever should have planned a party with pugs."

I ignored the last part and tried to focus on the matter at hand. "How do you know no one will notice?" I asked him. "What about any number of people, curators, assistants, from Nineteenth Century? How can you be sure they won't notice?"

"Elliot himself said that it was a really good fake, one that could get past a curator," Gil hissed.

"On an off day," Elliot interjected.

"Well, if this isn't an off day, I don't know what is," Gil said.

41

"I'm not sure about hanging it back up," I said. I wasn't. Gil narrowed his eyes at me.

"If a tree falls in the woods and no one hears it, does it make any sound?" he said. He blinked repeatedly over and over again, like a mole that had just emerged by accident into the daylight.

"That's not at all the same thing," I said. I looked over at Elliot. Our eyes met, but even as they did I had no way of knowing what he was thinking, no way of reading his blank face. But I believed that even in the midst of what was unfolding, never would Elliot think a fake painting was the same as a real one. I looked away from Elliot, for a lot of reasons, not the least of which was that to me, Elliot in his own taciturn way is kind of like the sun. It's never a good idea to look directly at him, and definitely not for a long time.

"I just want to be sure I follow," I said. "Are you saying we hang it back up and don't call the police because this happened during your event, on your watch?" I asked, and Max, still in my arms, started to breathe a bit more heavily. Then he snorted. Gil had not turned his head toward me when I asked him the question, but upon Max's snorting he did, and then he looked right at me with wild eyes.

And then he walked a few steps closer to me. His jaw remained locked as he spoke through clenched teeth, this time at a much lower volume. "It did happen during my event, yes, and yes, it will be awful for me and awful for the museum, but I'd like to point out to you that *you* were the one who discovered it." When he said "discovered," he reached up into the air above him and made quotes with his fingers.

"What are you saying?" I asked.

"Well," he began, stretching the word out. "Who knows what really happened? The only thing I know is that you"— he paused and pointed a long finger at me—"are the one caught holding the bag."

"I resent that. Completely," I snapped back.

"Yeah, Gil . . . ," Elliot began. Gil whirled back to face Elliot and cut him off.

"And might I point out to you, Elliot, that this all took place in your department. And that your department is doc-umented on the only piece of evidence we have." Gil pointed a finger at Elliot. Elliot (wait for it) paused, his mouth slightly open.

"I got that," he said.

"My watch," Gil sneered derisively. "Ha," he added. "Ha, ha, ha." I believed he was surely hysterical now. "My watch, yes. But your watch and your watch, too." He pointed again at both Elliot and me as he spoke.

"Look." Elliot stepped forward, between us. "I don't know what's happened here, obviously." Then, as he placed so much emphasis on the word "obviously," I caught myself wondering, doth he protest too much? "But what we do know is this: Someone took the real Fantin-Latour off the wall and, for whatever reason—I don't know what it is—instead of leaving a fake on the wall, left it in here with us."

I could feel Gil staring hard at me. I tried to ignore the weight. I waited instead for Elliot to continue, and eventually he did.

"It doesn't look good for any of us," Elliot said to me. "I have to say I'm with Gil. The best thing I can think of is to hang this up, buy ourselves a little time, before we implicate our department."

My inclination was to listen to Elliot. He was my boss, and even though I had made great strides in the past year in terms of no longer being in love with him, I still looked up to him. And it's not as if Gil was without some very convincing arguments.

"Okay," I said, after a long Elliot-style pause of my own. "I can see that maybe for the time being we don't go to the police. Okay," I said again. As I did, I thought in the midst of this of Ben, in Kinshasa, trying to make the world a better place and me, in New York, suddenly immersed in and possibly in danger of being unjustly implicated in an art heist at the Met. On top of so many other things, how bad would I look to my do-gooder boyfriend if I were sent to the clink? And, as important, if that happened, who would take care of Max?

"But we're not just hanging it back up," Elliot continued, slowly. "We've got to figure out what, uh, happened."

I listened to Elliot and tried to ignore Gil standing right there, and as I did I reminded myself that this, what was happening, a painting stolen from the Met, was bigger than me, bigger than each of us here wanting to save our own skin. I tried my best to concentrate on what we needed to do next.

"We have to look at the security cameras," I said.

"I looked at ours when I walked in; they're both dead," Elliot informed us. Gil whipped his head around from camera to camera to camera and back to Elliot.

"You don't say?" he said.

Elliot ignored him. "We're going to have to figure out how to get a look at the camera in the nineteenth-century wing," he said. I couldn't think how on earth we would be able to do that without rousing some serious suspicion. I only knew we needed to figure out a way, before anyone else did. For a while no one said anything. For a while it was as if we had all been stunned silent by the severity of our situation. Max, less so, let out a loud snort.

Gil began raking his hands through his thinning hair. "I've thought of something," he said as he worked at loosening his tie (bunnies playing drums) and then untying and removing it altogether, jamming it into his pocket. "I know a guy."

Gil whipped his iPhone out of another pocket and began pecking at it and scrolling. "You know," he said distractedly as his finger slid up and down over the surface of his phone, "some time ago, a very important friend told me that if I ever needed a private investigator, for any reason, there was only one person in New York discreet enough to call." He looked up at Elliot and then over at me, all wide eyes and expectation. "Thank God, I was smart enough to hold on to the information," he concluded, holding his iPhone aloft and giving it a quick shake. "I'm contacting him now," Gil said next, tapping at his phone for a while longer before slipping it back into his pocket.

"All right," Elliot said. He rubbed his hands on the front of his rust-colored corduroys and took his ID card out of a pocket. "Where's the sign-out slip?"

I stepped forward and handed it to him. He took it, looked at it, and slid it into his back pocket. "Okay, I'm going to hang it back up," he said.

"I'll come with you," I said. He looked up at me then, and for the briefest of instants, our eyes locked.

"No," he said. "Let's not draw any more attention than we have to. Also, I want us all to be clear," he said, directing his gaze at Gil. "We don't have a lot of time," he said next. "We can look for this, but not forever. Sooner rather than later we're going to have to turn this over to security, to the police, I don't even know." He closed his eyes and shook his head again. Out of the corner of my eye, I saw Gil wincing. He did not want to be known for this happening during his event. It could be that. It could be something else. My arms began to ache from the weight and effort of holding Max

46

this whole time. It was only then that I realized I had been. I set him down, and he scurried off silently in the direction of my desk.

"Gil, see if you can get your guy in here, like tomorrow," Elliot continued, taking charge of the situation in a way I had never seen him do before. The part of me that had already spent what in some cultures might amount to a lifetime swooning over Elliot, swooned just the slightest bit then, too. Gil took his iPhone out of his pocket and shook it in the air.

Elliot turned and walked back to the examination table. He picked up the small and beautiful and fake painting of pansies and held it from diagonal corners and headed to the door. Right before he left, he stopped and turned around.

"I'll be here at eight tomorrow," he said.

"I'll be here then, too," I said.

"I'll be here sometime after that," Gil said, and then there was a moment in which the three of us all just looked at each other again. We each knew that we'd all stepped into something we shouldn't have. There was, however, a finality to that moment, a determination, an unspoken understanding between the three of us, that we were in this together. I looked from Gil to Elliot and thought that these two men, for very different reasons—because I really disliked one and endeavored not to love the other—might be the last two people I'd want to be in cahoots with over anything.

Elliot turned and opened the door and walked through

it with the fake Henri Fantin-Latour. Gil waited a moment, maybe two, and then he left as well. And then Max and I were alone with everything that had just happened and everything that had only started to happen. There in the stillness of the Conservation Studio, at first the only sound I heard was the soft breathing of my pug in the background. Then, in the more distant background, the one that existed only in my mind, I heard it again. "None of this would have happened if Woody had gone straight to the police." I wondered who in this scenario was Woody Woodpecker. I imagined it was me.

chapter four

ha-ha-Ha-HA-ha

As I stepped off the sidewalk in front of the museum to hail a taxi on Fifth Avenue, I thought about what I had done. I had entered into collusion with a vile and officious man. I had entered into that same collusion with my boss, with whom I used to be in love. I had obstructed justice. I was helping to cover up a crime, and in the process I was committing one myself. I felt shaky, unsure of almost everything. I was only sure that I didn't want to take the bus.

The clear skies from earlier in the evening were gone. A light spring rain had begun to fall. The plaza in front of the museum was deserted, quiet, just starting to get rain-slicked.

I stood with one arm outstretched for a taxi and the other holding Max. I looked back up at the museum. Lights shone up its façade; flags hung down from its roof. I've always thought of this view as one of the best views in New York. This view had always reminded me that I actually worked there, at the Metropolitan Museum of Art. Just seeing it said I had done some good things in life, made some good choices. Yet as the events of the evening poured over me, as what we had just done spread out in my mind like an unwanted houseguest who had no intention of leaving, the view of the Met shining in spotlights, adorned with flags, glistening in the rain, didn't remind me of any of that. As a taxi pulled to a stop in front of me, as Max and I got into the back and I gave my address to the driver, I wasn't sure it ever would again.

The taxi wound through Central Park toward home. As it did, I leaned back against the seat and closed my eyes, and I thought that the only way through this was through it. And that meant figuring out what had happened to the real Fantin-Latour. I thought about what had happened, what I knew, and what I needed to find out.

The first thing I thought was that it had to be an inside job. *The Thomas Crown Affair* this was not. It was not as if a bunch of bandits had entered the museum and only made off with a Fantin-Latour of pansies. Someone had placed a fake painting in the Conservation Studio and then taken the real one. Or the other way around. I knew it had happened that night because a painting leaning up against a wall in the studio would not, could not have gone unnoticed for long, even without the help of my extremely intuitive pug. Someone who knew the ins and outs of the museum had likely done it. I thought of Gil, late to his own party and later lingering by the exhibition. I thought of Elliot not at his desk when he was always at his desk. I thought of his jumping to action when he had so rarely, in all the years I had known him, ever seemed like the kind of man to jump to action. Both Elliot and Gil could easily be described as knowing the ins and outs of the museum. But then again, I reminded myself, so could I.

The taxi pulled to a stop outside my brownstone.

Max and I walked into the dark and quiet vestibule and then up two flights and into the stillness of our apartment. In the darkness, I tripped over an African statuette I'd placed by the door a few days ago.

"Damn," I muttered, and I could feel Max below turning his head up toward me. I fumbled for the light switch and turned it on, at which point Max spied the same African statue and stared at it, shocked, as if seeing it for the first time. Not that it was anything like his reaction to the fake Fantin-Latour, but I got the distinct impression that Max did not like this statue, a small dark wooden figure, possibly a deity, I wasn't sure.

"No, no," I said gently to Max, reaching down to pet him. "We like the statue. We love it." I figured it was the best approach, seeing as our tiny apartment was quickly filling up with random, often rough-and-ready, sometimes kind of hideous pieces of art that Ben purchased from the people of Kinshasa and neighboring and distant villages. He did it to help Kinshasa, and he did it because he knew I loved art; he did it, he'd told me, as a way of staying connected. I loved the things he sent even though a great majority of them freaked me out. Max seemed to accept my declaration of love for our newest roommate and sauntered past it and into the kitchen. I followed him in there, gave him a treat— one of the new low-calorie ones I'd recently acquired as part of Operation Slim Down Your Pug.

After giving Max a late dinner and skipping my own, I got ready for bed and sat with Max for a while before pulling back the covers. I looked at a picture I had hanging in the corner of the room. Ben had given it to me just before he left. It was a black piece of wood with white lettering, a nice saying stenciled across it about making the right decisions in life, about embracing the ride. I hugged the pug he had left in my care and I thought of Ben, selflessly living in Kinshasa to try to help people, and shuddered again at the thought of what he might think of me if he found out about this, or if I was blamed for the crime. I knew I could never tell him about any of this. Ben was so far away from me, and now, on top of rarely being able to hear his voice, or see his smile, or look into his eyes, or be in the same room, let alone the same country as him, he felt somehow even farther away. As Max circled a few times at the foot of the bed and settled in with his chin resting on my ankle (Max is a fan of the elevated chin), I leaned over and took my laptop off the night table where I'd left it. The last time I'd been on it, I'd been searching for dog photographers for Max's portrait before bed. I powered it on to send an e-mail to Ben. But once it was on, I didn't know what to say.

A new wave of anxiety rose within me. I reminded myself that it could all still turn out okay. We had a private investigator coming to help us. We'd figure it out. As I turned off my laptop and put it aside again, it never once occurred to me to think that maybe there was a reason that line about Woody Woodpecker and all the things that wouldn't have happened had he gone straight to the police had kept popping into my head. I didn't see it as a prophecy, or as a warning bell, or even as a call to action. But that night, as I tried to fall asleep, I listened to the sound of Max's snores in the background. Right before I finally drifted off, I became convinced that his snores sounded exactly like this: ha-ha-Ha-HA-ha.

*   *   *

The next morning, though it was only Wednesday, I had the feeling I'd just been through a very long week. I stood at the front door, ready to go, leash in hand, pug-transport bag at the ready. Max stood at the other end of the room staring at me.

"Come on, Max," I said, lightly tapping the side of my thigh with one hand and jingling his leash at him with the other. Max tilted his head to one side and looked at me, perplexed. I wasn't sure what he could be confused about, considering he comes to work with me almost every morning, unless of course I've been alerted by Alan or Belle that they won't be at their stations—in which case he stays home, and a lovely neighborhood dog-walker comes to take him out (not once but twice) during the day.

In addition to being a perpetual take-your-dog-to-work pug, Max used to always accompany Ben and me out to dinner when the weather was nice and we could sit somewhere outside. I take him as often as I can to the New York City Pug Meetup Group so he can hang with his own kind. He eats a special prescription allergen-free food prescribed by the vet ever since he experienced what, looking back upon it, I can only now describe as a raging stomach upset. Max is what you might call a spoiled pug. But my guess has always been that a great many pugs are spoiled. How could they not be? They are, after all, pugs.

The leash jangling eventually got the message across, and Max charged across the living room to meet me at the door. Outside on the street, though the air was now crisp and clear, a perfect spring morning, it was still on the rainy side in my heart. We walked toward Central Park, passing a basset hound named Rocket and his person at the corner.

"Hey, Rocket," I said as we waited for the light. The guy with him, whose name I didn't remember, smiled at us. That's one of the things about having a dog in New York: A lot more people smile at you. I smiled back. That's another thing: It works both ways. Max and I crossed over Central Park West and into Central Park and headed toward the Great Lawn. I reached down and unhooked Max's leash and watched as he ran a few feet out in front of me. There are so many things that are wonderful about Central Park, to say nothing about living so close to it. But ever since I've known Max, the best thing might be the fact that dogs can be off their leashes throughout the entire park every morning up until nine A.M.

I draped Max's leash around my neck and balanced my load, with my handbag on one side and Max's necessary-for-museum-entering carrying case on the other, and set off behind him toward work. Our route was the same every morning, around the top part of the Great Lawn, and then around the back of the museum to the employee entrance on the north side of the building. Max knew the way and led it confidently. Max and I started most of our days this way. It was always one of my favorite parts of the day, and my money is on the fact that it's one of Max's, too.

Right then, Max stopped to greet his hands-down favorite pug friend, a nice fawn pug named Cooper. Max became exuberant and devoted whenever he came across others of his pug kind. Greeting a fellow pug always stopped him in his tracks. I counted on these pit stops to be sure Max didn't stray too far ahead.

"Hi, Cooper," I said as I caught up, and we rounded a corner and made our way under the bridge right by the museum.

Then, as happened far too often, Max and pretty much every other dog off his leash in Central Park made a mad dash—an unstoppable, spitting in the face of any amount of training you've been able to do, which admittedly in the case of many pugs can often be not much, dash—in the direction of a woman whom I have come to know only as Crazy Snack Lady. Many mornings Crazy Snack Lady can be found with her beloved and elderly shih tzu, who travels via stroller, near the back of the museum, quite close to the staff entrance Max and I use.

Crazy Snack Lady arrives at her perch on the top of a museum-adjacent hill armed with snacks she doles out to every eager dog, of which there are many. Word gets out among the canine population of the park. Spot Crazy Snack Lady at any given time, and she will be surrounded by dogs, some sitting politely and patiently, some very much not so, waiting for treats. Every time Max sees her I completely lose control of him. It fills my heart with fear at the prospect of losing Max in Central Park (pugs can run faster than you'd think when food is in question). And also, Max has a sensitive constitution and I really don't like him eating anything if

I don't know what it is. Crazy Snack Lady has claimed, on the occasion or two she has been queried, that the snack in question is either "chicken" or an unqualified "fresh," but I have my doubts.

We all have our moments, and that morning might have been one of mine. I was fast. I was on my game. I ran quickly and caught up with Max, much to his chagrin. I was able to pull him from the throng before he received any questionable amuse-bouche. I thought that this was good, not only that I'd prevented both the possibility of an AWOL pug and the ingestion of a mystery treat, but that I'd been quick and fast to react. I figured that with everything that awaited me at the museum, I was going to need to be.

As I dragged a disgruntled Max away from the throng, it occurred to me that maybe I should put Crazy Snack Lady on a list I needed to make of possible suspects. She was often lingering right by the staff entrance to the museum, an entrance I had already determined could have been used by the person who put the fake Fantin-Latour in the studio, the person I just might have caught a glimpse of running around a hallway corner last night. Whoever took the real Fantin-Latour and left the fake could have been someone who spent a fair amount of her time proffering treats (that were likely neither chicken nor fresh) within spitting distance of one such staff door.

I turned around and looked back at Crazy Snack Lady, still surrounded by—I counted quickly—six dogs, each with his tongue lolling out of his mouth. I added her to my list. I wasn't sure of her motive, other than the fact that everyone had a motive because who wouldn't like a Henri Fantin-Latour of pansies to call her very own? In my mind, no one.

The addition of a suspect to a nascent list comforted me more than might have been appropriate as I stooped down to face the not-at-all-easy task of wrangling Max into his bag. It took some doing, it always does, but at last he was in and we approached the entrance. Alan smiled and glanced down at my museum ID, but not at my bag, as we passed.

"Thanks, Alan," I said. He nodded. I loved the fact that Alan was willing to look the other way. Alan had never once given me a hard time about secreting my pug into the museum. Walking away from him and toward the Conservation Studio I realized, even though I almost wished I hadn't, that Alan knew the ins and outs of the museum, had a lot of cleared access, and maybe, like me, wasn't exactly a rules follower. I didn't want to think that turning a blind eye to the smuggling of an adorable and charming pug into work could be the gateway to taking part in a felony theft. But if I was going to do this right, if I was going to put everyone with means and motive and opportunity on a suspect list, I might need to consider adding Alan, and even the other guard, Belle.

Whether or not it is true, I like to believe that even though I smuggle a pug into the Metropolitan Museum of Art on a daily basis, I exist on a plane somewhere between completely insane and normal. In such a state of being, even I can see that someone who is willing to look the other way so that a dog can come into the museum might be willing to look the other way when it came to other things, too. The shaky logic pointed. And maybe it pointed to Alan. Of course, I knew that the very same logic could point to me, too.

I walked into the Conservation Studio. At first glance it seemed so bright and cheerful, in such great contrast to what I was sure would be the prevailing mood within it. I expected to be greeted by the ever-present Elliot, remembering as I did his absence early on last night. I was right: There he was, at his workstation bright and early, just as he'd said he'd be. Interestingly, so was Gil. My mind went to the night before, to Gil telling Elliot he'd be in after us.

Sometimes I worry a bit about the way I perceive reality, something I'm sure everyone worries about from time to time. Just to be sure the earlier Crazy Snack Lady diversion had not somehow taken a full hour longer than I had thought, I checked my watch. My watch said five after eight, the time I arrived at work most days. Something struck me about the fact that they were both here before me. Gil wasn't wearing his suit jacket; it made me think he hadn't just arrived. I noticed he'd had his initials stitched onto his shirt; they were about halfway up his torso, right underneath where a front pocket would be, had there been a pocket. There wasn't any pocket. I stared at the monogram until my eyes lost focus. I don't know why.

"Hope," Gil said, his gaze landing on the Sherpa bag slung over my arm. I clenched my jaw and tried to send out a vibe that said there was nothing at all in the bag. That did not, however, stop the rhythmic snort-snuff-wheeze, snort-snuff-wheeze that emanated from it. Gil raised a long, arching eyebrow. His heavy-lidded eyes bulged.

"Oh, no!" he exclaimed. "Is that one of the pugs from last night? I knew I was right about that. One got left behind, didn't it? And now it's loose and breaching our sacred spaces!"

"What?" I said, even though I heard him. "No. We've been over this already."

"Then what?" he said back, pointing at my bag as Max snorted from within it.

"I told you this already, it's Max. He comes here."

From behind Gil, I saw Elliot look up from his desk, rubbing one eye and then the other with his thumb.

"It's all right," Elliot said, and Gil whipped back around to face Elliot, and I thought, *Thanks, Elliot*. Then I went back to doing what I always do: trying not to think about Elliot any more than I absolutely had to.

I turned to head to my desk. As I did, out of the corner of my eye I saw Gil pivot once more in my direction. He jutted his lack of chin pugward and, enunciating every syllable, said, "Not okay." I chose not to address this as I took Max from his bag and set him down. Gil kept talking.

"Well, I imagine it's helpful to know that at least one person here has no shortage of experience getting things that shouldn't be gotten in and out of the museum," he said. I bristled, but I didn't turn back. I tried not to concentrate too much on Gil. I knew that when one is trying to figure something out—trying to crack a case, as it were—one likely needs to pay a fair amount of attention to a great many things, and that some of those things may not be very pleasant. Yet when faced with Gil, I felt it was important to direct one's attention elsewhere.

"All right," I heard Elliot say again, and then he said, "Hope," and I turned around.

"Yes?" I said.

"Hope," he repeated, getting up and walking out from behind his desk. "We have some news and it's weird."

"Weird?" I asked.

"Weird!" Gil echoed.

"Yeah," Elliot continued. "Gil got a look at the camera footage from Nineteenth Century from last night."

"How'd you do that?" I asked, momentarily forgetting my efforts to ignore Gil. I could see I'd have to do more of this in the days, weeks, however more to come.

"I know someone in security," he told me. He tilted his head, narrowed his eyes even more. I wondered if he wished he hadn't just revealed that to me. I raised an eyebrow at him. He raised one back at me.

"See," Elliot continued, "on the playback, you don't see anything. One frame, the pansies are there, and the next frame the pansies are gone. It's like a ghost took them."

"A ghost?" I asked, wondering if maybe Gil wasn't the only one coming unhinged.

"It's like it just disappears," Elliot clarified.

"Ghosts are very big right now," Gil added with an uneasy and high-pitched, some might say hysterical, laugh.

"That's vampires," I said to Gil. "And you're right, that's completely weird," I said to Elliot, unsure whether he was even telling me the truth. I wondered if maybe they were, somehow, unlikely though it seemed, in this together. In a much different way than they were in it with me.

"Can I see the video?" I asked the room.

"I destroyed it," Gil informed me. "We cannot risk anyone else seeing it. I thought it was for the best just to get rid of it." *Really?*

"Uh, yeah," I shot back. "For the best? Unless it wasn't, Gil." Unless, I thought, it was Gil who did it. As I looked at Gil and then Elliot, I thought it was Gil who had done it, and then I thought it was Elliot, too. On the topic of "for the best," I decided not to voice this opinion. But I filed it away. I definitely filed it away.

Max skittered out into the space in front of my workstation. "Hi, Max," I heard Elliot say, in a much softer tone than he'd been speaking. *Pug*, I thought, *the great neutralizer.*

It was as good a time as any to let them know of the role

I planned to take. "Well, whether or not I can see the tape, I'm still going to help," I said from my desk, directing my words toward Elliot and not to Gil. "I'm actually very good at this, at looking for things." I can't say for sure, or maybe it's that I don't want to say for sure, but I believe that right then Gil rolled his eyes.

"Now that we have Chaz," Gil answered, "I think the best thing we can all do is stay out of his way and let him investigate."

"Chaz?" I asked, even though I could deduce that Chaz must be the private investigator.

"Our private investigator," Gil replied.

"Right," I said. I kept saying that. We all kept saying that.

"We should stay out of his way," Gil repeated.

I do in fact aim to be neither defensive nor paranoid, but in that moment, in the cool clear morning light of the Conservation Studio, I wondered then if, in the English-to-Gil dictionary, "we" actually meant all of us or if it just meant me. I knew I would not listen to Gil. I knew I would somehow, some way, do my best to figure out who had taken the painting and replaced it in my department with a fake. The question was not whether I was going to get involved. The question was *how*. I sensed Max settling down at my feet. I tried anew to begin to wrap my head around how on earth a painting could have been stolen from the Metropolitan Museum of Art; how such a perfect fake could have been created in the first place; and how it could have wound up in the studio. I listened to the soft whistling of Max's at-rest breathing, and in spite of my ongoing aim not to become a fully crazy dog person, the type of person who will project just about any ability onto her dog, I found myself wondering if Max might have known what had happened long before anyone else. Maybe, I thought, Max always knew what was happening about a whole slew of things on a deeper level than people even have access to.

I looked down at him, first at the crushingly adorable section of tongue that always peeked out of his mouth and then into his eyes. I thought then that Max, long proven to be a superior and extremely intuitive being, might just prove instrumental in helping me sort out my suspicions. He looked back up at me and scrunched up his forehead so that the tops of his ears scooted upward. I winked at him. I considered the possibility of discussing the finer points of the case with him later.

Gil didn't say anything else. Neither did I, and neither did Elliot, for that matter.

I turned on my computer and pulled up my work log. I studied the things I'd planned for the day. I had set aside the morning for work on a Maxfield Parrish landscape that had recently arrived in the studio with surface damage. For the afternoon, I'd scheduled prep for the next acquisition meeting and had, in an annotation that made me feel very much like the slacker I feared I was soon to become, designated the three o'clock hour for researching Max's portrait. Under the heading "research portrait" I'd typed out "photographers," "dates," "diet plan," "groomer," and "pug exercise" (with a question mark next to it). I sighed. I hated to put the pug portrait by the wayside, hated to put anything that had to do with Ben by the wayside, but even I could see how I had to.

Like ripping off a Band-Aid, I quickly hit my delete key and erased the hour. I stared at the new blank block of space, and after looking over at Elliot and the still-standing-there-pointlessly Gil, I quickly typed their initials: "E. / G." Underneath I typed "look into M" (M for "motive"). As good a place as any to start.

"Hello, young friend!" I heard from the door of the studio. It was Sergei, the third member of the conservation team, calling out to Max as he entered. Sergei, the only one not involved in our possibly criminal, most definitely ill-conceived, and thus far poorly directed cover-up plan. As Sergei walked over to his workstation, Gil, Elliot, and I busied ourselves with pretending we were working. This was obviously the most difficult for Gil, seeing as this was not where he worked. To his credit, though, he whipped out his iPhone and pretended to send an e-mail.

Max scurried over to Sergei, circled his feet, and returned to me.

I looked at Sergei, our tall, burly sculpture expert, thinking again how he was the only one of us not in on it, and as

I thought that, it occurred to me that that could in fact make him a likely suspect. Yes, it was roundabout logic, definitely, but as with other things, I am oft of the mind that a person should take logic where she can get it. I turned back to my log and, with one touch of a finger on my keyboard, after the "E. / G." typed "S."

Though the Maxfield Parrish beckoned, though I had responsibilities to attend to and deadlines to meet, I was too distracted and possibly too overwrought to consider touching a painting in such a state. I turned instead to my e-mail. As is so often the case, the first e-mail in my inbox was from J.Crew. "Are you missing out?" it asked me. Lately J.Crew had been asking me that a lot. That day, for just an instant, the words changed in front of my eyes: "Are you missing something?" my e-mail now asked me. I was certain that my answer was yes, definitely. I deleted J.Crew, deleted a few others, and then right as I was about to turn away, another message popped in. The e-mail was from Gil: *No longer safe, obvs. Change of plans. We'll meet Chaz outside by the Manship bears. 10 minutes.*

I looked up and saw that although Elliot was still at his desk, Gil had gone.

I turned back to my computer and thought two things, in reverse order of importance. First, it struck me as odd that Gil would use the abbreviation "obvs" in an e-mail; even if he was sending it from his iPhone, it just didn't seem like anything he would do. Then I thought, why would Gil e-mail about anything that had to do with any of this? My fondness for it as a medium of communication notwithstanding, e-mailing was something that should, under all circumstances, be refrained from when you were a person who did not want to be found out. E-mail was so often people's undoing. I hoped it wouldn't be ours. I deleted Gil's note and deleted it again from the trash.

"Hey, Sergei?" I called across the studio. "Would you mind keeping an eye on Max?" It takes a village if you want to bring your pug to the Met with you. "I have to pop out," I added, as casual-like as possible.

"Sure!" he said, and smiled. I smiled back. And then without looking anywhere near Elliot's station, I gathered my ID, bag, and sunglasses—surely sunglasses were now an important part of my life—and headed for the door.

chapter five

Chaz Greene and Paul Manship's Three Bears

Stand on Fifth Avenue, face the museum, then turn left and walk around the side of it, into Central Park. Stay close to the edge and you'll find yourself in a small circular clearing of pavement with benches. At the center of this space is a sculpture by Paul Manship of three bears. It's a smooth, polished bronze with a large bear standing upright on its hind legs, a smaller bear crouching next to him, and then an even smaller bear, their cub, rounding out the group. It's finely wrought with a perfect patina, sentimental, and beautiful to look at. I've always thought there to be something distinctly comforting about it. This is the site Gil had selected for our meeting. This is where I met them.

I walked up to the sculpture to see that Gil and Elliot were already there, waiting. I didn't know how Elliot could have gotten there before me. They were both standing, facing the bears, with their backs to me. I walked up into the space right between them and faced the bears, too. I didn't say anything. Gil and Elliot didn't say anything. If I reached my arms out in a T, I would be able to graze each of their shoulders in the exact same spot, that's how perfectly spaced we were.

"Hey," I said eventually, for no other reason than a need to fill a silence.

"Hey," Elliot said back, under his breath.

We all waited. I was waiting for Gil to speak, to tell us what was going to happen next. And then I wished I weren't, because I didn't want to do anything, even if it was just inside my head, that would assign a leadership role to Gil. It was not that I wanted said role, it was more that I didn't want Gil to have it.

From behind us, someone cleared his throat. We all turned, the three of us at once, as if we were all carved out of the same piece of bronze, to see a man standing behind us. There was something about him that reminded me of Gil. He was shorter, stockier, darker than Gil, yet the resemblance was there.

"Chaz?" Gil said, tilting his head, taking a step forward.

"Indeed," said the man who must be Chaz. His voice was deep but his tone was oddly exuberant, as if he were shouting "Surprise!" at a birthday party and not secretly meeting three museum staffers right outside their place of employ to discuss a crime. The three of us, we must have looked so shifty to him. Though our intentions were good— I so badly wanted to believe that they were good—we were shifty.

Chaz and Gil shook hands. As they did, Elliot turned and walked a few steps to the side of the circle and sat down on one of the cement ledges. Chaz stepped back a bit and angled his stance so that he faced not only Gil but also me. I looked at Gil. His nose seemed to be almost twitching. I turned my head to the right away from Gil, away from Elliot, and made eye contact with Chaz.

"I'm Chaz Greene," he said to me, extending his hand. I stepped forward and shook it.

"Hope McNeill," I said, and as I let go of Chaz's hand, Elliot appeared at my side and shook Chaz's hand as well.

"Elliot Death," he said. Even as he pronounced it "Deeth," I couldn't help thinking of the word "death"—the death of our careers, or worse.

As soon as Chaz let go of Elliot's hand, he reached into his jacket—not a suit jacket like Gil wore, nor a red North Face pullover like Elliot did, but a green waxed canvas Barbour jacket that gave him a certain, if not Sherlock Holmes look, then at least a British effect—and took out a notebook. It was one of those miniature Moleskine note-books. I could tell because I like Moleskine notebooks, and I think sometimes it's much easier to recognize things that you like than things that you don't. Then, as if it had ap-peared out of nowhere, Chaz had a pen in his hand. He jotted something in his notebook. I wondered what it was—we hadn't talked about anything yet. Maybe it was about Elliot, or Gil, or me. I wanted the notebook. I thought I most likely needed one of my own.

"So," Chaz said, looking up again. "Gil's gotten me, uh, up to speed on things." It was the "uh." That brief stammer between words made me lose any confidence I might have had in Chaz. It vanished with the "uh." I looked harder at Chaz right then, Chaz with his nice jacket and his swarthy looks, and I noticed what might have been an ever-so-slightly-dim look in his eyes. And this is what I thought next: *Chaz is not the answer.*

It was as if Chaz had somehow heard me thinking. For an instant, he looked right at me with those eyes that only moments, milliseconds, centimeters of time before had seemed dim. For a flash they didn't, for a flash they seemed sharp, flinty, almost a challenge to any just-thought suspi-cions of subpar mental acuity. I considered, not for the first time since last night and surely not for the last, whether I had reached what could be considered a more-than-normal level of paranoid.

"Hope, is it?" Chaz asked.

"Yes," I said, "Hope." And though I long ago grew tired of any plays on words that sprang from my name, the next thing I thought was: *Hope. Hope for the best.*

"So," Chaz continued, tilting his head to his left, and narrowing his eyes a bit, too, "I, uh, understand that you're the person who first discovered the forgery?"

If a person could interact on a physical level with words or parts of speech, if I could run up and hug the "uh," I would have. I would have done this because it was that, and I think only that, which kept me from feeling really scared.

"That's right," I said.

"Right," Chaz echoed. And then out came the notebook and he took a while writing what looked like several sentences in it before returning it, along with his pen, to a pocket.

"All right then," Chaz said next, as soon as his detectively accoutrements were once again concealed from view. "Time is of the essence." As he said this, I noticed Gil looking down at his watch. He wasn't trying to hide it.

"The situation we have here," Chaz continued, something about his delivery making it seem as if he were reading off a prompter, "is not at all unlike a case of a missing child. The, uh, unfortunate fact of the matter here is that with every minute that ticks by, the likelihood of the painting being found is exponentially decreasing." I felt exponentially more anxious than I had since even last night. What were we doing, all of us, just standing there waiting? "Exponentially decreasing," Chaz repeated with a little nod of his head. "I'd like to start by asking you all some questions," he announced, just like a detective from a movie, a TV show, any sort of story that wasn't real but seemed to be.

"I'd like to look around the various places of ingress and egress to the museum," Chaz continued, and I paused for a moment in the midst of my stressing to think, *Who talks like that?*

"Okay," Gil said, standing firm in his spot. "Though you should know at this point that the likelihood of this being an inside job is high." I kid you not, at this juncture Gil looked right at me. I didn't even realize I was doing it, but I did, I looked right over at Elliot. Elliot was looking at the ground and, I was pretty sure of it, Chaz was looking at me. I felt a little queasy.

"But even so," Chaz continued, "I think the best place to start would be the main entrance. Then I'd like to walk through the Temple of Dendur Hall where the fete was held. From there, perhaps, the exhibition, and then to the Conservation Studio, the scene of the crime, right?" Chaz ticked off the locations in the museum dreamily, as if he were a starry-eyed and leisure-seeking tourist planning out the sights he would see for the day. Gil's beady eyes flashed first in my direction and then Elliot's. Everyone was after everyone. It had all become so *Lord of the Flies* so quickly. I don't know why, but I looked over at Elliot again. Our eyes met, and for an instant I felt like there were a million things between us, only none of it was anything that I could read.

I turned away to see Chaz fiddling again with his notebook before returning it to his pocket. There was something about that notebook, the way he handled it, that I couldn't stop noticing it. With that last flourish, Chaz straightened himself up and campily adjusted the lapels on his jacket.

"Also," he added, "I'd like to see the cameras in your department," he said to Elliot.

"Uh, yeah," Elliot said. Did he stammer it? As with so many things, I could not be sure. "The cameras in our department were compromised."

"When will they be fixed?" Chaz asked.

"Within the next few days," Elliot told him.

"Do you know exactly?"

"No," Elliot said, "not exactly."

"Well then, I'd like to see them as soon as they're fixed." Elliot looked confused and tilted his head at Chaz, and Chaz smiled back brightly at him.

"Shall we start at the front entrance, then?" Gil asked.

"Indeed," Chaz said, and then he started walking, almost marching, full of purpose, away from us and toward the front of the museum.

Elliot and I looked at each other across the cement clearing upon which stood a sculpture of three intrepid bears, with Gil to one side of us and the person we hoped was going to figure everything out walking away from us.

As Gil ran off after Chaz, as Elliot and I dispersed and entered the museum through the staff entrance at carefully spaced intervals, I knew on a much deeper level than I had known last night that I couldn't sit back and wait for this one. I couldn't wait for it to be solved. I couldn't wait for it to be okay. I had to go after it. I had to take charge.

chapter six

How to Hide a Pug

I didn't go right back to the Conservation Studio. I needed to go get myself a notebook. I told myself Max was good with Sergei for a little while longer. Sergei loved Max. Everyone loved Max. Except, of course, Gil.

But then I started to think that if Sergei was the culprit, as he could be, maybe it wasn't so good to leave Max with him. I almost turned around, until I remembered that Elliot had headed right back to the studio. By the time the rampant paranoia that had begun enveloping my brain sent me down the rabbit hole of "but if Elliot is the culprit . . . ," I was already well on my way. I stayed the course. It was not the easiest thing to do. But I assured myself that whoever took the real Fantin-Latour was in the business of stealing art, not providing substandard day care to pugs.

I walked quickly. I didn't go through the back corridors, stealth though that would have been. I went through the expanse of the first floor of the museum, past Greek and Roman Art, through Antiquities, and out into the main entrance. I paused at the sight of the great hall, took in the grand flower arrangement at the center information table, and scanned the crowds of visitors for Chaz and Gil but didn't see either of them. I passed a group of schoolchildren in uniforms, adorable even though one of them was complaining, loudly, that there weren't any dinosaurs. I walked by two women in their, I'd say, early twenties, less adorable. One was saying to the other, "I hate the Met; I always get lost here." I wanted to stop and tell her, *this is the best place in the world to get lost; you'll see so much*. I wanted to stop and tell the kids that though there were no dinosaurs here, there was everything else. The thought that I might have to amend that last sentence to something like "and almost all of it's real!" spurred me forward. I hurried through the lobby and into the first level of the gift shop.

My eyes darted from bookshelves stocked with everything from scholarly tomes to the most recent full-color exhibition catalogs. I walked past toys, board games, silk scarves, and T-shirts, all printed with images from the museum's collection, and straight to a kiosk filled with notebooks. There were no Moleskine notebooks. Alas. In lieu I reached out and grabbed the next best thing, a small lined notebook featuring William, the famed blue hippopotamus from the Egyptian wing. William is awesome. He is a fantastic-looking hippopotamus: adorable, a striking color of blue and, it goes without saying, breathtaking. William is an unofficial mascot of the museum, just the way Max is an unofficial mascot of the Conservation Studio. In fact, I find there to be a likeness of spirit between Max and William. Thinking of Max, back in the studio with, who knew, possibly an art thief, possibly two, I hurried with the notebook to the cashier. I paid for it and dashed with it back to my desk.

Back at the ranch/scene of the crime/Conservation Studio, Elliot was seated at his desk with his back to his easel, staring motionless into his computer screen. I wondered if he was reading an e-mail from Claire, his long-standing girlfriend. Claire works in advertising, I think, but am not sure. All that time when I was, let's say, smitten with Elliot and he never noticed me, I had tried not to think about Claire, as obviously Claire and her existence were troubling on several levels. And now I'd actually forgotten many of the details I'd once known about her. But whatever she did, whoever she was, she was not off in Kinshasa, trying to help the world by way of a law degree. I thought that if Elliot was not in fact the culprit, he could very possibly go home and tell Claire everything that had happened. It could be an ongoing thing; he could tell her everything that was happening, as it happened. For a sharp, shooting pain of an instant, I envied Elliot all the secrets he didn't have to keep. But then who could say why Elliot was staring, so listless. Maybe it was because he was in fact the culprit. Maybe it was because he was living with his regrets? But why? *M for "motive,"* I thought. It was nothing if not a very good thing that I now had a notebook.

"Hey, Elliot," I said.

"Hey, Hope," he answered, without turning away from his screen. "Max is cool; he's over with Sergei, I think."

"Thanks."

As I turned in the direction of Sergei's area, tucked away behind a corner, Max emerged from underneath my desk. So much for Elliot being good at noticing things. But then I imagine I already knew that that wasn't his forte.

"Hi, sweetie," I said, happy as always for a Max distraction.

"The colleague was very well behaved while you were away!" Sergei called from around his corner.

"Thanks!" I called back, and I thought, it couldn't be Sergei. Unless, of course, it could.

After giving Max some good scratches, assessing by the way he went right back to his bed that he had no interest in heading outside for a pit stop, I headed to my desk and settled onto my stool. I put my new, filled-with-the-possibility-of-blank-pages William notebook to the side for the moment and checked my e-mail. There, a reminder that Max's first swim lesson was scheduled for that night. I had never thought I would be the type of person to take a dog to swim lessons, but I'd heard from someone in the park that it was a really excellent way to trim down an overweight canine. I looked down at the pug. He had his head rotated around on the edge of the dog bed so that he could stare up at me; the rolls of fat on his neck made him look from that angle a bit more like a shar-pei or a walrus than a pug. I thought, *Yes, he really does need to lose a bit of his winter weight.* But truth be told, I didn't really want to go to swim lessons. I didn't think it would be a huge stretch to assume that Max probably didn't want to either.

"How about this?" I whispered down to him. "We're not going to go to swim lessons, but we will be vigilant with our walking, no exceptions." Max seemed okay with this, so I continued. "We are going to slim you down. Even with our other problem"—I whispered the words "other problem" a bit softer than the rest of it—"we are still going to get your portrait taken for Ben, for Daddy, for when he gets home."

* * *

Eventually, after I had dealt with the bulk of my administrative e-mails, spent perhaps longer than I should have comparing the pros and cons of Max's current vet-prescribed allergen-free dog food to some flashy organic diet brand (in an effort to still be weight-loss oriented, swim lessons or no), and spent a solid few hours filling out all the necessary paperwork for the Maxfield Parrish landscape and examining the damage, I placed my William the Hippopotamus notebook in front of me and, finally, opened it up. I looked over at Elliot, and then in the direction of Sergei, to make sure I wasn't being watched. One could never be too sure one wasn't being watched. Especially when one has devolved into a state of paranoia. The coast was clear.

I turned to a blank page of my notebook and continued what I'd started on my work log earlier in the day. I wrote *Alan*, *Belle*, *Elliot*, *Gil*, *Sergei*, and just because why not, *Crazy Snack Lady*, each on their own lines, with a space under each. On another line I wrote "Possibly anyone who was at the museum after hours on the night of Pug Night." I considered that that could include curators, assistants, any staffer who happened to work late that night, waiters and caterers from the party. And then I entered into a relatively brief but nonetheless deeply felt period of great despair. Fortunately for me this descent into despair coincided with five thirty, so even though it was much earlier than I ever left work, technically I could vacate.

I closed the notebook and slid it into the bottom of Max's carrying case for the safest keeping I could think of. I gathered Max from under the desk and went through the various machinations to make sure he was fully concealed in his bag. I headed out of the museum—and everything that was in it, and missing from it—for the night.

As I have mentioned, if you are the kind of person who smuggles your pug in and out of the national treasure of an institution where you happen to be lucky enough to work, you're going to have to take some precautions. First things first, you need a good bag, and more important, you need a guard who's not going to search that bag. And even if you have that, as I do, it's not as if you're home free. You have to make sure your coworkers aren't going to turn you in. (This, I'm beginning to see, applies to other things in life, too.) You have to be sure that people who do not work in your department, who do not fondly think of your pug as their colleague and welcome him daily with open arms, do not ever see your pug, because if they do they, too, could turn you in.

For this reason, even after we've left the museum, I never take Max out of his bag right away. I never set him down anywhere near the employee entrance. Instead I walk around to the opposite side of the museum from the employee entrance, the same side where you'll find Manship's sculpture of three bears. I always wait until we're under my favorite bridge, the Greywacke Arch. It's a beautiful bridge made out of the greywacke sandstone that it's named for and has a pointed arch. I always let Max out right underneath, just before we walk out in the direction of the Great Lawn.

I'm aware that this location could be all wrong, too close to the museum, that the likelihood might be too high that I might run into a fellow Met staffer and that said staffer might see me there with my pug and put two and two together. But it's the only place I know of on our route home that offers even a bit of cover. And I think cover is important, maybe more important than other things. I've always believed that with the art of pug concealment, as with everything really, you have to pick your battles.

Together Max and I emerged from the other end of the arch and out into the late April evening. As we did, I noticed someone sitting on one of the benches lining the path that approached the Great Lawn. I considered the weirdness that at the exact moment that I had been contemplating this very reality—running into someone from the museum while leaving the museum *avec* pug—I noticed someone sitting on the bench. And not only that, it was someone sitting on a bench with a pug. Upon closer look, I could see that at least it wasn't someone from the museum. Not technically at least. Though it was not anyone who worked with me there, it was someone I knew only from the Met. It was Daphne Markham, the museum patron from Pug Night, sitting right there, on one of the north-facing benches. Her pug, Madeline, was sitting right next to her.

It was Madeline who saw us first. Or rather, she saw Max first. She stood up, alert on the bench, and started to bark. She made the same "woo" sound that Max often did. I wondered then if maybe Madeline's bark was one of outrage. I wondered if she remembered Max's display from the previous night, the subsequent trouble it had caused. As if on cue, Max began barking back. He pulled on his leash and leaned the bulk of his barrel-chested weight against his harness as if he were less a pug walking home and more a sled dog showing off his skills. I followed after Max to Daphne Markham and Madeline, embarrassed because of last night's attack but not thinking fast enough to know of anything else to do. Max came to a stop right in front of them and squared himself off, staring up at Daphne and Madeline with his full attention. Madeline stopped barking, moved herself a few inches forward on the bench, and, leaning over its edge like Narcissus over a river, stared intently down at Max. I held fast to the leash, looked up, and smiled at Daphne. I worried that my smile, more self-conscious than anything else, might have come across a bit lamely.

Daphne, chic in navy blue pants, quilted ballet flats, and a trench coat, looked back at me and smiled as well. There was an air of glamour—of more than that, of elegance—about her. Her shiny silver hair was polished into a bouffant. You may hear the word "bouffant" and not think this possible, but it was a very attractive hairstyle on her. Her hair gleamed in the rays of light from the fading sun. Sitting next to her on the bench was a large quilted patent leather tote bag that perfectly matched her ballet flats. I wondered if it was her giant purse or if it was for Madeline. She sat there, so refined, so together, so expensive. She looked as she had at the Pug Night, as she did in every photograph I'd ever seen of her: as if she had spent a great deal of time getting herself ready. Recently, my horoscope had suggested that I take an extra twenty minutes getting myself ready each morning. I hadn't paid attention when I'd read it, but I thought of it again right then, and this time I thought that it might have been right. I could devote a few extra minutes to my overall look each day.

Madeline jumped off the bench and squared off in front of Max. I tightened my grip around Max's leash, just in case. Like Max, Madeline was of the short and stocky variety of pug and not the long-legged slimmer ones a person can also come across. She was a little smaller than Max, a little slimmer than Max, but to say someone was slimmer than Max was not setting the bar very high.

Daphne Markham looked down at Madeline and Max for a moment, just as I did, making sure no pug tussle was in the offing. After a moment, Daphne looked back up at me, smiled again, and raised her right hand just slightly. She gave a tiny tilting wave, just from the wrist like the Queen Mum.

"Ahoy," she said.

I thought, *Yes, of course, ahoy.* Daphne Markham is famous for a lot of things: for being a septuagenarian socialite, for being an heiress, for being a philanthropist, and for having an oft-photographed apartment on the penthouse floor of the Carlyle Hotel, to say nothing of her oft-photographed pug. She was also well known for greeting everyone, no matter who it was or what the occasion might be, with the salutation "Ahoy."

Even though I'd seen her up close just last night, I suddenly felt a little starstruck standing in front of her. For a moment, maybe longer, I forgot about the other things, about all the fast-forming worries that were only just beginning to wear me down. And then I remembered just as quickly. I don't usually think things like this, but right then, even though we were in the exact same place, I wanted to be in Daphne's world and not mine.

And though Daphne Markham didn't pat the bench right next to her gigantic and beautiful patent leather quilted bag and say, "Yes, dear, come and sit right next to me," there was something in the way she smiled serenely at Max and me that made me feel as if she had. I believe mental telepathy can work with pugs. I tried to send a mental message to Max to be sure not to attack Daphne or Madeline again. And then I reached down and picked him up anyway, lest this be one of the times that telepathy came up short. I smiled again at Daphne and said back to her, "Ahoy."

As Max squirmed furiously in my arms and Madeline attempted to hoist herself back up onto the bench but fell just short of succeeding, I sat down next to Daphne.

chapter seven

First Things First

I sat on that bench with Daphne and Max and Madeline for about half an hour that night.

"Hi, Maddie," I leaned down to say, hoping in some small way to make up to her the Max attack of the previous night.

"Oh no, dear," Daphne told me. "Madeline never goes by Maddie, though she will answer to Moosie."

"Right," I said, "of course." I didn't think Daphne's correction was at all weird. Instead, I thought that if Max's name weren't so straightforward and unshortenable, I'd probably find myself saying something similar on occasion. As I've hoped to make clear, over the past year of having Max in my life, the past three months of having a one-on-one relationship with him since the most unfortunate departure of Ben for Kinshasa, I have witnessed myself becoming a true dog person. I have witnessed this almost as if standing a distance outside the events as they unfolded, as I became preoccupied with dog foods and doggie gyms, with the connection I felt with the world because of Max, with the people in the neighborhood I never would have noticed and now exchange daily greetings with, all because of a dog. I have spent a great deal of time researching photographers to take a portrait of my pug. I have learned the right way to trim dog toenails. I have signed up for countless pug message boards and created a Dogster.com account for Max. I have done all this happily and in awe of Max's personality and spirit, in awe of how much love I feel for him. Throughout this I have been aware, albeit distantly, that when non–dog people think of the term "dog people," they sometimes think of crazy people. Sitting on a bench that evening with Daphne, someone with whom I had moments ago felt I had nothing in common, I felt we had the most important thing in common. As all my moorings felt as if they were drifting out to sea, I felt a wave of gratitude. Gratitude, relief, a kindredness of spirit. I think that's what it was. I thought, *Here is someone who, when it comes to pugs at least, is a little like me.*

"This is Max," I said. "He mostly just goes by Max."

Daphne smiled again and nodded at me. I believed it was with approval.

I went for it. I set Max down, and to my relief he seemed to forget about his prior ferocity-slash-bloodlust toward Madeline; in fact, he seemed to get a bit looser, a bit more relaxed once I put him on the ground with her. He looked at her, and, staying in one spot, he spun himself around.

"Ah, yes. Madeline does that," Daphne observed. I nodded. I smiled. I looked down and watched as Max pointed his nose skyward. It reminded me of something I'd been meaning to post on a pug message board.

"Actually," I began. "I've been wondering. Max's nose gets very dry . . ."

"Oh, yes. Pug noses get very dry," she nodded in agreement.

"What do you do for it?"

"Bag Balm," she told me. "It works wonders." Bag Balm, I thought, and stopped just short of pulling out my hippopotamus notebook in order to make a note of it. I thought it best to keep all things pug in my life, which really were all things good and pure in my life, as far away as I could from all things pansy in my life, all things bad and, I thought, possibly more than a little twisted.

Instead I asked, "Daphne, how's her snoring?"

"Torture," Daphne told me. "Real, real torture." I laughed. I knew exactly what she meant.

We watched our pugs play, and I was mostly happy. I

was mostly removed from the events at the museum, though of course I remembered some of them as part of my mind was fixated on the hope that Max would not repeat his recent Cujo episode.

"Dear," Daphne said, breaking the silence, and I thought it nice, charming, that she started so many of her sentences with "Dear." "I saw you last night, at Pug Night, yes?"

"Yes," I said, and looked away. I stared down at Max, hard, attempting to send a reminder telepathy about not attacking Daphne again, nor her charge. Max, I kid you not, looked right up at Daphne. A certain gleam in his eye made me nervous that he was considering the very thing I feared. I'd lived on the edge long enough. I reached down and picked him up and held him on my lap. I couldn't be sure, but I thought maybe he was lunging in Daphne's direction. Daphne didn't mention the attack, the affront, the scene. It was nice of her, I thought, especially since I was now sure she remembered it. *I'd* remember it. To this day, I can picture perfectly the exact facial expression of the standard poodle who'd chased down Max by the Bethesda fountain; same thing with the early-morning jogger who'd tripped over him by the bridle path.

"I work at the museum, in conservation," I explained, once Max was secure.

"So interesting," she said, and I thought that was nice. Conservation is not exactly the most glamorous department in the museum, not by a long shot, nor the most visible or high-profile or any of that. I appreciated the interest and, maybe, the approval.

"I know May Mlynowski," she said. I thought of my beloved former boss, May. I thought of her leaving last year to go on an extended sabbatical and of how much I had hated to see her go, and also how much I'd not exactly loved that she'd appointed Elliot as her replacement.

"I miss May," I said, looking toward the stone staircase that led to the obelisk, another side of which was visible from certain of the Met's windows. I said it without thinking, and wondered after I did if it was too personal to reveal. But I did miss May, a lot. May was a leader, a touchstone, a guidepost, someone to look up to, a fellow woman in the man-heavy Conservation Studio, in my man-heavy life. I wished May were here now. She could help so much with the pansies, with figuring out what happened to them. I looked over at Daphne. I wondered if she knew May well enough to miss her, too. I guessed that she did; May was the kind of lovely person who, were she in your life at all, you'd miss her once she was gone.

"Yes," Daphne said. "I miss her, too." She stared off at the Great Lawn and there was the same feeling, the same pug kindredness of spirit all over again. I suddenly felt like maybe Daphne could help me.

For an instant, a crazy instant, I almost took out my notebook and showed it to her. I caught myself, checked myself. *Hope, do not talk about a painting stolen from the*

Met with one of the biggest donors to same. And at that moment, though I would have loved to stay, I made an excuse to go home.

"Ah, yes, dear," Daphne said, looking down at her watch and gathering her tote bag up. "I must be going, too. But I hope I'll see you again."

"Me, too," I said, certain that my notebook, to say nothing of my collusion, was burning a hole in Max's bag.

Though my departure was hasty, I left Central Park that evening hoping I'd see Daphne and Madeline again, and even though I have never thought myself to be especially prescient, I had a very strong feeling that I would.

* * *

The Conservation Studio had become, literally overnight, the place I did not want to be most. It is the way of the world that because of that, it was as if I blinked and the next thing I knew I was back there again.

As I walked in and bent down to let Max out of his bag, I consoled myself with the thought that at least Max was there with me, too. This was immediately tempered as I looked around me and saw that Gil was there, too. And Chaz was there. And, of course, so was Elliot. Always, I thought, always Elliot. Even though, obviously, I should absolutely not think that. Ben, I reminded myself. Ben in Kinshasa trying to save the world. I looked at Max, waddling across the studio to look for Sergei, and thought that though I had made the necessary decision to scale back on some of the more fitness-oriented aspects of the preparation for the pug portrait, I would not forget about it in toto. Doing something nice for Ben, in the midst of everything else, would create nothing if not a nicer sense of balance. Balance is important in life. This is what I have always heard. But also, where was Sergei?

I walked first to my desk and put my things down. From behind me I heard Gil exhale.

"Why must you bring your pug in here and bandy him about?" he asked me from across the room. I turned around and looked at him; he was just standing there in a different monogrammed shirt, his eyes following Max's progress across the room. I looked away without answering.

Chaz, who'd been studying something in his notebook, looked over and said, "I like pugs." Max stopped his investigation of a corner and turned his head all the way around to Chaz. He stared at him with wide, happy eyes and an open-mouth smile. Flattery could get you everywhere with Max.

"Where's Sergei?" I asked Elliot.

"Not here," Elliot said blankly, as if that part had not been obvious to me. He looked up at me and blinked at me mildly. I wondered again if Elliot knew more than he was letting on, or, differently, more than I did. I settled myself at my workstation and glanced over at Chaz and Gil, each as far as I could tell seemingly unconcerned about Sergei's absence. I, however, was a bit concerned.

I looked over at Chaz, sitting at an empty desk. Like Gil, he had an iPhone and was intent upon it, typing on its screen. I was unsure as to what texting or e-mailing via phone was going to accomplish in terms of solving the crime. I hung back behind my desk and tried to watch what Chaz was doing without being so laser focused about it that he'd sense my gaze upon him. He bit down methodically on his bottom lip as he glanced at Gil, typed something, glanced at Elliot, typed something, and then—I looked down in the nick of time—looked over at me. I looked back up to see him tapping wildly away. I considered the possibility that Chaz was somehow not so much investigating *for* us, but instead, just investigating us.

Chaz leaned back in his chair, and in one motion he hoisted both of his feet up onto the desk and crossed one over the other. Still endeavoring to steer in a direction that would be clear of eye contact, I focused on his shoes. They were pointy at the tips, polished; they looked expensive.

"So," Chaz said, not to anyone in particular. I looked away from his footwear and noticed he'd had out his notebook again. "Let's talk about the video cameras, shall we?"

My first thought was, *But didn't we already talk about the video cameras? Aren't the video cameras kind of the only thing anyone has talked about?*

"What about them?" Elliot asked from his perch. As he did, Chaz opened up his notebook and poised his pen over it.

"You say the ones in this space were . . . compromised?"

"Yes. Tampered with. Dead. They're getting fixed." Elliot answered. "I told you yesterday."

"Yes, you did," Chaz replied. "But what I was interested in was, when will that be?"

Elliot turned, clicked at his keyboard, and looked up at his computer screen. He shook his head. "Tomorrow."

"To-mor-row," Chaz said slowly as he wrote in his notebook. Elliot furrowed his brow and regarded Chaz for what felt like a long time.

Gil cleared his throat. Somehow (how?) I'd forgotten about Gil. He craned his neck around, looking around the room. I tried to shake the thought that he was still looking for stray pugs intent on taking over the museum. Then Gil's gaze fell on Max, and he almost tripped stepping backward.

"Gil," Chaz asked, diverting his attention, "the cameras upstairs? You got a look at the cameras upstairs?"

Gil snapped to attention: This was his moment. His slightly hysterical moment. "I did! Yesterday. Bizarre! Painting there one minute, vanished the next." I saw Elliot wince at the word "vanish," and I think I might have, too.

"And that tape?"

"I destroyed it," Gil replied.

"That was good," Chaz said, and I for one was really surprised that he did.

"Why was that good?" I asked Chaz. I wondered if they were all insane.

Chaz looked back at me, clear-eyed. "Because we don't want any of this getting out while our investigation is on-going."

"Thanks, I thought that exactly," Gil said, pursing his lips and rotating his iguana head in my direction to look at me with every ounce of smugness he could muster. For a moment I wondered if it would be possible to sic the newly aggressive Max on him.

"Okay," Chaz said, not writing anything down. "I think I'll start with questioning everyone here, yes?" He looked up and over at Gil again, then ambled over to Elliot's desk and picked up a magnifying glass. He held it up to the back of his hand and peered through it, then stepped back, ostensibly startled at how close everything seemed. I had reached a stage in my life in which I was finding more and more that I had to remind myself of things. However, I knew I no longer needed to remind myself of my feeling that if this mystery was going to be solved, if this painting had any hope of being found, it probably wasn't going to be accomplished by leaving matters in the hands of Chaz.

"As good a place as any to start," Gil piped up to agree. Chaz nodded and walked into what had once been May's office and now was technically Elliot's office, though he'd never moved any of his stuff in there and rarely went into it. Gil looked after him as he went, slightly perplexed. After a moment of looking around to see if anyone had been watching, he strode into the office after Chaz. I wished that

I could hear everything that they were going to say. I often wished I could hear everything everyone was saying all the time. It would make so many things easier to make sense of.

I arranged myself behind my computer so that as far as I could tell Elliot couldn't see me, and then in what I hoped was as quiet and undetectable a way as possible, I sighed. I clicked my mouse at my e-mail like a lab rat in one of those lever/food pellet experiments.

Every now and then, when you want something, need something from the universe, the universe actually steps up and gives it to you. This is the only logical reason I could think of for what happened next. There, in my e-mail inbox, sandwiched between messages from Sephora and J.Crew and one from a dog photographer I'd reached out to in simpler, purer times, was an e-mail with a subject line in all capital letters: *I CAN HELP*. I'm not sure why I didn't immediately dismiss it as spam, as nothing more than one of those e-mails that pop up again and again with subjects like *Can I Trust You, Dear Sir*, but I didn't. Quite the opposite, I was drawn to it. I ignored both Sephora and J.Crew, two things I rarely ignore. I ignored the e-mail from the dog photographer and felt a twinge of guilt as I did, as if I were somehow ignoring Ben. I forgot any previously held beliefs I'd had about e-mail being the undoing of so many, and, less like a lab rat and more like a moth to the flame, I brought my cursor to that subject line. *I CAN HELP*, it said, and I thought, *God, I hope so.*

I looked at the From line; it read *MA100*, a name, not an e-mail address. Even though I didn't recognize it and even though you're not supposed to open e-mails from senders you don't recognize, especially at work, I clicked it open.

And once I did it read, simply,

If you follow, you'll have your answer.

And then on a second line, less simply, it read,

First things first: Up half, walk around, and there you'll see what happens after summer.

And that was it.

I knew, deep within myself, that the e-mail, every word of it, had to do with the pansies, the lost ones, the stolen ones, the fake ones, all of it. Yet even in the throes of my growing sense of desperation, I was able to see the possibility that perhaps it was all just a coincidence, a fluke, that there was a chance that this e-mail was just that, just some random e-mail that arrived on the day that everything else was already completely out of whack. But still I knew it had something to do with the pansies. I knew the way a pug knows it's going to thunderstorm long before it does. For a year I'd been saying that Max is the most intuitive being I've ever met, and I believe he is, but it was not until that moment, in the face of my all-encompassing faith in a strange, unsigned e-mail, that I had ever given myself credit for the fact that I'm more than a little intuitive myself.

I stared at it. I clicked on the name, but no e-mail address appeared, just the name *MA100*. Weird, I thought, but then, everything was weird. I hit reply and send without writing anything, just to see what happened. I waited. An instant later, an "undeliverable" error message came right back to me. I looked up, my gaze landing as it so often did on Elliot, hunched as he so often was over a painting. I looked to my right and to my left. Safety was important. Determining that I was not being watched, I printed the e-mail and deleted it from my inbox and again from my trash. I knew that double-deleting probably didn't do enough, knew that a record of this would be saved somewhere on a hard drive if anyone was looking for it. I shuddered at the thought of anyone looking through my e-mails for anything. I'm not the chattiest person. I do most of my conversing by e-mail. It's a scary thought how much I may have said over the years via the e. I wanted to stop believing in hard drives right then; I wanted it to be that hard drives didn't exist, that if I deleted the e-mail it'd be gone, and so I did.

I jumped off my stool, bent under my desk, whipped my hippopotamus notebook out of Max's Sherpa bag, and brought it with me up to my desk. I turned to a new, blank page of the notebook. I paused for just a moment. I wrote "MA100" up at the top and then copied out the entirety of the e-mail, looking anxiously, nervously, and probably a bit obviously all around as I did. I folded and tore the printed e-mail again and again into an obsessive-compulsive's dream pile of paper confetti. I looked for a while at MA100. MA, to me, always meant "master of arts," and I wondered if that was a calling card from Elliot, who, like me, had a master's in paintings conservation. Maybe Elliot was trying to tell me something? Except that MA could stand for a hundred, a million different things, and even if it did stand for master of arts, I'd say probably more than half of the people who work at the Metropolitan Museum have a master of arts in something.

With that thought, I looked down at my notebook with admittedly less enthusiasm than I'd only just previously had for it. I felt suddenly concerned that even though writing everything down could help, it might not be the answer. I was concerned above all else right then with the answer. I considered the very real possibility that I might need to bounce this off someone. I faced the fact that I might have needed to do that even before the e-mail came in.

I couldn't bounce this off Elliot—not yet. I couldn't bounce this off any of them. I took a deep breath and told myself to work, to focus on things other than the pansies. I turned to the newly arrived Maxfield Parrish and made sure it was arranged properly on its easel. I managed to spend the better part of the morning and a good deal of the afternoon, what felt like forever but wasn't, studying a corner in which some pigment had worn off through various magnifications. I typed another thorough and detailed-to-the-point-of-obsessive report on the damage in the hopes that I was in some small way being conscientious. I e-mailed my report to Elliot and willed the day to end. I looked up for the first time in what felt like ages and looked around the studio. Though of course one could never be sure, it appeared that Gil had gone. From the muffled sound of their voices, I ascertained that Elliot had now joined Chaz in his office. Sergei, for anyone keeping track of Sergei because surely I couldn't be the only one, was still MIA.

I looked down at Max, snoozing peacefully and noisily at once in his dog bed. I fished my cell phone out of my bag—my other bag, the one for carrying things other than Max and the hippopotamus notebook of inquiry and accusation—and thought I'd slip out a bit early and call my friend, my best friend, Pamela. Pamela could be the answer. Pamela was enthusiastic, ever optimistic, and rational. Clearheaded. When it came to so many things, Pamela was if not always, at least very often, right. These were all qualities I needed for myself, and for the pansies.

I slipped off my stool and bent down so that I was at the same level as Max. He was there, lying on his back with his legs held stick-straight above him, splaying out in different directions. His head was to the side and his tongue hung out of his mouth significantly more than it usually did.

"Hi, love," I said, and he whirled around. By no means do I wish to disparage the beauty and grace that is the pug, but when I say "whirled around," what I technically mean is that by way of a few labored, slightly spastic, and wheeze-accompanied jerking motions, Max managed to right himself and wind up on all fours, still in his bed. He stood staring back at me, his mouth open, his head cocked slightly to the right side, his forehead a bit lined.

"You ready for a break?" I asked. I considered just saying "bag" next, as if I had an obedient, trained dog, one who followed instructions, even just on occasion. Max stared at me for one moment longer and then turned and began running, full speed ahead, to Elliot's office. At the door, he paused for a moment and cocked his head in a way that I was sure was meant to express bewilderment at the notion that anyone could ever shut a door to him. Upon a closer look, I saw that Elliot's door wasn't completely closed. I tried not to think that such an observation could be at all symbolic or metaphorical. I needed to not think that; I had neither the time nor the emotional wherewithal to deal with such a concept. And then Max noticed that the door was a little bit open, too.

I watched as Max nosed the door aside and ran into the middle of Elliot and Chaz's question session. My mind flashed, as it sometimes did, to a documentary I'd seen about pugs a few years before. It was called *A Pug's Life* and in it, a great array of pug owners talked about their pugs. In one scene, a scene that has stayed with me most vividly, an art gallery owner in New York sat on the bleached-blond wood floor of his gallery as his pug snorted and chortled around behind him. The gallery owner looked at the camera clear-eyed, not sad or disappointed or disillusioned or let down, but simply factual about the whole thing, and he said, "I haven't been able to train him." That's a thing about signs. The hard thing isn't seeing them; they're actually quite easy to see and they're everywhere. The hard part, the part I so rarely get right, is figuring out what it is they are trying to say.

I hurried after Max into Elliot's office. As I walked in, I saw that Max was sitting with the entirety of his rear end on top of Chaz's shoe. Max did this when he liked someone. If Max liked a person who was sitting on a couch or some-where where Max could get to him, Max would crawl into that person's lap. In the event that the object of Max's cur-rent affections had a lap that was unreachable, he would try as best he could to sit his entire self on that person's foot. I looked at Chaz, who was smiling down at Max, and I won-dered if maybe Chaz wasn't all bad. And then, right as I thought that, Max looked up at Chaz and growled at him.

"Max!" I blurted.

Everyone—Elliot, Chaz, Max—looked up at me expec-tantly. I was thrown by the events so far, and further thrown by the fact that such a previously super-genial pug had begun to charge after some people and growl at others, others for whom he'd just professed love by way of shoe. I was very much at a loss for any other words. It was not the first time.

105

"Uh, sorry," I tried to say but mostly mumbled. I stepped into the office and hurried over to Max and lifted him off Chaz's shoe. Then I sprinted, with Max held at my side like a football, out of Elliot's office.

As soon as I was out of the office, I headed, with Max still in hand, squirming, straight back to my desk. I bent underneath it and snatched out Max's carrying case as quickly as I could.

Holding the bag open and in place with one hand, and balancing Max between my hip and the crook of my elbow, I stretched my fingers out and reached my hand around his "waist" and scratched his belly to distract him. Max, a tremendous fan of the scratched belly, gasped and snorted in delight and began bicycling his front legs at warp speed. Though there was a part of me that was more interested in Max's happiness than in anything else and hated to ruin his good time, there were other parts of me, too. These parts, the parts that had to get out of the museum, the parts that had so much stuff to figure out, the parts that couldn't quite grasp how deeply I was already mired in all sorts of wrong, and the parts that needed advice, won out. I seized the opportunity presented by my distracted pug and in one fell swoop stuffed him in his bag and zipped the zipper. Possibly criminal activity aside, I had not become hardened; my heart broke a little bit when I heard Max's one note of whimpered protest as he realized, a moment or two after it had happened, that, despite his brilliance, he was actually in his bag.

I took a moment to pet Max through the mesh and whispered, "I'm sorry, pumpkin," in as reassuring and calming a tone as I could muster. I hoisted the weight of Max over my shoulder. I didn't look back in the direction of Elliot's office or at any of the rest of it. I grabbed my cell phone off my desk and hightailed it out of the studio.

Just outside the museum, I left Max in his bag and turned to my phone. It was the real-life equivalent of "I'd like to phone a friend." Only, alas, this was not a game of *Who Wants to Be a Millionaire?* I scrolled through my contacts to Pamela. It was then that I remembered. I remembered what I should have thought of right away the moment I thought about Pamela. Pamela was just at the very start of a two-week trip to Paris. I couldn't believe I'd forgotten. Pamela's Paris trip had loomed large in my recent past. I'd considered going with her. *Oh God,* I thought right then, as I stared at the screen of my cell phone, as my shoulder started to ache from bearing the weight of my concealed pug, *I wish I'd gone with her to Paris.* If I'd gone with her to Paris, I wouldn't have been at Pug Night. Even though I somehow might have been roped in anyway, I believed right then that none of this would have happened if I'd gone to Paris with Pamela.

I walked away from the museum, all the way around it to the Greywacke Arch, and let Max out of the bag. As I walked him on his leash up the path, I tried to think of who else to call. So in need of advice was I that I considered calling my parents, even though being involved in an art heist is not the sort of thing with which I really wanted to bother my parents. Also, it dawned on me, faster this time, that my parents were whale watching somewhere in Alaska, and were unreachable, I believed, by phone. I sat down on the bench, let go of Max's leash, and watched as it trailed behind him. I held my cell phone with both hands and stared at it. It was no longer a cell phone. It was suddenly a useless piece of plastic. I tried to think who I, a person who had always been of the mind that one or two good, close friends was better than a slew of casual ones, could talk to about this.

There, in Central Park with Max wandering away in front of me, with the Metropolitan Museum of Art looming large behind me, I thought of Ben in Kinshasa, Pamela in Paris, and Mom and Dad in Alaska. Maybe I wasn't thinking hard enough about my resources, but right then I felt like there wasn't anyone I could really count on in New York. It was not a good feeling.

Pamela was my best shot. I told myself it wasn't entirely self-involved, to say nothing of entirely heist-involved, to bother Pamela in Paris. I did of course want to check in on how her trip was going. I counted six hours ahead.

I dialed Pamela's number and sat frozen in one spot as I listened to the ring.

"Bonjour!" she answered, and I thought how happy she sounded, and thought again how much nicer it would be to

be in Paris. Though I imagine that thought was not at all unique to my situation. I bet people, no matter where they may be, think that a lot.

"Hey, Pamela, it's Hope," I said. "I'm calling from New York," I added, unsure of why I did.

"*Bonjour!*" she said again. "*Comment ça va?*"

"I'm good," I lied. "I'm calling just to see that your trip was off to a good start," I lied again. "And I so wish I were there with you," I added, finally telling the truth.

"*Il est parfait,*" she said, and in this order I thought that Pamela sounded so happy and relaxed, and I envied her that; I worried that advice might be hard to understand if given all in French, and then most important, I thought, *If you tell Pamela everything she could be implicated, too.* And then, *What are you doing, Hope, don't implicate your friend.*

I exhaled heavily, away from the phone, so that Pamela couldn't hear, and resigned myself not to get her involved, for her own good. We talked for a few minutes more, Pamela *en français*, me in despair, before Pamela mentioned she was standing right in front of the Louvre. The Louvre. The mention of the museum made it all so much harder to resist, set me back for a moment on my myopic trail toward the answers. I changed my earlier tune. I thought a hypothetical couldn't hurt. A hypothetical was not an implication. This is what I told myself as I kept an eye on Max, wandering a bit too far in the distance, and scanned my mind for a good way to phrase it all. I didn't have one, so I just phrased it.

"Pamela," I said, "one quick thing. This may seem random, but just go with it."

"*Oui?*"

"Say something had been stolen . . . from the Louvre . . . and someone knew about it, right? But it was better, for a lot of reasons, that they not tell anyone?" I began.

"*C'est hypothetical?*"

"Yes, totally hypothetical." I assured her. It was for the best.

"*Combien ça vaut?*" she asked. How much is it worth? A sensible question; Pamela was always sensible. How much were the pansies worth? I wondered. I didn't know. I'd have to check, though I didn't know if that knowledge wouldn't only make things worse. I also didn't know how I thought this roundabout line of questioning was going to help me figure out the e-mail.

"A lot," I answered. "It's worth a lot."

"Hope," Pamela said, "is everything okay?" Her transition to English alerted me to the fact that I had perhaps failed at the light and breezy tone I'd hoped to achieve, failed altogether at the hypothetical, and that this, calling Pamela, was most definitely not the answer. I needed to wrap this up.

"Oh, of course, it was a silly Q, never mind, we'll talk soon. Have the best time," I rushed.

"Okay, Hope, but whatever's going on there, be sure to *faire la bonne chose.*" *Do the right thing,* I thought. Right, of course, always.

"Of course," I said.

"Are you sure you're okay?" she asked one more time before we hung up.

I wished I'd never brought it up, I felt silly, stupid, a little desperate, and very lost. I had no idea what to say, and so, for lack of anything better, I signed off with an overly cheerful, and completely fallacious, *"Oui!"*

chapter eight

Thursday in the Park with Pugs

By the time I'd tossed my phone into my bag and looked up again, Max was halfway to the Great Lawn with his leash trailing behind him like a friendly snake. I'd already learned the hard way, the fifty-dollar-ticket hard way, that a leash trailing after a dog does not a leashed dog make. And here we were, well past the designated ending of off-leash hours in the park. I hurried after my pug, hoping to catch up to him before any park police did. I tried to calm myself with the (perhaps uncalming) thought that at this point I'd already broken so many rules that an off-leash pug hardly seemed wrong, not against the backdrop of everything else.

I paused a few feet away from Max and took a breath. I wanted it to be the kind of breath that was cleansing, centering, the kind I'd learned once was key to relaxation and clear thinking. It wasn't.

I dashed the few steps left. As soon as I had the leash once again in hand, I sat down on the nearest of the benches that circle the lawn. Max sat down, too, right on my foot, just as he had with Chaz. I looked down at him, and he craned his neck around to look up at me in this very adoring and adorable way he has mastered.

"Are you trying to remind me of Chaz? Of why I came out here in the first place? Were you trying to get me to focus on the task at hand, the e-mail clue?" I asked/projected at him, and he stretched his head back farther, opened his eyes wider, and stuck his tongue out at me in a way that I was certain meant, "Yes, yes, that's it exactly." I wished, not for the first time, that Max could talk. I felt grateful that even though he couldn't say words, he was always proving that he was quite the master at nonverbal communication. I smiled my appreciation at the reminder and retrieved my notebook from the bottom of his bag.

No sooner had I opened it to the page across which I'd written the e-mailed clue did Max, only a moment ago so relaxed and admirably Zen, become suddenly agitated. He charged off in the direction of the Great Lawn. Unfortunately for Max, less so for me, his progress was cut sadly short by the other end of his leash, which I'd looped around my wrist. I grabbed the leash to take the sudden pressure off my wrist and I saw that Max's attention had been captured by another pug on the approach. I stood up, and as I did the notebook slid off my lap. I reached hurriedly down to get it. Not that I thought anyone was going to materialize from behind a tree or bush and snatch it, but even so, I did have the names of several of my coworkers written within it, along with an at-present-quite-cryptic clue. More than a lot of other things right then, the hippopotamus notebook was something I didn't want to lose track of.

As I retrieved it and looked back up, the approaching pug had approached. Max, still straining on his leash, was standing right in front of it. He was posturing with his thick barrel chest as if he were blocking the path like a bouncer. Even so, I could see the twitching of not only his tail but also his entire rear end, giving away his inherent nature: not so much tough guy as smoosh. As is often the case with dog people in Central Park, in all of New York, and my guess would be anywhere, I was so busy noticing the approaching dog, watching my own dog interacting with it, that it was a moment before I recognized the person on the other end of the leash. Then I did and it was Daphne Markham, wearing light pink Chanel, a lot of it, and carrying her tremendous bag. The pug that had so lured—enticed? attracted? threatened? I couldn't be certain—Max was Madeline.

"Oh," I said, a little jolted by the coincidence. "Hi."

"Ahoy!" Daphne said back to me, raising her hand and waving it in a grand, sweeping way. It was a gesture so different from her Queen Mum wave of the day before, and it seemed out of place, as we were now only a few feet away from each other.

"Ahoy," I said back. As soon as I said it, I wasn't sure if I should, if maybe Daphne was protective of the word, seeing as it was, after all, her catchphrase. I thought I saw something in her eyes when I said it. A flash of something, recognition maybe, I didn't know.

"Or, uh, not ahoy?" I added, feeling, as I sometimes did, a bit like a spaz. Daphne smiled kindly at me. We both, almost in tandem, let go of our pug's leashes. Max and Madeline scurried together underneath the benches and popped out on the other side, behind them. I turned around quickly to see them facing each other in a patch of dirt. A pug standoff, I thought, and for a moment longer I kept my eyes fixed on Max. I admit, I still wanted to be sure he wasn't going to attack.

"Sorry?" Daphne said, and it took me a minute.

"Oh," I said, trying my best to catch up with myself. I clutched the notebook in my hand, wishing I'd thought to put it away. "I just meant that I didn't mean to say 'ahoy,' if that's your thing." I heard the words coming out of my mouth and felt ridiculous. Of all the ways to start a conversation, this is what I'd chosen. It was something I had begun to do more and more lately: I wished that I could start again from the beginning.

"Oh, it is," Daphne said, tapping her hands together, as if she were starting to clap but not taking it any further than that first step. "'Ahoy' is my catchphrase. But I don't mind if other people like to say it." She paused and smiled at me. "You're right, though. I think at this point, after so many years of saying 'Ahoy' at people, I do feel that the very word is mine. And I shouldn't, you know. It's not as if one can own everything, can one?"

"No," I said. And then Daphne sat down on the bench next to me and reached over and patted my knee.

"But all 'Ahoys' aside," she said, and laughed softly, "don't you have your own catchphrase?" She inquired this of me with complete seriousness.

"Catchphrase?" I parroted, wondering if with everything else I was piling onto my plate I had room for a lesson, albeit a possibly good one, on personal branding from a septuagenarian socialite heiress museum patron? Probably not right now, I thought. "No, I don't think I do have a catchphrase," I said.

"You should think of cultivating one," Daphne advised me. And then she added, quite gravely, "Everyone should have a catchphrase."

"Yes," I agreed, nodding, because, really, what other options?

"A catchphrase," Daphne repeated. She nodded at me

again and then she looked off at the middle distance and added, "Everyone should have a catchphrase and a museum wing at the Met named after her."

A what? I waited a moment before inquiring, "A museum wing?"

"Yes, dear," she said, turning back toward me. "Everyone needs a museum wing named after her," she said, and again she patted my knee. She sighed. I wondered then if she was not as completely right in the head as I had previously deemed her to be, based solely on how much she enjoyed discussing pugs. But even with pugs aside, if pugs could ever be aside, I liked Daphne. What was not to like? I could think of nothing. She was elegant, she spoke in a lovely lilting voice, she seemed almost inexplicably fond of me, she was oft at the ready with a bon mot of advice, and she seemed to love her dog as much as I loved mine. And I know that's not a huge coincidence because I can't imagine that anyone who has a pug isn't madly in love with it, but I think what it was as much as anything else is that I was just drawn to Daphne.

"But then I imagine," Daphne continued, "you just have to try to control what you can." And knowing as I did all the wings at the Metropolitan Museum of Art, all the rooms and hallways and exhibition areas, and knowing that none of them were named after Daphne Markham, I dismissed any notion of Daphne not being fully with it. I put any thoughts of Daphne being not right in the head right out of mine. There was something she wanted and didn't have. I got that. Oh, how I got that. I felt close to her right then—closer, that is, than our present immediate proximity and shared love of pugs. Sometimes I lose sight of the fact that people, no matter how different they may seem, might actually be so alike. There, sitting in Central Park with Max and Daphne and Madeline, with eponymous museum wings and stolen paintings to be found and everything else, I thought—in a way that almost took my breath away—that everyone had things they wanted, things they might not ever have, but hoped for and tried for anyway, even someone like Daphne Markham.

"Right," I said, as if I were in complete agreement. "Absolutely." Though I was not at present at all desirous of my own museum wing, unless of course somewhere within it I would come across the actual Fantin-Latour as opposed to the fake one, I was no stranger to having things out there on the horizon that I wanted. I've never been a stranger to the quest.

Madeline and Max scurried up in front of us. Daphne reached down and scratched the top of Madeline's head. I did exactly the same thing to Max. After I scratched the top of his head, I used both hands to get behind his ears just the way he likes best. I don't think she had seen me do it, but Daphne leaned down and did the same to Madeline. Our movements were almost mirror images, like a water ballet only performed on a bench, with pugs.

"Well," I said, once cultivated catchphrases and museum wings seemed covered for the moment, "it's very nice to run into you again."

"Yes, well, I used to walk Madeline in the park every day at four thirty, but now because my Pilates got switched round, I've been walking her later, around five thirty."

I loved three things about that sentence, in order of appearance: that Daphne took Pilates, that she said "switched round," and that she was as much a pug-walking creature of habit as I was. I realized, a second too late, that I was still white-knuckling the notebook in my hand, holding on to it in a way that was bound to draw attention to it. Maybe that was what I wanted. I'm sure it must have been; from the start, all I'd wanted was someone to talk to. I wonder sometimes if, all along, it had only been a matter of time before I told Daphne all about it.

"What's that?" Daphne asked, looking down at the notebook in my hand.

It crossed my mind to say, "Oh, nothing. Oh, it's just a notebook," and slide it back into my bag. But I didn't. I looked at the notebook once more, as if maybe William the Hippopotamus would come to life, look over at Daphne, and answer the question himself. I opened the notebook, turned to the page across which I'd written out the e-mail clue, and then looked right at Daphne, straight on, and said, "I think it's a clue."

Daphne's eyes brightened at the word "clue," and then she reached her hands up and clapped a few times quickly. Both Max and Madeline, who had each moseyed slightly off again, turned around and barked at us a few times. Then both pugs charged back over to us, reminding me again of Pug Night. Max planted himself on Daphne's foot and craned his neck around in order to look up at us, wild-eyed. He looked first at me and then at Daphne and then back to me, and I imagined that he was saying, "Look, look, I like her now, too!" Madeline tried and failed to jump onto the bench and then, determined, busied herself with clawing at the bench as if she believed that if she scratched it enough, it might become easier to summit. I smiled. There was something at once inspiring and deeply humorous about her resolve. Stifling a laugh, Daphne swooped down and grabbed Madeline securely under her front legs and lifted her up and off the ground and then aloft in the air above.

"How's my gorgeous, gorgeous girl?" Daphne asked Madeline. Madeline, for her part, looked ecstatic and wiggled the entire lower portion of her body in what I believed was her way of saying, "Thanks for the lift." Then, as Daphne lowered Madeline onto her lap, I worried that the focus had been taken off my clue, that Madeline had, in no small way, stolen my thunder. I shifted my gaze down to Max, sporting one of his more attractive tongue-lolling-out-of-his-mouth expressions.

Daphne turned back to me, clapped quickly, and said, "Now, tell me." She widened her eyes and smiled. "What's this about a clue?" *Good,* I thought. *This is good.*

"Well," I began, "it's all a bit of a mystery to me at this point, which I guess is where the clue comes in."

"I do love a mystery!" Daphne exclaimed, and she began to count things off on her fingers as Madeline looked on, rapt. "I love an Agatha Christie. I mean, who doesn't?" she asked before moving on to the next finger. "I loved Nancy Drew as a girl, and what about P. D. James? I was just last week reading her book *Talking About Detective Fiction.* Have you read it?"

"No, I haven't," I said, thinking I wasn't at all sure why. Daphne leaned in an inch or two closer.

"Dear? Are you trying to solve a murder?" she asked, with what I feel safe in saying was probably too much glee.

"Oh, dear God, no," I said quickly. "No," I repeated. "No murder. I just need to find something that's missing."

"I see," Daphne said, looking less enthusiastic now that it wasn't a murder, and not terribly interested in concealing her disappointment. "Well," she continued, as if she were struggling to stifle a yawn, "can't win them all, can you?" Without realizing I was doing it, but doing it all the same, I tilted my head and looked at her funny. I don't think she noticed. If she did, she didn't care. "May I see your clue anyway?" she asked, and my brain lingered for a moment on the "anyway."

"Yes," I said, and handed over the notebook. As she held it upright in front of her face and squinted at the words I'd scrawled across the page—*First things first: Up half, walk around*—I told myself I trusted her. I told myself that at this point I had to trust someone, even if just a little bit. I first took a breath and then blurted it all out. "A forgery, an almost perfect forgery showed up in the Conservation Studio, and a painting is missing, a small painting. I'm trying to figure out what happened exactly, and of course, there are museum officials involved." I lied a little bit, lest Daphne get all Woody Woodpecker about the whole thing and suggest going straight to the police. I probably didn't have to; for some reason I couldn't put my finger on, it didn't seem like something she'd suggest. Regardless, I left out the name of the painting. I thought it was best.

I continued, "But seeing as it's my department on the line here"—*and seeing how it could very well turn out to be my ass on the line*, I thought but didn't say—"I need to figure out what happened to the real painting, where it went."

Daphne turned away from the notebook and looked at me, right at me, seriously, as if she were trying to figure something out, too. I realized I had believed that the moment I told someone about this, I would feel tremendously relieved. I didn't. I felt the opposite: even more flustered. But still, I soldiered on.

"I think that someone else wants me to figure out where the real painting is, too, because this arrived today, this clue.

It said if I followed, I'd have my answer," I explained, gesturing at the notebook now resting in Daphne's lap. Daphne picked the notebook back up and stared eagle-eyed at it again. She turned back to me and began to speak.

"I went to a benefit once at the Met and it was a scavenger hunt. It was divine." For a bad moment I feared this was an unwelcome non sequitur. I had begun to suspect that Daphne might be prone to the non sequitur.

I looked at Daphne and waited—politely, I hoped. Daphne looked back at me, moved her head from one side to another, blinked a few times, and looked as if she were waiting for me, too. She exhaled.

"Dear," she said next. "Did it occur to you perhaps that maybe this clue has something to do with a scavenger hunt?" She handed the notebook back to me, and as I held it in my hands and looked down at it, she leaned over to point to the words, specifically touching her index finger down on "up" and "around."

"See, those," she said, "those are direction words, and they remind me very much of the clues we had at the fundraiser scavenger hunt. It was divine," she repeated, and I thought in a rush, *fund-raising, Gil,* and that Daphne might be on to something. And then I looked up at her and thought, of course she must be on to something. I held the notebook closer to my face, peered down at it, and thought, *Yes, yes, scavenger hunt.*

"Thank you," I said, turning to face her. "Thank you so much."

"Well, don't thank me yet. I could be entirely wrong," Daphne demurred. I was tempted to ask her if the directions looked familiar, if they jogged any sort of memory for her, if the clue was similar in other ways to the clues she'd received at a fund-raising event and if perhaps she knew if Gil—Gil!—had had anything to do with those clues. I held back; I didn't ask her that. I was at once so much less flustered. I was grateful—energized, thrilled—that I'd thought to show Daphne my notebook, or that the universe had thought to show her my notebook, whichever it actually was. But still I hesitated to get someone so close to the museum any more involved than necessary, not just yet. Though a part of me wanted this all done with as quickly as possible so that I could go back to my life in which my only illegal activity had been smuggling my pug into the museum, I thought that now that I'd been shown the start of the path, I might be able to find my way on my own. I thought, *Don't look a gift horse in the mouth*, or rather, *Don't look a gift socialite heiress museum philanthropist in the mouth*.

I closed the notebook and put it away. There would be time to study the clue in this new light later. I turned back to face Daphne.

"Thank you," I said again, and because I wanted her to know it was really heartfelt, I continued. "Just so you know, I've really needed to talk about this, and for all these different reasons, I haven't been able to talk to anyone, so, thanks."

Daphne smiled back at me. "My pleasure," she said. "And also, dear?"

"Yes?" I answered.

"I've always found, with scavenger hunts and of course with much bigger things, too, with all aspects of life, it is always—and I do mean always, dear—important to listen to your inner voice."

I nodded. *Inner voice*, I thought, perhaps without fully wrapping my head around what exactly it was. "Inner voice," I said out loud, as if maybe the act of doing so would make it so that I might be the type of person who not only heard her inner voice but knew how to listen to it.

"Yes, listen to it," Daphne said, with a nod of her own.

"Listen to it," I repeated.

"You'll be surprised once you do," Daphne continued, "how many other things will make sense." She gave me a wry smile. Right then, I believed her to be Yoda—a much more elegant and beautifully attired Yoda, but still, in her way, Yoda.

"And I'd remember this," Daphne continued. "No matter what anyone tells you, what you always have to do in these situations is consider the very high likelihood that the butler did it." She nodded her head authoritatively, and I noticed a gleam in her eye.

"The butler did it?" I asked.

"Always worth looking into," Daphne said, and she looked at me so seriously for a moment and I didn't know why. I looked back at her and tried to process what she had just said. There were no butlers at the Metropolitan Museum of Art, but even as I thought this, I wondered if this was the universe's way, via Daphne, of suggesting I extend my search into the various dining rooms throughout the museum. Only, and I was sure waiters would be with me on this one, I didn't think a waiter, even a waiter in the private members' dining room, was anything like a butler. I checked anyway.

"Do you mean waiters?"

She didn't consider it for very long. Her answer was quick. "No, that's not what I mean."

I looked back at Daphne, at Madeline stretched out on her lap, gazing up at her with an adoring pug look on her face. I looked away from them and down at Max, who still had himself planted firmly on top of Daphne's needlepoint loafer. I noticed by looking at the loafer not covered completely by my pug's hindquarters that the design on the front was a skull and crossbones. *Interesting choice,* I thought. I also thought, *Yes, Max, I totally get it, you like Daphne now.* I turned back to Daphne and said, "I've never known anyone who had a butler."

Daphne looked out across the Great Lawn, absentmindedly massaging Madeline's head as she did so. Madeline closed her eyes three-quarters of the way and swayed and pressed back into Daphne's palm, giving off the appearance of a large pug bobble-headed doll. After a while, Daphne turned on the bench to more fully face me and said without a hint of snobbishness or condescension, more just matter-of-factly, "Yes, I'm sorry, dear. I suppose you haven't."

Madeline jumped off Daphne's lap and sprinted a few feet away, and Max jumped up off Daphne's loafer to run after her. Daphne and I sat there together for a while longer watching our pugs sniff at a nearby tree. We didn't say anything more about clues or butlers or the fact that there weren't any butlers at the Met or elsewhere as far as I knew.

Though part of me wanted to go, to do nothing so much as lock myself in a room with my notebook and a pen and maybe a map of the museum until I figured everything out, that part of me took a backseat to the fact that sitting there with Daphne watching my pug have a playdate was lovely. I needed a little bit of lovely. My mind had been in over-drive, possibly ineffectual overdrive, for the better part of the past three days, and I relished simply sitting for a little while. And that was all it would be. In about the amount of time it had taken me to settle, to relax, I remembered.

I remembered that later on I had a date to Skype with Ben, scheduled a week ago. Ben could rarely get access to a laptop or an Internet connection, so a Skype date was a rare treat. I wondered how I could have forgotten it for a minute, let alone the better part of a day.

I shook Max's leash at him and called out, "Max." He looked up at me. I believe he considered coming over to me, but ultimately he chose to stay focused on Madeline and the yonder tree. I got up from the bench and turned to Daphne. "This has been so nice sitting here with you," I said. "But I've actually got to get heading home now."

"Ah, yes, I think I should, too," Daphne said, getting up alongside me, at which point Madeline, followed closely by Max, ran up to us.

"Okay then," I said as I bent down to hook Max's leash to his collar, "Bye." I raised one hand in the air.

"Ahoy!" Daphne replied gleefully, and if I hadn't just had a conversation with her in which she'd seemed so sharp and so intuitive, if I hadn't been so energized by the fact that I was sure she'd been the very first crack in my case, I would have maybe applied the word "batty" to the way she had just blurted out "Ahoy," a greeting, even though we were saying good-bye.

"'Ahoy' can mean good-bye, too," Daphne said next, and I thought of Chaz, the way he'd looked sharply at me the moment I'd thought him dim, and I wondered if this was maybe one more thing I didn't know—the fact that everyone I'd met recently could read my mind. "I like to think of it much in the same way the Italians think of 'Ciao,'" she told me. "It can mean two opposing things. Both hello and good-bye at once." I nodded in agreement. That appealed to me, one word with two divergent meanings, just like how the same thing could be right, and still wrong.

I smiled back at Daphne and Madeline. I hoped Max and I would run into them again soon, and then I said to her, "Ahoy."

chapter nine

Ode to a Grecian Chick

"We're going to see Ben as soon as we get home!" I said to Max in order to hurry him through the last leg of our cross-park journey home.

As we walked together into our building, up all the stairs, as I finally turned the key in the door, I got a glimpse at my watch. It was, somehow, much later than I had thought. That kept happening. I unlocked the door and Max went charging into the living room, all "Daddy's home" in the way he used to do when Ben lived here. As the front door slammed behind us, a tribal mask that had recently arrived from Ben fell off the wall where I had only just hung it. Max stopped and stood stock-still in front of it. He tilted his head at it.

"That's from Ben," I said, with as much assurance as I could. "You remember: Now we know Ben's thinking of us." Though that last part may have been blurted out a bit too fast in order to actually achieve the soothing quality for which I'd been aiming. I dove for my laptop on the desk, bringing it with me to the couch as I powered it on. I hoped it wasn't too late. I thought how good it would be to see Ben, to talk to Ben. It always was, even if it wasn't in person. But today it would be even better. I relished the thought of a block of time that didn't have anything to with the museum and the Fantin-Latour. Ben might only be able to see me through the lens of his Skype, but if I had anything to do with it, he wasn't ever going to see me through the lens of my obstruction of justice and criminal activity.

Max jumped up onto the couch with me, all exuberance and joy. As I opened Skype, it was almost as if I could already see and hear Ben saying, "Hey, buddy! Hey, buddy!" to Max through the computer screen, the way he always did. Hands down, Ben had mastered the enthusiastic hello.

My Skype screen was dead. I'd missed him. I exhaled heavily, and as I did, Max, always so aware of everything that was happening around him, exhaled in exactly the same way. On the couch next to me he circled three times and then flopped down and curled himself up into a ball. I wished I could do the same thing.

"I know, honey," I said. "I know." I clicked over to my e-mail and there, as I'd hoped, was an e-mail from Ben.

Hey, it began. *Sorry I missed you. Would have loved to see you and your pug coworker. Everything's good. This is hard. Thanks again for taking such good care of Max. I miss you. I love you. Two months, Ben.*

I shook my fist at the computer. I exhaled and typed back. I missed him, too. I loved him, too. *All is well here, too,* I lied. And then I signed off: *Two months, Hope.*

I tried to console myself that maybe right now wasn't the best time to talk to Ben anyway, because if my conversation with Pamela had been any indication, I ran the risk of being completely weird. Though I shuddered at the thought of posing such a lame hypothetical via Skype to Ben—so, say you're dating a lawyer and you're involved in something totally illegal, right? If that lawyer happens to live in say, the Congo, are you somehow less reprehensible?—it was a small consolation. I flipped the laptop closed and put it down on the other side of me from Max. Max popped up, surely sensing that with this activity over before it began, dinner could be next.

"Who's a good boy? Who's a good boy?" I asked him, trying to evoke the way Ben sounded when he greeted Max, but it came out sounding less like Ben and more like Daphne, inquiring of Madeline, "How's my gorgeous, gorgeous girl?" Pugs, with all their outstanding qualities, do call up these kinds of questions.

I fed Max dinner, giving him a few more pieces of grilled chicken mixed in with his kibble than usual. Max always has either grilled chicken or poached salmon mixed in with his meals; otherwise he doesn't eat them. I didn't prepare my own dinner anywhere near as lovingly. I took a microwave dinner out of the freezer, and even though it was an organic microwave dinner, acquired from the newly opened Trader Joe's, I was loath to think about how many dinners I'd been eating out of a cardboard box lately. But still, it was late, and it had been a day, to say the least, and so I took out a hint of aggression setting the timer on the microwave and ate.

As soon as I was done, I went to the newest African mask, which had been lying in the corner since we'd walked in. I picked it up and placed it on the desk, angling it against the wall. I looked at it for a moment. "Hey, Ben," I said. No answer.

"Hey," I said, turning back to Max. "I guess let's look at the clue a little bit longer." I've learned a lot of things from Max. Among them, that when you live alone with a dog, you tend to talk to him about a great variety of things. And not only that, you do this and it helps. No matter what the problem. I walked across the room to grab the hippopotamus notebook from where I'd stashed it and brought it back with me to the couch. Max sprawled on my lap and looked up at me. I angled the notebook behind him and opened it up to the page with the clue.

First things first, I read out loud. *Up half, walk around, and there you'll see what happens after summer.*

I stared at it for a moment. Then, trying not to disturb the already softly snoring Max, but still disturbing him a little, I got up and crossed the room, went into the kitchen, and poured myself a large glass of wine. As I took a long first sip, I was more than a touch surprised I hadn't done this the moment I'd walked in the door. It had, after all, been a day. It had been a few days, come to think of it. I walked back to the couch, took one more sip of my wine before putting it on the coffee table, and returned to my notebook. I was not, however, with my notebook or my glass of wine for long. In somewhere between three and five seconds, I think, just like Max, I drifted off to sleep.

*   *   *

I had a dream that night, a really vivid one about Ben and Max and dinner and the heist. In the dream, Ben didn't live in Kinshasa, but the painting had still been stolen.

In the dream I walked into the living room and sat down on the couch right in between Max and Ben.

"Do you want to order from Burritoville?" Ben asked me. Granted, since this was a dream and all, it would have been nicer had Ben turned to me and said any number of things: "I'm back from Kinshasa for good." "We're going on a trip to Cabo." "Will you marry me?" (Whoa! Where did that come from?) But since you can't control dreams any more than you can control life, my dream about Ben began with a burrito.

"No, I don't think I want a burrito," I said, even though I am generally of the mind, and so is Ben, that who wouldn't want a burrito from Burritoville?

"I could make chicken," I offered, and Max, who had been noticeably unfazed by the mention of Burritoville, a word I am certain is part of his vocabulary, jumped up between us and fixed me with a stare.

"Ode to a Grecian Chick?" Ben asked, and smiled, referencing my chicken dish, one of the few items in my repertoire. Max spun around on the couch and faced Ben. In the dream, as in life, Ode to a Grecian Chick is a favorite of both Ben and Max. It has olives and feta cheese and tomatoes. It's almost impossible to mess up, so unlike other aspects of my life outside this dream.

I made my way into the kitchen and cubed chicken and sliced olives and tomatoes and waited for the pan to heat up. I started throwing ingredients into the pan. Max ambled into the kitchen, as is his way if anything at all is going on in that room. And he looked up at me, just as he so often does. And then he started to talk. Really. He started to talk.

"First things first," he said to me. "Up half, walk around." His voice was a little scratchy; it sounded older than his one and a half years, but there was also something lilting and lyrical about it, and something, just like Max in general, that was very, very sweet. And the thing was, because this was a dream, and also because I think I've often thought of a moment like this ever since I met Max, it wasn't weird at all. I didn't question. I just started talking, too.

"The clue?" I said.

"Yes," he said, and he sounded very serious, very—dare I say it—wise. "Sometimes repetition can be helpful," he suggested.

And so, because why not, I looked right at him, and I repeated it. "Up half, walk around. Up half, walk around."

"Up half, walk around," Max said again, and continued to look up at me. I didn't dare take my eyes from his. And then, just like that, it hit me. "Oh my God, Max," I said. "The mezzanine?"

"The mezzanine," Max said, and he nodded.

"The mezzanine!" I said back to him again, much louder. Max didn't say anything. I was the one who spoke next.

"Oh, shit!" I said, jumping back from the sauté pan and leaning down to plant a kiss on the top of Max's head. "That's it! Of course! 'Up half' has to mean mezzanine, right?" Max didn't answer, but he didn't have to.

Then Ben, the wonderful dreamlike, non-Kinshasa-living Ben, walked into the kitchen and said, "Hope." I turned and saw his expression. It was more perplexed than anything else. Before I could answer him the smoke alarm went off.

Only it wasn't the smoke alarm, it was the wake-up

alarm trilling from my night table. I realized I had spent the entire night on the couch with Max, and then I remembered the dream.

"Max?" I said. I waited for a moment, just in case he had a response. I mean, of course I had to check. Surely anyone would? Max didn't say anything. As much as I have at times thought it might be nice if Max could talk, I was almost relieved that he didn't say anything then. Max, never a jump-out-of-bed type, looked at me for one more moment, then curled back up and went to sleep again.

I sat there on the couch, in the early morning, still in my clothes from the day before, and replayed the dream in my mind. *Mezzanine,* I thought, *mezzanine.* The Metropolitan Museum of Art does indeed have a mezzanine. There's a hidden-away quality to it; it's very nooklike and one of my many favorite places in the museum. Much of the museum's collection of contemporary art is there. Damien Hirst's bisected shark in a fish tank is there. I hoped that this had nothing to do with Damien Hirst. The word "mezzanine" buzzed through my brain like that first springlike day after a long winter, the one where it seems like every last pasty person in New York is wandering around dazed in Central Park in shorts and flip-flops. Like those days, though it was pale and weak, cautious and possibly fleeting, for a moment everything felt right, for a moment it felt like I was on to something.

I remembered what Max had told me, how repetition

could be helpful, and so I repeated it a few more times in my head. Over the din of Max's snoring and the alarm still beeping from the sleeping alcove, the words *what happens after summer* popped once again into my head. An answer so obvious, so clear, so definitely the right one was there. Autumn happens after summer! I closed my eyes and pictured the museum's mezzanine and as I did, I saw Jackson Pollock's painting *Autumn Rhythm* hanging there.

I jumped up. Max opened one eye and looked at me. I gave him a thumbs-up and said, probably louder than he appreciated at this early hour, "Answers!" Max, sensing my enthusiasm, or maybe just ready for breakfast, roused himself. I ran to my night table and turned off the alarm. I flew into the shower. I couldn't wait to get to the museum.

chapter ten

Friday Morning
at the Museum

As soon as I was out of the shower, I hurried back into the living room and grabbed my cell phone to text Max's sometime dog walker to see if he was free. I didn't have to wait for long. I'm convinced that Max's dog walker has a microchip embedded in his brain that allows him to text back simply by thinking of a response. He's that fast, and even better, he was available to walk Max the customary two times that day. Though I was understandably loath to leave Max at home for the day, I thought it might be easier at the museum without him. Who knew what I might discover now that I had (hopefully) solved the clue. And also, the two long walks Max would get with his walker would be an excellent start to the exercise regime I'd been not exactly on top of implementing. I thought of the pug portrait for Ben I really needed to remember not to forget.

I took a taxi to the museum to get there as quickly as I could. Even though there aren't that many stops between my apartment and the museum, just a straight shot across the Eighty-sixth street transverse of the park, it was a ride that felt interminable. I felt anxious, eager, rushed even though no one was rushing me. I leaned back in the taxi and looked not at the scenery whizzing by outside my window, but down at my lap. I brushed countless little black pug hairs off my light gray dress and wished for the thousandth time that Max didn't shed copiously, everywhere. In addition to his power snoring, Max is a world-class shedder. It is a wonder that the pug has any hair left on his body. And then, because the visual of a hairless pug is not a nice one, I made myself stop thinking along those lines.

The taxi pulled to a stop outside the museum at last. I paid the driver and sprinted into the museum. I sped to the south side, to the stairs that would lead me, halfway up, to the mezzanine. I walked up the half flight of stairs and then, on the landing there, I paused. A few more steps and I'd be there. A few more steps and I'd be looking at Jackson Pollock's *Autumn Rhythm*. Though my pace had been fervent since the instant I'd woken up that morning and though I'd been raring to go since long before that, I needed a moment. I stopped. I took a deep breath. I let it out. This may have already been made apparent but I can at times be dramatic, and right then, I was.

I ascended the rest of the staircase with a sense of great purpose. I closed my eyes and walked around the corner. I opened them. And there it was: Jackson Pollock's tremendous canvas, gray with white drips and black drips, all frenetic energy to match the energy of my quickly beating heart. I stood directly in front of it and looked up at it, all genius and brilliance and madness at once. I stayed there, standing in front of the painting, and kept looking. Maybe it was some sort of small mercy that it took me a moment to realize that was all I was doing: standing in front of a painting, monumental though it was, and looking at it.

No lightbulbs went off. Neither answers nor missing Fantin-Latours appeared to be forthcoming. I looked over to the wall label for the painting and read over the title, date, dimensions, and medium. I turned to the page of art historical information typed up on a bigger card next to the wall label. I read every line twice. My heart raced and my mind raced and I hoped against hope (oh, the pun, it was so intended) that there would be a secret message, some sort of answer, anything that would lead me somewhere. I read every line again. But there wasn't anything, there was only text detailing Pollock's process, the painting's importance and great art historical significance. Nothing at all about a Fantin-Latour of pansies and who might have stolen it.

There were only words I'd already read so many times before.

It was like watching a movie you'd already seen, the kind of movie that at first you're excited to see but then soon enough you say to yourself, "Oh, I've seen this before." That moment when enthusiasm gets lost somewhere in the middle of disappointment. It was like that but it wasn't; there was one big exception. When you see a movie for the second time, you know everything that's going to happen; you know what the ending is going to be. As I stood alone in the museum in the early-morning stillness, alternating between staring at Jackson Pollock's drips and looking around the empty, silent room, I had no idea about the ending. I couldn't come close to saying what was going to happen next.

I endeavored to stay positive. I took care to remind myself that sometimes, a lot of times, things don't fall into place all at once. This is true in life and in art heists. As I turned to make my way back to the Conservation Studio, to the center of all of this, I hoped that though Jackson Pollock's *Autumn Rhythm* had not been the answer to everything, it could turn out to be the answer to something. It wasn't the final piece of the puzzle, no, but that didn't mean it couldn't be a part of it.

A piece of the puzzle, I thought again. I closed my eyes and heard Daphne telling me about the scavenger hunt here, the one she'd said was divine. Scavenger hunts were a process. One clue led to another. Like so many things, answers led to more questions; not everything happened at once.

I turned back to the painting and looked all around me to make sure I was still alone. I was. I continued scanning the room for something, anything. Something that would lead me somewhere else. Anything that would lead me to the answers. I laid myself down flat on the floor and looked one way and then the other, a foolproof way to find lost earring backs and a great many other things, but yet it did not unearth anything at all from the spotless, shining museum floor. I walked the length of the painting and then flattened myself against the wall, peering as best I could into the space between the painting and the wall.

There, I saw it: a small sheet of paper, folded in thirds like a miniature letter, tucked perfectly between the Pollock's frame and the wall. I looked left and looked right. Still pressed up against the wall, I walked sideways, a few steps closer to the painting. I reached behind the frame with the edge of my pinky and dislodged the paper, then scurried after it as it fell to the ground. I picked it up and held it in front of me: a thick, heavy stock paper; I unfolded it. There—maybe it was a gift from the universe, or maybe it was just from someone who'd decided to help me catch a thief—was another clue. It was written in black ink, in a beautiful script. It was just one word: *William.* I breathed in. I believe I may have grinned. This was good. This was too good. There was only one thing it could be.

On the first floor of the museum, in the Egyptian wing, there is a statuette of a bright blue hippopotamus from the Middle Kingdom Dynasty. He is unofficially called William. He is the very hippopotamus on my notebook. I pulled my notebook from my bag and looked at William the Hippopotamus on the cover. I knew William; of course I knew William. Anyone who had anything to do with the Metropolitan Museum of Art, or had even just popped into its gift shop once, just as I had a few days ago to buy my notebook, knew William.

I thought of the real William. I could almost see him. I would go to him! I raised one hand in the air in triumph. I felt closer to something. I felt hopeful. I looked all around me again because even though I was spurred by this victory, buoyed even, I was still completely paranoid. I refolded the thick paper and slid it behind the last page of my very now apropos hippopotamus notebook. I held the notebook tightly in my hand. Though I wanted, obviously, to go right to William, I knew I needed to first make an appearance at work. I turned and headed in the direction of the studio.

Outside the door, I took yet another moment. To compose myself. To wash any look of exuberance or even (possible) triumph off my face. I didn't think it could help matters in there to walk in late, appearing all pleased with myself about something. I still stood firmly by my earlier decision not to tell anyone who might be in there anything about my clue. Now clues, plural. I couldn't trust Gil or Elliot. And Chaz, I wasn't so sure I had any faith in him.

I smoothed down my hair and then the front of my dress. I slid my ID card and walked into the studio. Elliot was there, of course. He was standing in front of the stationery closet, with both of his hands in his pockets, staring at the shelves of office supplies and art restoration materials, razors, bottles of pigments, loupes, an almost uncountable stash of every imaginable type of paintbrush. It was just a supply closet; there was no stationery in it at all, but our old boss, May, had always called it the stationery closet, so I always had, too. I called it that even now, long after she'd left. I thought about how things might be different now if May were here. I wondered if May would have gone straight to the police. May would never have allowed such a toxic, festering environment to go on unchecked. May would tell me where Sergei was, or at least she'd care that he seemed to be missing. As Elliot took his hands out of his pockets, stepped back, and sighed before slowly pushing the stationery closet door shut, I wondered if he even called it a stationery closet. I suspected he didn't. The stationery closet was a good thing, and Elliot, I very much believed this, didn't recognize a good thing when he saw it.

As the door of the stationery closet, or supply closet, or

whatever the hell it was now called, clicked into place, Elliot turned and saw me standing there behind him. I needed to talk to him. And also, I needed to think about his motives. I needed to get an answer to the now-burning question, where the hell was Sergei? I knew I needed to do this, and soon, but first I wanted to document my clue. He tilted his head slightly and furrowed his brow.

"Hi, Hope," he said. The way he looked at me, so squinty, made me think that if Elliot was not the culprit and, like me, Elliot had his own ongoing investigation, I was a prime suspect in it.

"Elliot," I said, forgoing any salutation at all because when faced with the choices of "Hi," "Hello," "Hey," or even "Good morning," I was unable to decide which one might sound the most innocent.

As I turned and walked over to my workstation, I was surprised to see Chaz by the back door of the studio, dusting the doorknob for fingerprints. It was not as if I was aware of some new technological advancement in the gathering of fingerprints; I had no way of being sure that detectives don't still dust for fingerprints all the time, but there was something in the way that Chaz hunched over the doorknob, gingerly brushing at it, that struck me as archaic. Fingerprint gathering from that door struck me also as pointless, seeing as I was the only person who ever used it. And then it didn't seem archaic or pointless at all but, rather, anxiety producing and slightly scary. The only fingerprints

Chaz was going to get off that door were going to be mine! Though the answers remained elusive, the angst did not.

"Hi, Chaz," I said.

"Hi, Hope," he said, turning around and looking at me, jutting his chin out in my direction, a substitute wave as he never removed his gloved hands from the doorknob. I lingered for a moment on his gloved hands. The gloves he wore looked exactly like the white cotton gloves we wore to handle works on paper.

Chaz must have followed my gaze because suddenly he held his hand aloft, smiled, and said, "Borrowed a pair!" I smiled back. Chaz didn't turn back to his task. Instead he tilted his head just slightly to the left. He knitted his brows together, and I realized that he was looking at me in exactly the way that Elliot had been looking at me a moment ago. I stared back at him as, with his right hand, the one he'd held up in the air, he made the shape of a gun.

"Chk-chk," he said as he pointed his "gun" at me and pantomimed pulling the trigger.

I turned quickly away and hurried over to my workstation. Before I could get there, however, I heard the beep go off indicating that someone was entering through the front door of the studio. I stopped. I felt a little frozen as I heard the soft metallic whoosh of the door opening and then clicking shut again. There was Gil, resplendent in a three-piece navy blue pinstripe suit. Once again, just in the way that pugs know that it's going to thunderstorm long before it does, I knew exactly what was going to happen next. First Gil craned his neck and looked around the room. He walked a few steps and peered over a partition, possibly scouting for a rogue pug. Then Gil tilted his head just slightly to the left and furrowed his brow. He looked at me the same way that Elliot and Chaz had looked at me, in that way that relayed something more than a garden-variety suspicion. I'd worked at the Met for years with nary a criminal thought; I'd called Elliot the moment I suspected the fake, when, really, if I'd wanted to steal the painting, why would I have left such a calling card—and for that matter, why would anyone?—but, still.

I felt dizzy. I didn't know which way to look. My paranoia was on a crash course with my persecution complex. If their logic was what I thought it was, their logic was totally twisted. But I'd been seeing for a while now that logic could often be. As I stood in the middle of the room where I had worked for so many years, I worried deeply that they'd all blown past suspicion. Suspicion was somewhere in the rearview mirror and they were fast approaching certitude. And the certitude they were speeding toward was this: Someone had stolen the Fantin-Latour and that someone was . . . me.

chapter eleven

Keep Track

I swiveled my stool more fully in the direction of my computer. As soon as I had my mouse in my hand, I clicked immediately on my e-mail program and clicked the send/receive button there a few times in a row. Nothing.

I opened up my bag and took out my notebook once again. I opened it up to a new, blank page, grabbed a pen, and wrote "*Autumn Rhythm*, Jackson Pollock, 1950." I wrote the name of the painting before I wrote Jackson Pollock's name because if there are two types of people, those who think the artist is more important than the art and those who think the art is more important than the artist,

I'm camped in the latter group. I didn't write about William yet; I wanted to be sure. I wasn't sure I needed any of this, but I wanted to keep track. I closed the notebook and looked up. I saw that Gil had, thankfully, vacated the premises.

Gil's absence made me feel ever so slightly more relaxed, but no sooner than it did, I saw that Chaz had taken his iPhone out of a pocket of his blazer and was typing something on it. The anxiety and stress returned like one of those cats that people drop off miles away from where they live, but still they find their way back. I considered the merits of calling out across the room, "Yes, you're over there dusting my fingerprints, but that's not helping! I'm the only one who ever uses that door, and I used it the night of the crime, but not to commit the crime!" I'd worked in this room for the entirety of my career; my fingerprints were all over the joint. And to make matters worse, I was using words like "joint."

I wanted to leave immediately to go straight to the Egyptian wing, straight to William, but I looked up at Elliot, hunched over an easel, looked over at Chaz, bent once again over that doorknob, and remembered the way they'd all looked at me just before. Something inside me—perhaps it was my inner voice!—told me that the best thing I could do was act the way I would act on a regular day, a day when everything wasn't flipped on its head. The best thing I could do was not draw attention to myself, and if that meant staying at my desk and not taking off for distant Egyptian parts of the museum, then so be it. I determined to stay at my desk as long as Chaz was here. As soon as he'd left I'd go see William. In the meantime (oh, the meantime!), I tried to be conscientious. I turned to the Maxfield Parrish. I focused. I put in solid work studying the tear, comparing color shades, contemplating pigment, and eventually preparing to mix a matching shade.

Art restoration can be a tricky business. Doing it properly takes a great many things: education, training, years of practice. It also takes focus, engagement, and a sufficient amount of enthusiasm combined with the right balancing amount of steadiness. I had my education and my training. I had my years of practice, but after a few hours, I felt so far away from any of the rest of it. I turned away.

As I'd been doing for the entirety of my career at the Met, I looked up, across the room, at Elliot. I'd believed for so long, throughout all of the nonrequited-love years, that not talking to him was the best way to go. Yet things were different now. Maybe everything was different now.

I climbed down from my stool and walked the length of the room. I stopped in front of Elliot's desk. I stood there for a moment, for what felt like forever, until Elliot looked up at me.

"Elliot," I said.

"Hope," he said back.

I spoke softly so Chaz couldn't hear. "I think we need to

talk about this." Elliot looked sideways, almost a parody of what a person who was both suspicious and under suspicion would do.

"I just don't think now is the time." He said it without very much of his usual pausing hesitation at all. It didn't take him a hundred years to consider every nuance of what had just been said. He was much less contemplative and thoughtful than his usual self. "Okay?" he said. He was brushing me off, I knew this, but I stayed the course, or tried to.

"I'm wondering. Do you have any sort of plan, any thoughts on what we should do?" I wanted an answer to that question and also perhaps an indication whether he, too, had been the recipient of clues. If Elliot had clues, it would mean both that he hadn't done it and also that I wasn't losing my mind.

"My plan is to let Chaz do his job," he whispered to me. It was almost a hiss. "And to hope for the best."

"Hope for the best?" I parroted.

"Yes, Hope," he said. I didn't know if he was using the word as my name or as a verb. I wasn't sure it mattered. "Sometimes that's all you can do."

Elliot looked away from me and back down to the surface of his desk in front of him. I followed his gaze, and there, on top of a pile of books, I saw something. It was a catalog from Tiffany's, and not Louis Comfort Tiffany but Tiffany's, the store. A sapphire-and-diamond engagement ring adorned the cover, and a yellow Post-it note marking a page I couldn't see stuck out from the top. Engagement rings? Elliot looking at one? I felt a pang in the part of my heart that had spent so very long pining after Elliot. I pushed it aside and thought one thing: Engagement rings are expensive. If I knew anything, I knew that art conservators are not rolling in a lot of excess expendable income. Maybe Elliot needed money. The letter M crashed into the forefront of my mind. M for "motive." And then I knew something else: Elliot was not getting taken off my list.

Elliot followed the direction of my gaze, and I saw his jaw tense as his eyes landed where mine had. *Aha,* I thought. It was not the most sly or most stealthy or most wily question I could have asked or should have asked right then, but ask it I did. "What's that?"

Elliot reached to a different area of his desk and grabbed a Jasper Johns exhibition catalog and placed it on top of his pile. Taciturn and removed once again, he paused for a few long moments and then didn't even look up at me as he answered.

"It's nothing," he said. And with that he turned and swiveled to his easel. He looked back over his shoulder at me as he did. I turned around to return to my desk, and as I did, I almost walked straight into Gil, who must have just that moment sidled right up behind me.

"Gah, Gil!" I said and stepped back, almost falling over onto Elliot's desk.

"Hope!" Gil replied, recoiling. I shook my head, as much to get the image of Gil's face out of it as anything else, and hurried back to my own desk.

"I just came to say that I can't imagine what a nightmare this is going to be if this gets out," Gil exclaimed hysterically to the room. "I can't believe this has happened!" *Not helping*, I thought, and then wondered if his outburst seemed just a bit staged. Gil wasn't getting off my list anytime soon either. I climbed up onto my stool and swiveled to my easel, thinking that I needed to go back to Elliot's desk as soon as he was on one of his rare-but-becoming-much-more-frequent excursions outside this room. I needed to have a look around. I tried to put it out of my mind for the moment and dug in for an afternoon of Maxfield Parrish.

Chaz remained with us in the studio, wandering around, looking over our shoulders, brushing things with his ridiculous brush. I lost track of time in the white-hot glare of the interminable wait to go to William the Hippopotamus. After I'd eaten a street vendor pretzel at my desk, and nearly gnawed off my hand from impatience, Chaz walked over to me.

I looked up. I wondered if now would be our interview, or worse yet, if now would be the time he'd say, "I've looked at this from every angle and the only thing that makes sense is that you took the painting. Oh, and by the way, Elliot and Gil are with me on this, too." I think I might have gulped.

"You know," he said, in lieu of anything else or worse,

"I realize I haven't given you my cell phone number. You should have it in case anything, anything at all, suddenly comes up."

"Oh," I said, relieved. "Yes, right." I grabbed my cell phone from my bag. As he rattled off his number, I typed it into my phone and saved it in my address book as "Chaz Mobile."

"Do you want mine as well?" I asked.

"No, that's okay," he said. I wasn't sure but I thought that maybe as he said that he threw a meaningful glance Elliot-ward. I tried, if not to ignore him, then at least not to let it freak me out.

"See you all tomorrow, then!" Chaz said. I held my breath as he, at last, left. I waited ten, fifteen minutes longer and then, from the cover of my desk, I surreptitiously checked for my hippopotamus notebook inside my handbag. I grabbed my ID and threw in my phone as well.

"Back soon," I said, more to the universe than to Elliot. And finally, finally, I all but sprinted across the museum to see the hippopotamus up close.

* * *

All around me were treasures from Egyptian dynasties. There in front of me, the beautiful blue hippopotamus. I stared into his deep, soulful eyes. I admired him. I admired his soft, wise expression and his flattened ears, his sweet and docile look. He reminded me of a pug. Maybe in some parallel dreamlike universe, the same one where Max and Ben and I could all have dinner together, and Max could chat it up, William the Hippopotamus was the leader of all the pugs. Maybe that was true. That, however, was not going to help me find the pansies.

I looked around the room for another clue, any clues. I looked again, closer. I didn't see anything. I turned in a slow circle to see if my eye would catch on anything that could help me, anything that maybe I had missed. There were still a few stray museum staffers and maintenance crew, so I couldn't lie on the floor to look for clues that way, or even really flatten myself against any of the display cases. I sighed.

Keep track, I reminded myself. *Keep track.* I took my hippopotamus notebook out of my bag and, right underneath the line on which I'd written out *Autumn Rhythm*'s details, I copied down William's details, too: "Hippopotamus, Egyptian, Dynasty 12, ca. 1981–1885 B.C." And then I saw it. Like a matchbook balancing a wobbly table, a piece of paper folded into a square stuck out from underneath the base of a bench in the center of the room. I got down on my hands and knees and pulled at the edge gently. I slid it out, and it was the same type of paper I'd seen before. I stood up, looked around me, and unfolded the page. Directly in the center of the sheet it said in script, *Head Sand Archive.* I had no idea. I had my work, once again, cut out for me. I folded the page back up, slid it into the back of my note-book, and hurried from the room.

As I took a shortcut, cutting through the Arms and Armor hall, I remembered how, years ago, when I had first started working at the Met, I would always get lost. That never happens to me anymore, not even in the labyrinth-like configuration of Arms and Armor.

I turned a corner that came right after a row of chain mail made for horses. There, lingering in front of a case filled with knights' helmets dating from fifteenth-century England, was Chaz. I stopped short. He stood with his hands in his pockets and was swaying back and forth from the balls to the heels of his feet. And though I could not see what it was he was looking at, something about his body language and his relaxed stance made it seem that he wasn't really looking at anything. I didn't want him to see me. I started to turn around, hoping that I could remain unseen and simply walk the other way. Before I had even barely moved, when really all I had done was think about moving, Chaz turned around and saw me.

"Hope," he said. He didn't say it loudly, not as if he'd been surprised or startled, but rather casually. His tone lacked any sense of urgency; it seemed almost as if he'd somehow expected to see me there.

"Chaz," I said, taking care to try to smile, to let that smile be a part of my voice. I wanted to look like someone who had every right to be wandering around the museum, which of course I was. I didn't want to look like a startled or paranoid or, worse than that, guilty party. Because I wasn't. I wasn't the problem; I was part of the solution—regardless of the fact that as the days ticked by, even I had to remind myself of that with increasing frequency.

Chaz didn't say anything for a while. He stood with his hands still in his pockets and stared at me. It was a while that was outstandingly long. Maybe it was one minute, maybe it was two. This might not seem like a lot of time, but go stand in an abandoned stretch of the Arms and Armor wing of the Metropolitan Museum, where, though it is subtle, there is something undoubtedly sinister in the medieval air. Stare at someone—someone who could be at that very moment building a case against you. Do that and one or two minutes will seem like forever to you, too. Chaz stood with his hands still in his pockets and stared at me. And then, he smiled at me.

"Nice to see you," he said, and something about the way he said it made my heart speed up even more than it had already sped, and that was saying something. I got a terrible unexplained feeling, and as I did, I remembered the way Max had growled at Chaz. At the time, I hadn't known what to make of it and wondered if Max just ran a bit hot and cold when it came to Chaz. There, then, as a score of knights looked on, I suddenly thought that maybe Max had growled because he suspected that Chaz did not wish me well, or worse yet, that maybe Chaz had evil in his heart? I wondered for the first time since this had started if maybe I was in the early stages of a nervous breakdown. And then,

Chaz, hands still in pockets, turned and walked past me. He ambled, really, as if down a garden path on a perfect, lazy summer day, in the direction from which I'd come.

As Chaz disappeared around a corner, something about the dim light of the after-hours museum made him seem ephemeral. A chill ran through me. And then, as if that weren't enough, I had the distinct—crazy distinct—feeling that someone had just run around the corner behind me. I whipped around, the weight of my handbag hitting me on the hip with the force of my momentum. No one was there, but I'd learned enough at this point to know that just because I couldn't see something didn't mean it wasn't there. And right then, standing in the empty museum, with Chaz down one corridor and who knew what else down another, I really started to flip out. I turned around and ran full speed ahead through the deserted, half-lit hallways back to the Conservation Studio.

I wanted nothing more than to barrel into the studio and barricade the door behind me. No stranger, however, to the school of You Can't Always Get What You Want, I had to stop right before I reached the door. I had to find my ID card. I had to try, even if I had no chance of succeeding, to take a few deep, calming breaths. I didn't think it could help anything, least of all my desire to appear innocent, to barge into the dead silence of the Conservation Studio in a full-on hysterical state in front of Elliot, who would surely— maybe?—still be there. I placed my bag on the floor and, still deep breathing without even a touch of the desired result, I reached up to smooth down my hair. In situations of either duress or humidity, to say nothing of those that are made up of both, my (red, wavy, generally I'm a fan of it) hair does go the way of extreme frizz. I attempted to smooth the front of my dress, thinking as I did how it felt like a lifetime ago that I'd pulled it out of the closet that morning.

I took one more ultimately ineffectual breath and swiped my ID card. I walked into the studio determined to do what had been steadily becoming more and more difficult to succeed at: act like a normal person in front of Elliot. *You can do this,* I said to myself. Only, as the door swooshed closed behind me, I realized I didn't have to. Elliot's workstation was empty; his computer and overhead lights were turned off. Every last piece of equipment in the studio had been powered down for the night. Granted, it was a Friday night, and granted, it had been a very long week for all of us. But still. Where in the hell was Elliot?

I flipped the row of light switches over by the door and waited there while the dim hum of fluorescence vibrated around me and the section of the studio that was home to my workstation lit up. And then, because I'd gathered all my things and turned off all my equipment before setting off to see William, and because the last thing I wanted to do was stay in there alone, I turned the lights back off and left the studio.

As I headed out of the museum, past the other guard

Belle, she glanced down at my handbag and smiled and waved me past.

"Thank you, Belle," I said, thanking her for the fact that even if Max had been with me, she'd have waved me past.

"Good night, Hope," she said. And then I thought, *Oh, God, is she on my list?* I thought of the Sherpa bag–encased pug I usually had with me and wondered if the trouble I courted every day that I smuggled Max into the Metropolitan Museum of Art was ultimately worth it. For a moment, the thought of Max alone all day, even with his two visits from the dog walker, made me, in the midst of my hysteria, deeply sad. I was, however, coming around to the possibility that there are things in life that are a lot worse than a fleeting sadness, deep or not.

As I hurried away from the museum, darkness was gathering all around me. I walked underneath the Greywacke Arch, where I would have let Max out had he been there, and found myself hoping I would run into Daphne and Madeline once again.

I didn't.

chapter twelve

It Gets Worse

There's a spot in Central Park. If you walk around the Great Lawn to the bottom, there is a turtle pond. From there, proceed up a hill until you pass a statue of a Polish king. It's a good statue. Keep walking up that hill, to the top of it, until you get to the road that cuts through the park; you're right around Seventy-ninth Street. Someone told me once that this is the highest point in Central Park. It's not. But even so, even though it's so obviously not the highest point in the park, I actually once believed it was.

On Saturday morning, Max and I were standing right at this spot, about to cross the road. The sun was already bright in the sky; both the events of the evening before and the new cryptic clue were still heavy on my mind. I leaned down to clip Max's leash onto his collar. He stuck a long, curling-up-at-the-end tongue out at me. I smiled at him and stood back up, and as I did, the sun was in my eyes. I raised my hand to shield my eyes from the sun, and for a split second I couldn't see anything. It was one of those trick moments in which time seems to stop and you feel like you're watching someone else's life instead of taking part in your own. I don't know if it actually happened this way or if this is just how I'm remembering it, but right after that, nothing seemed real. It was like believing a place was the highest point even when you had perfectly good evidence all around you that it wasn't.

Shoop, shoop, shoop. The sound came from behind me and got louder. It was the sound of someone expelling air as he accelerated, participating in some athletic pursuit. I turned away from Max to look behind me and saw just that—a man, in bike shorts, a bright green golf shirt, and a tennis visor, sprinting up the hill. It took me a moment longer to realize that the guy charging noisily up the hill like an exercise-crazed banshee was someone I knew. It was someone I knew well. It was Evan Russell, the last man I dated before Ben. Evan Russell, the last of the ex-boyfriends. It hadn't ended horribly; there were no meteors, no explosions, nothing burst into flames, no hearts were irreparably broken. Though that's not to say that it ended particularly well. But then I've never really believed people when they say things ended well because, really, how could that be? If the ending were going so well, wouldn't it eventually get to the point where you'd reconsider the merits of staying?

I looked at Evan. It was the first time I'd seen him in more than a year. I'd never once run into Evan since the night we broke up. Though I have come to believe that a lot of the time this is not the case, New York will sometimes work in your favor. Every now and then this city of eight million people will actually feel its size. Evan looked up. As eye contact was made, as he made one last athletic, exerting, exasperating shoop sound, a glint of recognition appeared in his eyes. I thought how I now had an excellent boyfriend and his beautiful pug, and here was Evan all alone with only his pursuit of athletic endeavors to keep him warm at night. And then I thought, *Only, my excellent boyfriend lives in Kinshasa right now*. But still, I did have the pug.

Evan bent down and placed his hands on his knees, looked up at me as if he were about to say, "Hut one, hut two," but instead said, "Hope. Hi. Long time."

"Hi, Evan," I said, achieving, I thought, the calm, cool collectedness that had so often eluded me when we had been together. I cursed Kinshasa and wished I could look at Evan, tilt my head just ever so slightly to the side and reach out to touch Ben's arm. "Evan," I would say, "I'd like to introduce you to my boyfriend, Ben." Instead I looked down and said, "This is Max." Evan stood up to his not-very-impressive full height and wiped the palm of his hand on his shorts as if he were going to shake Max's paw. He didn't.

"Nice to meet you, Max," Evan said, and I actually thought that was nice.

Even though Ben was there only in spirit, I thought, *See, Evan and I were never meant to be together. Evan and I were only meant to break up.* I felt happy seeing him—not happy to see him, per se, but yet happy in the knowledge that it had all worked out for the best. Perhaps I should not have thought that. Sometimes happiness doth goeth before a fall. I heard another shoop-shooper coming up the hill.

The other shoop-shooper crested the hill and came to a stop right next to Evan. She put her hands on her knees, too, just as he had. She was wearing very short Nike running shorts. She had the legs for them.

I think it was some sort of self-protective reflex. I looked away from her, from her next to Evan, and looked down at Max. Max looked up at the woman in short shorts standing next to Evan. I looked back up at her, too, just as she brought her left hand up to her face and stuck a stray strand of hair behind her ear. She was wearing an engagement ring.

I believe that Max knew a split second before I did that this woman was Evan's fiancée. I didn't want to, but I compared myself to her, and then I compared myself to Evan, and then in lightning-speed record time I compared me and Ben to Evan and this woman, and despite the staggeringly small amount of data I had to go on, despite the fact that I knew this wasn't any sort of contest, in that moment I felt like Evan had won.

I didn't want to be Evan's fiancée; not in a hundred million years would I want to be Evan's fiancée. But what it was, was that Evan and this woman standing next to him with her running shorts and her engagement ring lived in the same place. They not only lived in the same country, they lived in the same city, and were here in the same park together. I thought that I wanted to be in the same place as my boyfriend. And then, then I thought that maybe having a boyfriend wasn't enough. I wanted a boyfriend who lived in New York.

I let my gaze linger for what I imagine was a moment too long on her engagement ring. It was a very pretty engagement ring, cushion cut, a nice size. Evan's fiancée, I did not yet know her name, turned her head, ponytail swinging, and crinkled up her nose at Evan as she smiled. He looked at her in a really nice way, in a way that I don't think he even once, in all the many months we were together, had ever looked at me.

"Hope," Evan said to me, tilting his head just slightly in the direction of this woman who had just run up the hill and right into the middle of what could have been a perfectly nice day. He rested a hand lightly on her arm. She reached out and touched his hand. She gazed over at him, quite adoringly. "Hope," he repeated. "I'd like you to meet my fiancée."

Marisa. It turned out her name was Marisa. She was pretty, not hugely intimidatingly pretty, other than the terrific legs, but regular pretty. She looked nice and, as her running shorts implied, probably much better suited to Evan, an exercise nut, than I had been. It didn't make it better.

Somehow, some way, I managed not only to congratulate them but also to inquire as to when they were getting married.

"Next March," Evan told me.

"No, honey," she, Marisa, said sweetly, reaching over and placing a hand on his stomach. "Since it's April, now we can say *this* March, right?"

"Right," Evan said, gazing at her, and then I think I might have been blinded and, I hope, rendered invisible, as a ray of sunshine refracted against one of the facets of her ring. I thought of a conversation I'd had recently with Pamela in which she had wondered out loud how long you actually just date someone at our age, before you know definitively one way or the other whether it's the real thing. As I lingered for another too-long moment on the way Evan's fiancée gazed at him and the way he gazed back at her, I knew there were things I wanted in this world other than finding a stolen painting.

A few horrible minutes later, we all said good-bye. Max and I turned in one direction toward Cedar Hill, and Marisa and Evan started doing wind sprints back and forth on the path that leads up to the Belvedere Castle.

I stopped walking and looked down at Max. He noticed and stopped, too. He looked up at me. I didn't know what else to do. Even though the run-in had served as a giant spotlight on the fact that there were things I wanted other than finding the Fantin-Latour, I still really wanted to find the Fantin-Latour. But I didn't want to go to the museum because it was so likely that Elliot would be there. For all I knew, Elliot would be there and Gil would be there and Chaz would be there, too, and they'd all be waiting for me, a trap.

"We're going to keep walking, Max," I said out loud to him. Sometimes that's all you can do: keep walking. And so we did.

*　*　*

What seemed like hours later, but couldn't have been hours later because Max does not generally put up with walking for hours on end, I realized I'd followed Max, without even noticing it, right to the museum side of the Greywacke Arch. I steered him away from the Met, which he seemed to be quite drawn to. I pulled him back underneath the bridge. Though it was the last thing I needed to remember right then, I remembered how once, a long time ago, I'd worried that nothing would ever work out for me and I'd wind up a crazy pug lady with no teeth living underneath the Bow Bridge, a different, even more picturesque bridge elsewhere in Central Park. I shook the thought from my mind, quickened my pace, and emerged, in a way that I wanted to think right then was symbolic, from underneath the bridge. I felt Max's pace quicken at the other end of his leash. Not a moment too soon I saw Daphne and Madeline sitting together on one of the benches at the turn in the path. Madeline was sitting up on the bench with Daphne, and she saw us first. She sat up straight and then stood. She looked at the ground, padding back and forth from one foot to another. As she jumped down to the path and ran toward us, Max strained on his leash.

"Hey, Madeline," I said.

Daphne was already smiling up at me as we followed Madeline up the path to her. "Hi, Daphne," I added.

"Hope. Ahoy, dear," she said, and something inside me swelled up a little bit with, I'm not sure what it was, happiness I think, at running into her, at being the recipient of her affection. She patted the bench next to her, and I, perhaps a shade too eagerly, sat down.

"It's nice to see you again," I said. I wondered if maybe something like that, something about seeing people again—Ben, Evan, Daphne, Elliot—would become my catchphrase. "Sorry I had to dash off last time; I was expecting a call from Ben." Daphne looked back at me blankly, and I realized that in the few times we'd talked, I'd never even once mentioned Ben to her. I felt a pang at that realization. The world in which Daphne knew me had been, thus far, a world without Ben. I wished I hadn't phrased it that way, even if only in my mind.

"Ben's my boyfriend," I explained. Kinshasa or not, I still smiled when I said his name.

"I see," Daphne said. I wondered if the universe did.

"Daphne," I told her, "you were definitely on to something with the scavenger hunt."

"Oh, wonderful, dear," she said. "I'm so glad I could help."

"You did," I said. "It was good advice. I'm glad I took it."

"Then I'm glad you took it, too," Daphne said. "Like Mr. Markham always said, you have to see the things you want in life and take them. You have to always think of life as a bull and grab it by its horns, dear."

"Oh, Mr. Markham?" I asked.

"Yes, Mr. Markham," Daphne said, looking out across the Great Lawn as she did. "He's been gone for some time now."

"I'm sorry," I said.

"Thank you," she said,

"Is it lonely without him?" I asked, and then didn't know if I should have.

"Yes," she said. "Sometimes. But I always have my pugs, and my art." In spite of the very things that made up my present life, or maybe because of them, my first thought was, *It's not enough*. I looked at Daphne then and she smiled back at me, and I wanted nothing so much as to lean over and pat her knee as she'd once done to me. And so I did. "I'm sorry," I said.

"Thank you, dear," she said once more, and then, with a quick shake of her head, again a movement that put me in mind of the Queen Mum, she leaned in toward me. "Now, tell me, where are you in your search? Any further clues?" She brightened at the word "clues," and I thought of how nice she was, how very willing to help. I didn't think I should yet, but I thought that if things got any worse than they were, I could tell her more about the Fantin-Latour. Museum patron or not, I felt right then that other than of course Max, Daphne was the one person I could confide in.

"Well, I'm still at a loss, but that could change," I said. A little bit of optimism can always help. I tell myself this. "I've still got things to work on."

"Yes." Daphne nodded. "Things can always change." And then she turned directly to face me and said, "Ahoy." I wondered if she had to go, if she was saying "ahoy" as good-bye. I didn't want her to go. I felt better about the prospects of my case when I talked about it with her, better just from sitting with her. I'd grown so fond of her in such a short time. Yes, I do believe that all pug people may be kindred spirits on some deep pug-influenced level, but this was different; this was more. I turned slightly on the bench so that I was facing her more directly.

"Do you have to go?" I asked. Daphne looked back at

me and didn't say anything, and I wondered if maybe I'd imagined it, if she hadn't just said "ahoy." "I, uh," I continued, "I thought you just said 'ahoy'?"

"I did," she said, her eyes wide and bright as she smiled back at me.

"Oh," I said. "I thought you were saying it because you had to go, as in good-bye?"

"Yes, that's it," Daphne said. "I do have to go." And with that she looked down and began to gather her giant quilted patent leather tote bag around her. Madeline snorted from below us, a long-drawn-out inhaling snort. I felt a little frantic, and I think that was because when you realize that for a million different reasons, the one person you can talk to is a senior citizen socialite you just met via your pug, you want to make sure you'll talk to her again.

"I'll be here Monday after work, around six?" I said. Daphne, like everyone else in my life recently, inclined her head to one side and appeared to be contemplating something.

Her eyes brightened, and she said, "Oh, yes, most likely. But just so you know, dear. We do go to the bar every weekday at four."

"The bar?"

"Yes," she said. "The Bemelmans Bar at the Carlyle Hotel. Every day at four."

I thought that even though I hadn't been very good at it lately (oh, the neglected Maxfield Parrish), I did still have a job. And until I was accused of art theft by Chaz and hauled off to the clink, hopefully I'd have it a bit longer. Unfortunately, meeting up with Daphne and Madeline at the Carlyle at four o'clock on weekdays would prove difficult. And also: Dogs at the bar at the Carlyle? Even if those dogs were pugs, I had a hard time picturing it.

"You bring Madeline to the bar at the Carlyle?" I asked. Daphne didn't answer me immediately. I had at some point during my own interior monologue lost Daphne's attention once again to Madeline. I looked up quickly and located Max, a few yards away by a tree. Madeline was now in Daphne's lap, and Daphne was gazing down adoringly and scratching Madeline behind one ear and then the other, the same way I did to Max. I got a flash of myself forty years from that moment, sitting on a park bench with a pug who was not Max but would probably spend a great deal of time being compared to Max—because surely I was destined to spend the rest of my life explaining to anyone who wanted to listen, and most likely to a few people who didn't, that I had a pug once, Max, and he was one of the great ones.

Daphne turned to me and said, "Of course I take Madeline to the bar at the Carlyle. For one thing, she lives at the Carlyle."

"Right," I said. I knew that.

"It's so convenient."

"Of course," I agreed.

"And after all," Daphne continued. "The Bemelmans

Bar features all those beautiful murals of Madeline from the book *Madeline*."

"Right, of course," I said again, as if that explained everything. Maybe it did.

"It's among Madeline's favorite books," Daphne said. I nodded. I had this sensation not unlike déjà vu but different. I felt like everything that was happening to me had happened before. Only none of it had. It had all happened to someone else.

Daphne moved her hands from behind Madeline's ears to underneath her front legs. In one quick motion she lifted her into the air in front of her and laughed. Then in her lilting voice, she inquired of her pug, "How's my gorgeous, gorgeous girl?"

The universe giveth and the universe taketh away. I reminded myself it was important to never lose sight of that. Though I had been taken by Daphne's natural affinity to clue solving, and though I had only a moment ago felt Daphne to be a great calming influence and very possibly the answer to many things, I looked at Madeline suspended in midair, her bottom half wiggling rhythmically from one side to the other, her tongue hanging out the side of her mouth, and as even the most devout must do at one time or another, I acknowledged the need to sit down at some point in the very near future and examine my faith. In a lot of things.

Daphne stood up then and placed Madeline on the

ground. Max ran back over to us, barking. Daphne smiled down at him, and right before she turned in the direction of Fifth Avenue, she said, "Ahoy."

"Ahoy," I answered back, almost a reflex, if perhaps at that moment a slightly lackluster one.

"Yes, dear," she said, her voice more serious. She looked right at me with what I would have thought was great meaning if I'd had any earthly idea of what the meaning could be. "Ahoy."

chapter thirteen

The Moosie Monster

By four o'clock on Monday afternoon, I was no closer to figuring out the latest clue. I'd neglected the Parrish, neglected the pug portrait. I'd rummaged through Elliot's desk when he went to the bathroom and I'd neglected to find anything.

As I sat on my stool in the late-afternoon light of the studio, I felt knocked sideways by a powerful punch of what-the-hell-am-I-doing-ness. It was the ambiguity. It was the paranoia. It was Gil, Elliot, Chaz, maybe even Sergei. It was Ben. It was Kinshasa. It was the answers, the elusive answers, the answers I felt like I might never find. I needed to solve the third clue. And though I sensed that the best way to do that might be to set forth throughout the museum and see what jumped out at me by way of *Head Sand Archive*, I didn't do that. I gave in to the part of me that doesn't always do the best thing. I took a deep breath and went with a sudden impulse to not try to figure anything out for a minute.

Maybe it was true, maybe a watched pot never does boil. I turned off my computer. I acknowledged that at some point in the near future I needed to sit down and have a long, long talk with myself about my previously stellar but now seriously compromised work ethic. Near future, I told myself; not now.

I wrangled Max and without even bothering to say anything to Elliot—I actually wasn't sure Elliot and I were still talking—I headed for the door. As we walked past the stationery closet and Max let out a low growl from his bag, I wondered if Chaz could possibly be in there. I didn't stop to investigate.

Once we were outside, I didn't turn into the park. Instead, I walked across the vast expanse of the plaza in front of the museum steps and I headed south, in the direction of the Carlyle Hotel. I walked as quickly as I could without breaking into a run.

I hightailed it across Fifth Avenue like a pug after a fake painting. I walked down Eighty-third Street to Madison Avenue before letting Max out of his bag. Max often takes the sniffing of every spare inch of concrete very seriously and also to the extreme. That day, he didn't. He seemed to share my sense of urgency. He walked out in front of me with purpose, comporting himself in a way that was both not very typical and, as a bonus, quite speedy. Max led the way down Madison Avenue, past Agnes B, a shop that I would most definitely frequent if only I had more funds to allocate toward clothing, and then past Peter Elliot, a shop at which Gil Turner most likely spends a great deal of time. I turned my head away from the window, but not before my gaze landed on a row of madras bow ties, and hurried down the street.

Keep your eyes on the prize, I told myself, like I meant it. Eyes on the prize. The only thing was, there were so many definitions of the word "prize." The prize was, of course, figuring this whole mess out and finding the missing, real Fantin-Latour. But even as I thought of the pansies, now as illicit as the poppy fields that were impossible for everyone to cross in *The Wizard of Oz*, I knew that the word "prize" could be applied to any number of other things: to somehow breezing through these last few months of Ben in Kinshasa; to reuniting with my former work ethic and life balance; to helping Max become less rotund, at least slightly; to getting his pug portrait taken for Ben. As I waited at the light at Seventy-sixth Street across from the entrance of the Carlyle Hotel, I wondered how many things a person could keep her eye on at once before she lost everything.

The light changed, and Max and I walked into the hotel and made an immediate right into the Bemelmans Bar. I'd been here before, but not for years, and certainly never with Max. I paused for a moment at the doorway and let my eyes adjust to the darkness. The flickering candlelight made the bar seem like it was evening even though outside it was a bright and sunny afternoon. I could feel Max straining on his leash, pulling me in the direction of a corner booth where Daphne sat with Madeline beside her. Daphne saw us and raised a hand in greeting, and we crossed the room to meet them. A few heads turned; the bartender idly followed our cross-bar progress with his eyes. But it was as if nothing were out of the ordinary, as if people walked through famed New York bars with pugs every day. But then of course it was ordinary here because in Daphne's world a pug, Madeline, was in fact in this bar every day.

Madeline sat on her banquette perch next to Daphne, studiously watching our approach. Once we reached the table, she jumped down to Max's ground level and the two squared off for a moment and then circled around each other and went about their now-customary pug sniffing. Though Madeline roamed free, I held fast to Max's leash. After his recent outbursts and wild cross-room dashes, I thought it best.

"Ahoy, dear," Daphne said, smiling.

"Ahoy!" I answered back.

Daphne glanced at the leash in my hand with a look

that I believed was meant to convey that here, in her world of pugs-in-glamorous-hotel-bars, it was fine if not down-right expected to unleash the canine. I stayed frozen in my spot, clutching Max's leash like a deer in the headlights. Only the headlights were flickering candles illuminating different sections of Ludwig Bemelmans's Madeline mural on the wall. Regardless of Daphne's nod leashward, I felt uneasy about letting Max loose; I was all too aware that one unclipping action could set off a chain of events that would send everything hurtling toward the bad place. But as Max and Madeline settled down underneath the table, the worries I had about Max's comportment began to subside; in their place rose an observation of how murky the line between right and wrong could sometimes be for me.

Before I had even sat down, a waiter appeared at the booth as if from nowhere. He positioned himself directly in front of Daphne, which was next to me. He didn't even seem to notice the pugs. My gaze fell on the bowl of potato chips on the table and memories flooded back to me: the best chips in New York, salty, crispy perfection. Suddenly I had no idea why I didn't come here more often.

He looked first at Daphne. "The usual?"

"Oh, yes, thank you." Daphne beamed up at him. The waiter then turned to me with a forward-thrust chin and raised eyebrows. Though I had already determined that waiters were not the same as butlers, I thought right then of Daphne's previous, very possibly out-of-left-field assertion that it was always important to consider the possibility that the butler did it. The waiter was still looking at me. I looked back at him. Still, the waiter looked.

"Oh, uh," I said, and though I knew not what it could be, I said, "I'll have the usual as well."

The waiter bowed just slightly in my direction and retreated to the bar. Another appeared with a silver dog bowl. He put it on the floor, right next to Max and Madeline, and then opened a small bottle of Fiji water and poured it in.

"Thank you, Cooper," Daphne said. Cooper smiled and drew back as well. I thought how Max knew a pug named Cooper.

I finally sat down and smiled over at Daphne. I hoped to appear cheerful and carefree, as if I'd cruised out of work well before the end of the day just because I'd felt like it and not because I'd been sure that my head might explode if I didn't. I could feel the smile coming out wrong, remembering that in the poker game that is life, I'm not always the most skilled and savvy player. Perhaps as good a reason as any why I never should have gotten myself this far involved in a life of crime. Daphne tilted her head at me in the same way I'd seen Jack Russell terriers do at every sound they hear in Central Park, in the way I'd seen pugs do when food or loud noises presented themselves, in the way that I'd seen almost everyone in my life do when they looked at me recently.

"Is everything okay, dear?" Daphne asked me. For a

while now I'd known full well that everything was pretty far from okay. I don't know what it was. Maybe it was the disorienting feeling in the bar that it was nighttime even though I knew it to be day. Maybe it was the fact that I was sitting with my pug in a bar. Maybe it was just because I liked Daphne, but for the first time, I said it out loud.

"No," I said. As I did, Madeline reached out her tongue and began to lick my ankle. The waiter returned with two Cosmos, each arriving with a silver ice bucket in which sat a decanter of what looked to me like an entire other Cosmo. Two Cosmopolitans before five o'clock. And this is what I thought: I thought, *Nice usual.*

Daphne raised her glass. I raised mine, taking care not to slosh any of my drink over the edge. "Cheers, dear," she said.

"Cheers." I took a large, quite fortifying sip of my drink. Daphne took a daintier sip from her glass and, the moment she returned it to the table, looked back up.

"What is it?" she asked, and I didn't answer right away. Suddenly, it was too big a question. And then I knew.

"I think it's everything," I said. Daphne nodded. She nodded as if she understood precisely what I meant. She didn't say anything. I looked around the bar. It was easy to separate the tourists from the afternoon regulars. The afternoon regulars went about having their drinks. The tourists glanced in the direction of the pugs, pointed at them, and whispered to one another. All around us there was the sound of ice cubes clinking against the sides of glasses, the muffled din of conversations, the breathing and snorting of Max and Madeline below us, but I heard nothing.

All I heard was silence. I sat there on the banquette next to Daphne and looked at her. I blinked a few times in the way that I imagine people tend to blink when they have no idea what happens next.

"Tell me everything," Daphne said.

If it's possible to think breathlessly, possible that thoughts can come out winded, mine did. *Yes, yes, of course I will.* I thought it all together as if it was one word.

And then I did. I told her everything, or at least a great deal of it. I think when you are defining "everything" in the context of things told to other people, it's never exactly that. I think the closest you can get to everything is that; close to it. That's what I told her.

I left out the feeling I had of being alone in New York. I left out the fact that this had happened at her party, at Pug Night. I didn't want her to take it the wrong way. I spent some time on Ben, on what had begun to seem like the never-ending trip to Kinshasa. But even as I spoke of him, as I said I loved and missed him, I knew that I was glossing over him, speeding ahead. I still had my eye on the prize, and the prize had become defined; the prize had become only the pansies. The prize was only figuring out what had happened to them, finally understanding all the things that must have gone wrong (or depending on your perspective, right) in order for a painting to have been stolen from the Met. Inside myself I shuddered at the realization that I had, in the course of only a week, transformed into a woman possessed.

I spat it all out. I told her about the Fantin-Latour. I said the name Fantin-Latour out loud. I told her the real details of the missing pansies. I told her how there were not in fact any museum officials involved. I told her that we had not even glanced on going to the police. I told her how we were covering everything up and trying to figure it out ourselves, and I told her that was why I'd been trying to figure out the clues.

Daphne listened intently with wide eyes, nodding encouragingly at all the right places and offering up a few studied "I see"s. As everything came out, Madeline began clamoring for attention, clawing at the banquette, her toenails leaving grooves in the leather. I looked down again as Madeline hoisted herself, had momentary purchase on the banquette, and then slipped down once again. Daphne turned her attention away from me and looked down at the scrambling and flailing Madeline. In spite of my great love of all pugs and my particular fondness for the oft-maligned-when-it-came-to-reaching-higher-surfaces Madeline, I looked down and thought, *Must you, Madeline?*

"The moosie monster!" Daphne exclaimed. "The moosie monster, have you fallen?" she asked, a rhetorical question if ever there was one. And then she reached down and lifted

Madeline up onto the seat between us while Max stayed, rather disinterested in Madeline's departure, in the space underneath the table. I worried that Daphne's focus on my story had been completely lost even before I got to my most recent, most stumping clue. As I had taken recently to doing, I worried that everything was lost. Madeline made her way noisily onto Daphne's lap and gazed up at her, and Daphne looked down at her and said, "I love you very, very much. There are few things in this world I love as much as you." Madeline inhaled mightily with a snort I was sure was of both agreement and appreciation.

But then, thankfully, Madeline, apparently satisfied and subdued by this expression of love, curled herself up into a ball. Daphne looked back at me, and in the flickering of the candlelight her blue eyes looked purple. I remembered the purple of the pansies and I ignored the moosie monster and continued. I soldiered on for so many different reasons, not the least of which was the fact that sooner or later, someone else, someone other than Max, was going to notice that the Fantin-Latour hanging in the museum was a fake. I kept talking.

Before I knew it, I had my notebook out on the table between us. In the ongoing spirit of there is no such thing as telling someone everything, I left out my suspect list and went right to the clue, the third one, obviously, the one that had thrown me just a little bit over the edge.

I showed her the page where I'd written the answers to the first two clues, and Daphne's eyes lit up. I explained how I was writing everything down, as so far it was the only thing I could think to do. Daphne looked down at my notes and nodded with approval.

"Yes, yes," she said, reaching over and pointing at a line of my notebook. "You write everything in your notebook. Neatly, neatly. Skip lines."

"Yes, yes." I nodded. I read the clue out loud to her. "Head Sand Archive."

Daphne took it all in without shock or judgment. I didn't regret telling her. I wondered why I hadn't told her more, sooner.

She looked at the clue. She looked up at me. "What do you think it means?"

"I don't know," I said.

"Have you asked yourself questions?" she asked me. I thought how probably I'd asked myself a million questions, but I wasn't sure I'd ever waited to hear the answers.

"I don't know," I said again. It was as truthful an answer as anything.

"You must," she said. "Look at it and ask yourself questions. Ask the right questions, dear," she said. She paused before adding, "A successful sleuth, and come to think of it, a successful person, always asks the right questions."

I nodded. I didn't say anything. I tried to let it sink in.

Max's leash fell off the banquette. Granted, not a big deal at all, but for whatever reason—reflex maybe, frustration at other things—as I reached down to collect it from the floor, I muttered under my breath, "Aw, shit."

"Don't swear, dear Hope," Daphne said. "It makes you seem far less lovely than you are. And you're lovely. You should never lose sight of that."

"Um," I said, thrown for a moment, "thank you."

And then, suddenly, as if some sort of switch had been flipped, for a relief-washed moment, I forgot about the pansies, about all of it, and the only thing in my universe was Daphne telling me first not to swear and then that I was lovely. I wanted to be someone who never swore again. I wanted right then to be someone who had beautiful, perfect manners, someone who never even thought about cursing because that is what Daphne wanted for her. I wanted to be someone who was even a modicum as lovely as Daphne envisioned me to be. I'm very impressionable that way, and also, it was true, I cursed too much and rarely for good reasons.

"You're right," I said.

Daphne smiled over at me and offered this suggestion, "Just do what I do. Just say 'shoot.'" I tried to look at the bright side, to think that if there wasn't going to be so much in the way of concrete advice about my third clue, at least there was some advice of the Emily Post variety. I have at times felt like someone who might benefit from some advice of the Emily Post variety, so there was that.

"Aw, shoot," I said, and Daphne smiled and nodded. I nodded back and said, "Aw, shoot," to myself and tried to make it stick so that the next time I was unpleasantly surprised, I'd be sure to say, "Aw, shoot," instead. *Very good*, I thought, feeling, as I'm sure everyone does at one time or another, momentarily British.

"Maybe it'll become my catchphrase?" I said, only partially joking. Daphne paused and seemed to consider this. She looked at me carefully, and then she smiled. It was a smile that I would have described as wry.

"Maybe it will, dear," she said. "Maybe it will."

Daphne looked down at Madeline, who was sitting patiently looking up at us. Daphne beamed at her. "Aw, shoot," she said to Madeline. "Aw, shoot."

And then I watched as Daphne swooped down and scooped Madeline up off her lap. She held her aloft in almost exactly the same way that Mustafa held Simba aloft at the start of *The Lion King*, except Daphne held Madeline facing toward her as opposed to outward in the direction of, for the sake of this scenario, the pride lands. I looked at the soft pink roundness of Madeline's belly and listened to Daphne laugh before commanding, "Guard your neck!" and pulling Madeline to her. Then Daphne kissed Madeline right on that softest spot of the pug neck. "Guard your neck!" she cried out again, and repeated. Madeline snorted softly, and wiggled.

Max, surely feeling horribly left out at this point, came right up to my feet, sat on one of them, and looked up at me with alarm. I leaned down and picked him up. I did not hold him aloft, nor did I caterwaul any unfollowable edicts about his neck and the fact that maybe he should guard his. But I did kiss him right there, on the softest spot of his neck.

chapter fourteen

This Is Your Last Clue

That night I had another dream about Max. I was in the museum sitting by myself in the exact center of the grand central staircase. No one else was there. It was completely empty and close to dark. I had the sense that I'd been sitting there alone for a while, and then I became aware of someone beside me, to my right. I turned. I think I expected to see Max, or maybe even Daphne, but it wasn't either of them. It was William the Hippopotamus. He was out of his display case, out of the Egyptian wing, and sitting right next to me.

"Hi, William," I said, half thinking he might not only

look up at me, but also answer. He didn't. I didn't touch him or move him, and then I was looking ahead again. And then Max ambled into view in front of me. He came from out of the same side of the museum as the Egyptian wing, on a path that led directly from the Temple of Dendur Hall. His pace was slow, methodical. His gait was confident; he was composed. In the dream he didn't look even an ounce over-weight. He stopped directly in front of me at the bottom of the stairs. And then, step by deliberate step, he began his ascent. It took him a long time to reach me.

When he was just one step below me, Max turned and walked over so that he was right in front of William. He got down on his belly in front of William. His front paws were stretched out and his back legs were tucked up underneath his body. He bowed his head and he looked just like the Sphinx.

"Hi, Max," I said. He unbowed his head and angled it toward me.

"Hi, Hope," he said. He said it so sweetly and the sound of his voice was so wanted, so needed, so welcome, that I can remember even in the dream being close to overwhelmed by the urge to pick him up and hug him. I smiled at him. He got up from in front of William and walked to my other side. He climbed one more step and sat down beside me.

"Hope," he said, craning his neck to look up at me.

"Yes," I answered.

"Head Sand Archive."

"Ah," I said, nodding. "The clue."

"How about this. Who sticks their heads in the sand?"

"What's that?" I said, intrigued, much more than intrigued.

"It is actually very easy if you think about it," Max said next. "Think about it."

I didn't get excited about it in the dream, not right away. Mostly, if I can remember how I felt in the dream, I was just thrilled that Max could talk to me again. But as soon as he said that, in a very hokey lightbulb-going-off way, the lighting in the dreamlike Met got brighter.

"Ostriches stick their heads in the sand," I said to Max.

Max moved a few inches closer to me and stuck a paw out to touch my leg with it. "Ostrich," he said, and then, "Archive."

*　　*　　*

I woke up the next morning and I looked at Max. As I did, I remembered everything about the dream. It was so vivid. "Ostriches stick their heads in the sand!" I said to him, and he opened one eye and looked at me. Before I'd even pulled back the covers, I thought of a whimsical and charming work on paper in the Met's collection: a drawing of an ostrich by Picasso.

Head Sand Archive. *Oh my God*, I thought. Because of their fragile nature, works on paper can't be exhibited, exposed to light, for long stretches of time. The light is not good for them, so they are rotated and only brought out for exhibition periodically. Picasso's *Ostrich*—I was almost sure of it—was not on view. Picasso's *Ostrich* was . . . wait for it . . . in the archive!

It was so exciting! I sat bolt upright in bed and said it out loud: "The archive!"

Max lifted his rear end in the air in a perfect Downward Dog, and looked at me with the ever-present tilt of the head.

I jumped in the shower, wrangled Max, and hightailed it to the museum with still-wet hair. My great sense of urgency can be conveyed through the fact that I didn't blow-dry. Although I do not consider myself a high maintenance person, I am a realistic one. I know very well that my frizzy hair looks very bad when it dries naturally. I avoid it at all costs. My main excuse for forgoing exercise is so that I don't have to wash and reblow my hair, an excuse I honestly see as having a great deal of legitimacy.

*　*　*

As soon as I'd arrived in the Conservation Studio, as soon as Elliot was nodded at, as soon as Max was nestled into his under-desk dog bed and my notebook was once again grabbed from its hiding place inside the Sherpa bag, I burst out from the secluded staff hallway and into the museum. I followed what I was sure was the right path, the shortest route to the archive where modern works on paper were stored, and slid my ID card through the door in front of it. It all felt, cliché aside, very much as if it were Christmas Eve. Only it was a Christmas Eve in which danger, the hope of catching a thief, the fear of losing your job and being blamed for a crime you didn't commit danced in your head instead of visions of sugarplums. I walked into the cool darkness of the room, took in the rows and rows of vertical files, the smooth surfaces shining in the dim glow that emanated from the computer screen by the door. I went to that computer and typed "Picasso" and "Ostrich" into the database to locate the drawing. As soon as I'd called up its location, I hurried through the room to the correct vertical file.

I put on the white cotton gloves I'd brought with me from the Conservation Studio; as I did, they reminded me of Chaz and his ridiculous fingerprinting. I slid the designated drawer open and took out the *Ostrich* and laid it down on the smooth surface of the top of the file cabinet. I put my open notebook next to it, but not too close. I turned on a special low-wattage light, and looked. I took a breath, steeled myself for the moment when it would all hit me, third time's the charm and all that. I studied the drawing in case I could find any clues within it. I didn't see anything. And then, third verse same as the first: I began to look around for another clue. I got down on my hands and knees and searched the dark corners of the room. I peered behind file cabinets. I pulled open the file drawer where I'd found the *Ostrich* and slid my hand all the way to the back. There it was.

I pulled out a small piece of familiar heavy paper, folded in thirds once again. I opened it up to see the script handwriting. The first line read, *This is your last clue*. There was something about that declaration that was comforting to me, just as there was something about it that was so unsettling. And then, the second line: *Not a ballerina, but close*. And then a third: *Red, blue, birds in pairs of two*. It seemed like quite a lot to go on. I tried not to get overly excited. I reminded myself that a great many things in life could seem like quite a lot to go on at first and then somehow turn themselves around.

I took out my notebook and placed the clue in the back. I turned to my "solved clue" page. One line after "Hippopotamus," I wrote out in block letters, "*Ostrich*, Pablo Picasso, 1936." I put the *Ostrich* away, took one last look throughout the room just to be sure I wasn't missing anything additional, and turned back to the studio.

As I walked, I wondered if maybe it had something to do with animals. But that didn't make sense because of *Autumn Rhythm*. I knew I needed to look harder. But even as I knew that, it was as if I could see enthusiasm walking out one door and doubt walking in another. I wondered what would happen if it turned out that this was all a maze that didn't let out anywhere. What if I was wrong to place so much importance on this scavenger hunt? I knew I was following my intuition, but what if my intuition was for shit? I mean, for shoot? Then what? Max has never chased his tail. I can't say that I've known any pugs that have chased their tails. I tried not to think that maybe this whole time I'd only been chasing mine.

As I approached the door of the studio, it slid open. Chaz walked out.

"Hi, Hope," he said, and smiled at me.

"Chaz," I replied. I turned and watched his progress down the hall. Only after he'd turned a corner and disappeared from view did I slide my ID and walk in. It was silent inside, empty except for Max, asleep on the floor beside my desk.

"Hi, Max," I said very softly. He opened one eye to look up at me, and then closed it. I climbed up onto my stool and endeavored to get myself into the right but so elusive frame of mind to think not only about my newest clue, but also about the other Max in my life, the Maxfield Parrish. I stashed my notebook. I swiveled with determination to my easel, but no sooner than I had, I heard the door to the studio beep and click and whoosh open. I turned and looked up as Elliot walked in. Elliot didn't turn right away and walk across the room to his own workstation. He stood there, right in front of the door, and looked at me. And I think he looked at me kind of funny.

"Did you just get in?" he asked me.

"No," I said. "I've been here for a while," I sort-of lied. "Did you just get in?"

"No," Elliot answered, turning away from me even as he kept talking. "I was here earlier, but then I went up to go look at something." Look at something? It could mean nothing. It could mean everything. Maybe the trick was accepting that there wasn't any way to tell. Unless, of course, there was.

"Elliot?" I said.

"Yeah?" he said. He stopped walking and turned around to face me again.

"Just wondering something," I began. "What do you think of when you think of the Jackson Pollock in the mezzanine? Just off the top of your head."

"East Hampton," he said without much of a pause to think at all. Interesting, I thought. "The Springs," he elaborated.

"And the hippopotamus? William?" I pressed. This time he hesitated.

"Egypt," he answered eventually. "And blue," he added, looking at me hard.

"Thanks," I said. It was all I could do not to duck under my desk to retrieve my notebook. I sat there not ten feet away from Elliot and clenched my teeth. He stood facing me, looking back at me. I saw his jaw muscle flex.

"Hope?" he said.

"Yes?"

"Does this have something to do with the Fantin-Latour?" he asked, and I wondered again if maybe Elliot had clues, too. I still didn't feel I could risk telling him anything. There was still too big a chance that he was the culprit, and even if he wasn't, I had begun to feel that he might be the enemy.

"I can't say," I said.

"Strange questions," he mused. I couldn't tell if he was baiting me. Paranoia, I was learning, can be hard that way. When it's everywhere, when you can't shake it, it makes other things so much harder to see.

I nodded at Elliot. I couldn't think of anything else to do. I remembered Daphne telling me that in life you have to ask the right questions. I thought how that was made so much harder when you have no idea what those questions might be.

I turned away from Elliot. I turned the new clue over in my mind. I looked down at Max, into his eyes, just to be sure he wasn't going to pipe up with some wisdom that would jog the clue-solving part of my brain. *Focus, Hope,* I told myself. *Focus.*

"Fucking hell!" I heard Elliot call out from across the room. I swiveled quickly around to see him standing underneath one of the security cameras.

"What?" I said.

"This camera, the other one, too. Broken again." I looked up at the camera above Elliot and then over at the one across the room. Neither one had the lights they usually had on. I got up from my desk to take a closer look. Max came, too. I looked at the camera at the far end of the room first and then walked over to where Elliot was standing. Both cameras, upon inspection, were missing their lenses.

"Oh, God," I said.

"They just got fixed," Elliot announced, turning as he did to face me.

"When could this have happened?" I asked.

Elliot didn't answer my question. Instead he shook his head and said, "Hope, I don't want to think this. I really don't. This whole time I haven't wanted to think this, but these cameras were fine yesterday. You just said you were here all morning. I wasn't. I mean, what's next? Does another fake show up in our nonmonitored, security-free studio? Does another painting go missing? It's . . ." He trailed off and let the things he wasn't saying speak.

"But, no," I sputtered. "I actually wasn't here either. I just said that I was."

"Where were you?" he asked me, angrier and more animated than I'd ever seen him.

"I was in the archive. Where were you?" I shot back, sounding so much angrier than I'd expected. Elliot put his hands up, as if it were a holdup.

"I can't deal. I really can't. I'm going to take a walk," he said, and turned toward the door. I watched—confused, angry, and in spite of my outraged sense of being wrongly accused, more than a bit suspicious—as Elliot stormed out of the studio. If the door weren't the kind of door that slid open, I was certain he would have slammed it. I stood there under the once-again-compromised cameras with Max, staring at the door that Elliot had just walked through, counting to ten and trying to gather my thoughts. Eventually I stormed back to my desk, with Max at my heels. I sat heavily on my stool. But just as couples should never go to bed angry, furious art restorers should not work on paintings. I turned to my computer.

I was glad that I did. A bright spot. There, right underneath an Important Message about an extended sale at JCrew.com was an e-mail from Ben. It was quick, only three words: *Skype at seven?* But those three words might as well have been "I love you." The end of the day couldn't come fast enough. Elliot and I did not speak again once he returned, and somehow, mercifully, the end of the day did at last come. As soon as the clock struck six, I packed up Max, powered everything off, and waved over at Elliot as if it were just another day, even though it really, really wasn't. I didn't even look to see if he waved back as I headed for the exit.

As soon as I stepped outside the museum, the skies opened up and a downpour started. It was impossible not to think, *How apropos.* Pug exercise efforts once again thwarted, I quickly abandoned any thoughts of a cross-park walk and jumped into a taxi that would speed us home.

chapter fifteen

Oh, Universe

I went immediately to the couch with my laptop. Max jumped up right beside me. I set the laptop down on the coffee table right next to a pile of gravel that had recently arrived from Ben. The logic, I think, was that it was something he saw every day, and so I loved it if only for the thought, and for the added bonus that it was not as scary as some of the masks and statues crowding the apartment could sometimes appear, especially when you ran into them in the dark.

Max stretched out across me and I angled the laptop so that he could see the screen as well. I turned Skype on, made sure everything was ready to go, and only then did I realize I had some time to kill. And I knew just how to kill it. I set the laptop down on the coffee table and retrieved the hippopotamus notebook. I opened it up and held it so that Max could see, too. He seemed interested, and, well, one never knew.

I still felt queasy from the run-in with Elliot, the unspoken but still very spoken accusation. I thought of Elliot saying, "I don't want to think this," and how that meant that he already did. It was all the more reason to solve this, to figure out who did this, to find the Fantin-Latour. I pulled my fourth and ostensibly last clue from the back of the notebook. I unfolded it and stared at it. I flipped through my notebook, studying all the notes I'd taken. I wondered if matters could be helped if I took some more notes. As may have by now become apparent, I'm a big believer in the power of taking notes. I needed a pen.

I never got to the pen. The Skype went off. Dear to my heart though it had become, I tossed the hippopotamus notebook aside in a flash. I repositioned Max, grabbed the laptop, hit enter, and then, thank you technology, there was Ben.

Ben's image came onto the screen and he looked, well, not like Ben at all. He looked as if he'd lost his umbrella and walked miles in the pouring rain. He looked awful. Granted, the looking-awful part could have been just from living all these months in Kinshasa, which I had never once imagined to be easy. But let the record show that the second I saw him, I knew the way he looked had to do with something else.

"Hey there," I said.

"Hey there," Ben said back. Max heard his voice and jumped up and started pawing at the laptop. I restrained him as gently as I could, lest he disconnect us.

"Hey, buddy," Ben said, without even an ounce of his usual Max-directed enthusiasm. He leaned forward and ran his hands through his hair, even though Ben's hair, very short and more wiry than anything else, isn't really the type of hair one can run hands through. I know, I've tried.

"Hope," he said, and the way he said it, I knew. I knew it wasn't going to be anything good. I knew the way a pug knows it's going to thunderstorm long before it does.

"I don't know how to say this, so I'm just going to say it."

"Okay," I said. I braced myself as possibilities ricocheted through my mind. In the last fraction of a moment before Ben started to speak, I had an image in my mind of a scene from an old black-and-white movie in which some character looks up only about a split second before she gets hit by a train. I knew there wasn't anything that I could do. I knew there simply wasn't time to get out of the way.

"I don't think I'm going to be coming home in two

months," he said, and even though I'd known that what he was going to say was not going to be good, it had not actually crossed my mind that it was going to be that.

"What?" I said, even though I'd heard him.

Ben inhaled. And then he exhaled. "I don't think I'm going to be coming home in two months." He said it again, even though it was the last thing in the world I wanted him to say. I closed my eyes. I wanted it to be anything but that. I wanted it to be that he'd—somehow—found out all about the Fantin-Latour. I closed my eyes and wished for him to say he'd found out and was disappointed I hadn't gone straight to the police. I closed my eyes, but Ben didn't say any of that. I opened my eyes.

"You're staying longer?" I asked.

"Yes," he said. Yes. It was the worst word in the entirety of the English language. Yes. Ben looked through the computer screen at me. He looked like he was about to keel over, and I felt that on that at least, on the keeling-over part, we were on exactly the same page. He didn't say anything. I didn't say anything. I felt on the verge of crying but somehow kept it together. I didn't ask why, I didn't ask what it was that made him want to stay. I tried to remind myself that Ben being in Kinshasa was about making the world a better place, that it didn't have to do with me, that not everything did. I knew as I did that these were things I shouldn't need to remind myself.

But still, I blurted out, "I don't want you to keep living

in another country." I could feel any small semblance of rationality I had left seeping out of my body along with those words. Ben leaned back from the screen a bit.

"It's not like it's forever. There's just more work to be done than originally anticipated. It would be for five months more, six tops."

There was a silence. A long one. "Five or six months?" I said.

"I don't even know," Ben said.

"Don't even know what?" I asked.

He took a steadying, I'm-calm-and-in-control-of-my-emotions breath. I envied him that breath. And then I think I might have, even if it was very briefly, hated him for that breath.

I looked into my laptop at him and swung on a pendulum of emotions. I looked at Ben and he looked back at me, and for a moment I thought about Evan in Central Park, and Elliot and his Tiffany's catalog, and Pamela and her thoughts on long-term relationships. I thought how it had taken me so long to find Ben, how after so many years of dating in New York City, I'd felt as if I'd been through a war by the time I did. I think I had, this whole time, held on to the perhaps seriously unrealistic belief that just because I'd waited so long to find him, as a reward for that, everything between us would be perfect.

I looked at Ben and felt right then that just as there are certain people who don't have a head for math or science, there are other people who just don't have a head for long-distance relationships. I knew I had to say I supported him and believed in him and wanted him to do what was best for him and for the world. I knew I had to say that, but still, I didn't.

We looked at each other for one more moment, through my laptop, across six thousand, three hundred, seventy-eight miles, and a world away. I thought of a song that had been playing on the radio constantly. It said how there were 86,400 seconds in a day to turn it all around or throw it all away.

"What are you thinking?" Ben asked.

"I'm thinking I need some time to think about this," I said.

"Take time," Ben said. "Take all the time you need."

"Well," I said. "I've got time. Five or six months of time, right?"

Ben ignored that. "I'll visit," he said. "You'll visit."

I thought again of how, in life, you need to ask the right questions. I wondered what question would be the right one to ask now. Is this definite? Is this going to be okay? Are you fucking kidding me? That last question I thought could be addressed not only to Ben but also to the universe.

"For now, it's just six more months, right?" I asked in lieu of any other questions. "It's not like tomorrow you'll call me and it'll be a year?" Ben smiled at me, a little but not really, not like he meant it. Something inside me tightened into a ball, a small one, and I thought that maybe I was going to throw up.

"Right," he said. Nothing was. Again I thought of asking the universe, are you fucking kidding me? And then the only thing I could hear inside my head was Daphne saying, "Hope, don't swear."

"Shoot," I said, and Ben looked at me funny.

"What?" he said.

"Nothing," I said back. He wouldn't get it.

I thought about Ben never coming back, about Ben calling me every few months to say he was staying longer. I wondered if it made me more shallow than I'd ever realized that right then I wished I'd blown out my hair that morning.

"I'm really sorry, Hope," Ben said, and I nodded. I exhaled. All this time I've been saying that this is okay, having a boyfriend who lives in another country. Maybe I want more than that. Maybe it's okay to want to have more than waiting at home with my art and my pugs, even if it was just the one pug, and even if the pug wasn't technically mine.

And then, admittedly a hundred moments too late, I thought of Max. I said, "Max!" Max, still next to me on the couch, stretched out a paw and swatted me on the lap with it. "Max will stay with me, right?" I asked.

"Of course," Ben said, and something else occurred to me. I thought again of asking the right questions. I was not sure if what I was about to ask was one of them.

"Ben?" I said anyway.

"Hope?"

"If this doesn't work out? Max will always stay with me, right?" I asked.

"Of course," Ben said again. "But Hope, I want this to work out."

* * *

Later that night—after we'd finished Skyping and I'd turned off the laptop and begun to try to wrap my head around the fact that Ben would be gone "longer"—I stayed on the couch with Max and thought about my first date with Ben, the one where Ben, Max, and I went sailing off into the sunset. We did in fact go sailing on our first date, only it hadn't been as the sun was setting. It had been closer to two thirty in the afternoon. But still, in my memory and in my heart, I always remembered it as the three of us sailing off into the sunset.

I have always believed in happy endings. My favorite books, my favorite movies, my favorite songs, they are always the ones that have happy endings, the ones in which characters are sailing off into the sunset, running through airports to find one another, taking off on a plane together. In all the time I spent trying to get to my own cinematic, storybook happy ending, I don't think I ever once considered what happens next. I don't think I ever once entertained the possibility that everything doesn't always work out after all. Maybe planes crash. Maybe boats sink. I had no idea.

But even then, as I sat alone in my apartment with my long-long-distance boyfriend's pug, staring into the eyes of an African tribal mask, I wanted to believe that they didn't. And I think that sometimes that's all you can do: Believe that they didn't.

chapter sixteen

Solving for Why

If ever you feel you have been done wrong, make a Court Yard Hounds station on Pandora and know you are not alone. That's what I did, but even so, waking up the next day felt terrible. I had a remarkable headache. There was a part of me that wished I'd handled it better. There was a part of me that wished I'd handled it worse. I didn't know in which direction I wanted to go. I didn't even want to think about it; I couldn't think about it. I shook my head to bring some action to not thinking about it, but because of the afore-mentioned major headache, it really did nothing to help.

I padded out through the living room to the kitchen and made coffee. I brought it with me to the couch and sat drinking it there as Max roused himself from the bedroom and came out to join me. There, in the corner of the couch, was my hippopotamus notebook, right where I'd left it last night when the Skype had gone off. With one finger I pulled my notebook closer and looked at it out of the corner of my eye. I did this so as not to feel like I was going too quickly from despair-over-relationship to godforsaken art heist, sure that it would give me some sort of emotional whiplash. With everything else I now had on my plate, I was sure I didn't have the wherewithal to deal with that.

I opened up the notebook in front of me and pulled out the fourth and final clue. I knew as I did that I would carry on, that I would stay the course, that I would keep trying to figure out what had happened to the pansies. I wondered if that was less about tenacity and perseverance than it was about the fact that right at that moment I felt like the pansies were all I had left. And Max, I reminded myself. I had Max.

Not a ballerina, but close. Red, blue, birds in pairs of two. Ballerinas made me think of Degas. Of course. I tried to think of works by Degas in the museum that were of subjects other than ballerinas. There were many. It could be anything. I told myself if I looked hard enough the clue would mean something. I had perhaps once or twice during the night denounced love and thought to myself, "Get thee to a nunnery"; suddenly I thought, "Get thee to the paintings database." Get thee to the paintings database and look through every single Degas in the museum's collections until something makes sense.

*   *   *

I hurried through the apartment getting ready for the day and walked quickly across the park to the museum. I had to hurry Max along on our cross-park journey, as he was of the mind that morning that he wanted to sniff everything. On a good day this made me anxious. Right then, it made me want to chew my hand off.

When I walked into the studio, Elliot was there before me. As I nodded at him it was easy to believe for a second that everything was the way it used to be, that none of this had happened. Then I saw that Gil was there, wringing his hands and pacing dramatically across the studio floor, and I remembered that nothing was the way it used to be.

"Hope!" Gil called out to me, the laser focus of his beady eyes burning into my pug-transport bag.

"Gil!" I called back, determined not to be deterred by him and to get to the database.

"Elliot told me about the cameras." I stopped walking. I turned to face Gil. He stopped walking, but still he was wringing his hands. "I have to say, I am really quite concerned." I looked away for an instant, over to Elliot. He looked up and met my eyes, but I couldn't read at all what was in them.

"I'm very concerned, too!" I said. It came out sounding much more frantic and exasperated, and actually Gil-like, than I had intended. Max was snorting from inside his bag, and so I set it down and let him loose. On sight of him, Gil gasped, and turned, and marched from the room.

I set Max up under my desk and grabbed my notebook. The moment my computer was on, I blew right past my e-mail and logged on to the database and started studying the list of works by Degas. And then, there: a work dated 1860–62. *Young Woman with Ibis*. I didn't have to go to the visual; I could see it clearly in my mind. It was a painting of a woman staring out over a blue metropolis, with two birds—two birds!—one on either side of her. *Red, blue, birds in pairs of two*. I didn't bother saying anything to Elliot (it was better right now not to say anything to Elliot) as I grabbed my notebook and set off for the Modern Art galleries.

I walked quickly there, through several rooms, before I located the Degas. *Young Woman with Ibis*. The red birds seemed to rest right on the woman's shoulder. It made me think of Snow White, when she sits in a meadow and all the forest animals gather around her. This, for some reason, is an image that has popped up in my mind at very different times in my life. I wondered whether this, combined with my recent recollections of Woody Woodpecker, meant I should perhaps be concerned about a preoccupation with cartoons. I didn't know. I only knew I didn't have time to start thinking about that. The red birds almost looked like hair, and I thought of my own red hair, and it occurred to me then, for the first time I think, that these clues had each been tailor-made for me.

I opened my notebook, turned to what I had perhaps too optimistically started to think of as my "answer page," and wrote "*Young Woman with Ibis*, Edgar Degas, 1860–62" across the page in all capital letters, just after the others. And then I did everything I had done before. I scoured the room for other clues, even though I'd been told there'd be none. I pressed myself against walls, waited for a lull in the crowd, and tried lying on the floor in a search for an answer. I didn't find anything. Nothing.

Nothing! I hoped for something to hit me. Hit me, hit me, I almost said it out loud. But the only thing that did hit me was the possibly very delayed realization that I'd spent the last week running all over the Met in a dither thinking that every clue I received from God-knows-who and blindly followed like a lemming was going to lead me to an answer. Only I was worse than a lemming because there were no other lemmings running with me over the cliff. I was alone.

I indulged myself in a very brief moment of despair. I closed my notebook and headed back to the studio, to Elliot, to Gil, and for all I knew to Chaz, but also, thankfully, to Max. I felt as if one of the red birds from the painting I'd just been standing in front of had flown right into my head. It struck me there with the sure and fast knowledge that everything had stopped making sense. I turned and headed to the studio.

Yes, there were so many questions left to ask, so many questions left to be answered, but right then only one question seemed to matter. How is a person supposed to have the presence of mind, the calm rational clearheaded type of thinking necessary to solve a mystery, when her life is, piece by piece, falling apart?

I've believed for a long time, for forever maybe, in a power greater than myself, in the thought that the universe will get involved in your life and will help you when you need help. I've believed the universe will occasionally show up and point you in the right direction at those times when you have no idea which way to go. But what if that belief had always been wrong? What if the only part that's right is that, yes, every now and then, the universe will show up. But sometimes when it does, it's really just intent on screwing with you? Although I suspect the universe doesn't have that kind of time, I now believe it to be a theory worth looking into.

I went to my desk, got on my stool. I wondered a bit where Sergei was.

"Where's Sergei?" I asked at one point.

"Not here," Elliot answered, without even the slightest swivel on his stool. I took Max out for a pit stop. I brought him back in. I worked for uninterrupted hours on the Maxfield Parrish, and the moment the clock said five thirty, I got up from my desk. With Max and my notebook both tucked safely in his bag, along with the sobering knowledge that there'd be no more helpful clues (or possibly not helpful, but maybe only distracting and misleading and taking one's attention off a different trail that they should have been on all along!), I left. I tried to steel myself and tried to look at the positive. I just didn't know where it was. I wanted to think that none of this meant that I was out of luck, out of time, and out of ideas, but rather that now it was go time. And I really think that someone in a better frame of mind than I was at the moment would have succeeded in that effort.

*　　*　　*

Right after the Greywacke Arch, right after Max had been freed, I saw Daphne and Madeline sitting together on a bench, the one I'd come in so short a time to think of as their bench. I'm not always a living-in-the-present type of person. As much as I would like it to be, it's never really been my bag. I have more of a this-thing-reminds-me-of-that way of looking at the world. In the reverse of the way that seeing Elliot at his desk on a recent morning had made me think that everything was the way it used to be, seeing Daphne and her pug there was like a bright spotlight on the fact that, actually, nothing was.

"Ahoy!" Daphne said.

"Ahoy," I said back.

"How are you today, dear?" she asked, and I was tempted to say, "Oh, you know, same shoot, different day," but wasn't sure the translation would work. So instead I smiled and said, "Oh, fine."

"And how's your mystery?" she asked.

"It's okay," I lied. I don't know why. I think I wasn't ready to say out loud that after everything I'd hit on nothing but a dead end. Saying it out loud would make it more assaulting and true than it already was.

Daphne turned to me with that slight tilt of her head that reminded me of Max, of so many other things, and a concern in her eyes that didn't remind me of nearly enough.

"I've been wrong about so many things," I blurted out. I don't think in the moments before I said it that I knew that was what I was going to say. But as soon as it was out there, it made sense, it was true. Maybe I was close to figuring out what had happened to the Fantin-Latour. Maybe I was as far as I'd ever been. I had no idea. Zero. I only knew that I felt like I was losing it.

Daphne looked concerned. She was good at that. She nodded at me as if she understood. I didn't know if she did, if she could. But even so, whatever it was—the illusion of understanding, the perception that I was, to someone at least, making sense, made a tremendous amount of difference to me. I took a deep breath and asked a question that I realized I'd needed to ask for a while.

"What if it turns out that I was wrong about Ben, too?"

Daphne nodded again, and then she smiled a comforting smile. She reached out a hand and placed it on my arm. It was there, standing in the middle of Central Park with my new pug friend and our two pugs, that, for the first time since all of this started, for the first time since I had become embroiled in this art heist, for the first time since the rug of my life had somehow gotten pulled out from under me, I burst into tears.

Daphne leaned over and rubbed my arm. She smiled at me kindly. "It will all turn out okay, dear," she told me. "I can assure you that it will. Everything will be okay," Daphne said again. I really wanted to believe her.

chapter seventeen

I Know You're There Because I Can Hear You Breathing

It was a beautiful summer day and there was one pug sitting by himself right in the middle of the Sheep Meadow in Central Park. He was a fawn pug, one of the stout and stocky pugs, all at once porcine and rotund and well muscled, my favorite kind of pug. And then there was another pug, right next to the first one. This second pug looked the same, only he was a black pug just like Max. I blinked and there were two more pugs. I blinked again and there were even more pugs. And more. They were everywhere, pugs in lieu of sheep, stretching out across the Sheep Meadow, all different shapes and sizes, all of them sitting still, at attention.

They were all staring straight ahead, intently, as if everything were ahead of them, as if everything in their line of vision were a treat they had to be sure they didn't let out of their sight.

More and more pugs kept appearing; they didn't walk up or run into the scene, they simply materialized. They were not there, and then they were there. Soon, there were hundreds of pugs, multiplying like an invasion of magical, amazing aliens. The New York City skyline loomed large behind them, and in the background, from some hidden speaker, someone started playing Michael Jackson, "Take the world, and make it a better place." The pugs didn't sing along, but they swayed in time to the music.

And then Max was there, right at the front of the pack, just off a bit to the side. He looked over at me, and he said, "Hi, Hope," just in the way he had before, and then I knew it was a dream. He said it so sweetly that even in the dream, even in the presence of all those many pugs, all I wanted to do was grab him and hug him and hold on to him.

"Hi, Max," I said in lieu.

"Look up and down, Hope," he said.

"At all the pugs?"

"No, not that."

"Then what?" I asked.

"Let me put it this way," he said back, his voice full of both wisdom and patience. "When you're looking at something, turn it on its head. Don't look at it the regular way, look up and down."

"Max?"

"Hope?"

"What do you mean?"

I waited, holding my breath, for him to tell me. He stuck out his tongue and for a moment he wasn't a dreamlike pug guru; for a moment he was just Max again, and I forgot that we were in the middle of a pug-filled Sheep Meadow and that he was about to tell me something I was sure I really needed to know. I looked at him and said, "Look how cute your tongue is." He snorted at me.

* * *

I woke up. It wasn't a beautiful summer day anymore. It was the middle of the night at the end of a rain-filled April, and I wasn't in Central Park with hundreds of pugs. I was in my apartment with just one pug, and except for that, alone.

I got out of bed and padded into the living room and to the couch. Max appeared sleepily in the archway, looked around the apartment, and then jumped up to join me. I picked my notebook up from the place on the couch where I'd left it the night before. A more presently positive person might have said to herself, "Ah, look, a benefit of Ben being gone, I can leave my things strewn all over the place if I feel like it." I didn't.

I missed Ben. I was mad at Ben. I reached across the couch to the cushion where earlier I'd tossed my phone. I held it in front of me, looked at its screen, stared at it for a while until the edges around its rubberized case got blurry. It was four A.M., ten A.M. in Kinshasa. I thought how easy it would be, two touches of the screen and I'd be calling Ben. I could say a lot of things. I could say, "Come back." I wondered if there was nothing I could do to make him want to come back, if the only thing I could do would be to make him not want to come back. I rechucked the phone to the far end of the couch. I turned my attention back to the hippopotamus notebook.

Beside me, Max stretched out a paw in the direction of my lap. Then he tried to nose his way under my arm and take the place of my notebook. I tried, as gently as I could, to keep him sitting next to me and not on my lap.

"No, see, Max," I said. "I need to hold my notebook here in my lap and look at it, and that's kind of hard if you're sitting in my lap, right?" I looked at Max, hoping he might see reason and stay where he was. He looked back up at me and inhaled heavily again, a deep soulful sound from the back of his throat. I feel like he does that when he wants something. "And also," I added, not taking my eyes from his, "I don't know why you're snorting at me."

I slid Max back beside me, took out all my clues, unfolded the thick cream sheets of paper and looked at the script writing across each of them. I studied the clues and then I turned to the page in my notebook where I'd written the works of art that the clues had led me to, one after the other. Max sidled back over again and onto my lap. He looked up at me as I stared at the page. I tried as hard as I could to ignore him and concentrate.

For a moment, nothing. And then, everything. Max turned his head away from me and toward my notebook as if he were studying it, too. He reached out again with his paw and this time it landed right on the open page. Max's paw landed right on the A of *Autumn Rhythm*. He kept his paw pressed firmly on my notebook. I could feel the bulk of his weight pressing down on it. I moved it away. I looked at the page again, at everything I'd written across it:

AUTUMN RHYTHM, JACKSON POLLOCK, 1950
HIPPOPOTAMUS, DYNASTY 12, CA. 1981–1885 B.C.
OSTRICH, PABLO PICASSO, 1836
YOUNG WOMAN WITH IBIS, EDGAR DEGAS, 1860–1862

And then I remembered, so vividly, every detail of the dream. Max sitting in the middle of the Sheep Meadow and saying to me, "Let me put it this way. When you're looking at something, turn it on its head. Don't look at it the regular way, look up and down."

I stared hard at the notebook, as I'd taken to doing with possibly alarming frequency. Only this time something was different. I read the page as Max had told me I should. I read the page from top to bottom, rather than left to right, and as I did, as my eyes stayed close to the margin, right where Max's paw had just been, I saw something there. If I read the clues from top to bottom and stayed close to the margin so that I focused on the first letter of each work of art—*Autumn Rhythm, Hippopotamus, Ostrich, Young Woman with Ibis*—this is what I got: AHOY.

Ahoy.

I let out a yelp. Max jumped up and let out a yelp, too.

I closed the notebook. I opened it back up again. *Ahoy*, I thought. *Ahoy*. Daphne. Daphne? It couldn't be. Only, of course, it could.

I looked at Max and everything in my brain went backward, backward to the night when this had started, the Pug Night. I could see it all as if it were happening a second time: Max attacking Daphne at the party, Daphne looking down at him and saying, what else, of course, "Ahoy." Daphne and Madeline dashing out of the party. I could see Max charging across the Conservation Studio and barking like mad at the fake Fantin-Latour. Daphne sitting next to me in Central Park. Daphne saying "Ahoy," explaining to me that everyone needs a catchphrase. Everyone needs a catchphrase and a museum wing named after her is what she had said. I could hear Daphne saying to me, as if she were right there, "A successful sleuth, and come to think of it, a successful person, always asks the right questions." In trying to solve a mystery and, most of all, in life, it's important to ask the right questions.

I asked a question even though I already knew the answer. Is Daphne the culprit? And then without yet knowing how it could possibly make sense, only that it did, I was saying the answer out loud.

"Yes," I said, my voice louder than it would be in conversation, filled with equal parts elation at finding the answer and dread at what that answer was.

Max started to bark. I looked over at him.

"How smart are you?" I asked him.

I sat frozen, overwhelmed by this new information. It was funny, or actually it was the exact opposite of funny, but for an instant, I forgot that Ben didn't live here, and in that moment, I worried that I'd woken him up. I don't know why or maybe I do, but for the moment after that I imagined I was listening to him shuffle the small distance from the bed to the archway. Then it was almost as if Ben had appeared in the doorway and turned his head to one side.

"Everything okay?" he would have asked me if he'd been there.

"Everything's fine," I would have said, even if it wasn't anywhere near true.

I shook my head. This was not helping anything. It was four o'clock in the morning, nine days after this had begun, and now, I hoped, there were only a few more hours left to go.

"Ahoy," I said to myself, to Max, to the African artwork in the room. "Ahoy," I said again. I turned to Max. He looked at me. "Max?" I said. He didn't answer me, but I kept the conversation going anyway. "We're going to have to wait a little while longer, but then," I continued, nodding to him, to myself, "we're going to have to go."

*   *   *

I waited until seven, and then I couldn't wait anymore. Once I had my shoes on, had located my keys, and had Max's satchel in hand, I attempted to issue a command to Max and have him actually obey it. I shook the bag in his direction and with more firmness in my tone than usual, said, "Bag!"

Max ran up to me and nosed his bag as if he wanted nothing more than to get in it, nothing more than to be an obedient pug. I thought it likely that this was the first time in his life that he'd been so inclined.

"Thank you, Max," I said as I hooked his leash on and slung his bag over my shoulder.

At the bus stop, as I prepared to secure the pug for the cross-park journey, I thought maybe not the bus. Even though I needed to get to Daphne, even though I needed to talk to her urgently, I admitted to myself that I needed the proverbial minute.

"Okay," I said out loud to Max, and together we set out across the park.

It wasn't Elliot; despite all the weirdness and vagueness and the Tiffany's catalog, it wasn't Elliot. It wasn't Gil, even though I will admit I would not have been chagrined if it had turned out to be Gil. It wasn't Alan, or Belle. It wasn't even Sergei, even though still, I wondered, where the hell was Sergei? In the distance, I saw Crazy Snack Lady standing behind her shih tzu *en stroller* with a pack of hounds gathered around her. I ran up to Max and clipped his leash onto his collar to avoid an episode. It wasn't Crazy Snack Lady either. I accepted this with only slightly less disappointment than I'd felt when I accepted it wasn't Gil. It was Daphne. The question was no longer who was it, it was how did she do it. And why.

I stayed in the park and walked south to Seventy-sixth Street. Our path was so close to the place that used to be Pug Hill that I was sure that if I got up on a bench I'd be able to see it. It was the place I'd always gone whenever I needed to see pugs, before I'd met Ben and before Max was my charge. I'd gone there whenever I needed to think, and I'd always done my best thinking there. I hadn't been there in so long; surely the connection was obvious. I needed to go back there soon. Later. After.

Max and I left the park and walked to the Carlyle, to the entrance on Seventy-seventh Street, the one for residents. A doorman stationed on the sidewalk right outside opened the door for us, and another, standing behind a lectern inside, looked up at me and Max as we walked in. He smiled, in a "and how can I help you?" way, and I tightened my grip on Max's leash. I both worried it was far too early for a visit and hoped I'd at least catch Daphne at home.

"Hi," I said, holding Max close on his leash. I did this, I realized, out of concern that Max might inexplicably attack. Though even as I did, I suddenly knew that nothing had been quite as inexplicable as it had recently seemed, especially Max's behavior.

Max hadn't been attacking anyone without reason. He hadn't been set off willy-nilly as I'd thought. It could all be explained, it was all so easily understandable now. It all made so much sense as long as there was a willingness to accept that Max was a genius. Maybe Max had been barking at the answers. Maybe he'd been trying to show me the answers all along. I've always believed that pugs exist on a purer plane. I've always, always believed that pugs know things people don't, can see things people can't.

I looked down at Max and smiled in amazement. He'd barked at the fake; he'd barked at it like crazy. He'd barked at Daphne the first time he met her, and come to think of it, other times, too, only I'd thought it had been at Madeline. All along, all the barking had been either at the fake or at Daphne, and that had been all. Fine, so he'd been a little off base when he'd growled at Chaz, but maybe that was just because he sensed that Chaz was involved as he was the official (though perhaps useless) investigator.

"Hi," I repeated to the doorman. "My name is Hope McNeill, and I'm here to see Daphne Markham."

"Yes," he answered. "Mrs. Markham is expecting you."

"Thanks," I said, and only after he'd directed me to Daphne's private elevator did I think, how could she be expecting me?

Together Max and I walked across the marble expanse of the lobby to the mahogany-paneled elevator, and together we rode up in it, almost in silence, except for the sounds of pug breathing. As the elevator sped upward, I didn't think anymore about the heist or my attempts to solve it. I didn't think of all the people I'd wrongly accused in my mind and in my hippopotamus notebook. I just thought of what I would say to Daphne. How I'd break it to her that not only did I think she'd taken the painting, but someone else thought so, too, and had gone to great lengths (lengths perhaps annoyingly great) to let me know that.

As the letters PH filled the electronic display at the top of the elevator, the doors opened, not into a hall or even a vestibule but right into Daphne's apartment. I stepped out with Max, who, of course, barked once upon entry. Genius pug! Madeline charged across the wood floors of a great expansive room to greet us. I put Max's carrying bag down right by the elevator and bent down to pet Madeline and say hello. I looked down at her, the Moosie Monster, the gorgeous, gorgeous girl, and I felt sad. Of all the things I could have, should have been feeling right then, more than anything else, I felt sad.

I heard the elevator doors slide shut in a whisper behind me. And then three things happened in quick succession, one right after the other, so that I felt as if I were the weaker fighter in a boxing match, getting pummeled one time, two times, three times, right in the face.

First, I thought again about the doorman downstairs saying that Daphne had been expecting me, and it occurred to me that he hadn't even buzzed me up. Then Daphne appeared. She walked up a few steps from an enormous sunken living room and met me on the landing by the elevators. She took a breath, and as she exhaled a sly smile spread across her face, and she said to me, "What took you so long?"

And then, finally, my line of sight skipped over the vast expanse of Daphne's living room, just barely took in the chintz, the antiques, the tremendous baroque mirrors, the six massive almost floor-to-ceiling windows that looked out over the treetops of Central Park all the way to the Great Lawn where we—Daphne, Madeline, Max, and I—had spent so much time together. It was as if the whole room went dark and I were a speeding car with its brights on, hurtling past everything and right into the farthest wall, and then up that wall to where, just to the side of a lamp, there was a painting.

The placement was what a decorator might call subtle. It was not right above a sofa or a mantel, but just above and to the side of a small skirted table; it was almost touching a lampshade. It was in the sort of place where you might not even notice it. But notice it I did. I noticed it because it was a small painting of pansies by—and I knew this from across the room, I would have known it a mile away—the nineteenth-century French painter Henri Fantin-Latour. Max ran to the painting and sat right underneath it, looking up at it peacefully. He wagged his tail.

I've found in life that though things so rarely make sense, there will still be moments in which suddenly, like a baseball crashing through a plate-glass window, everything you didn't fully understand will all at once fall into place. And when that happens, you may find that, much like the owner of the shattered window, you'll wish the moment hadn't happened at all.

At first I didn't look at her. At first I just stared, transfixed by the Fantin-Latour casually hung to the right of a lampshade as if it were a whatever picture of pansies. I rushed across the room to it. I stood right in front of it. I stared at it. I examined it. Without asking permission, I removed it from the wall and looked at the back. To my eye, to my gut, this was the real Fantin-Latour. I felt Daphne come up beside me. I turned to face her.

"You?" I said. "It was you?"

"Yes." She nodded. It was not at all a nod to the gravity of the situation, or to what she'd done, or to the fact that she'd been at last found out and would soon be brought to justice. It was more of an expectant nod, an agreeable nod, a "yes, as a matter of fact, I would like sugar in my coffee, thanks for asking" nod. It was as commonplace and casual as any reaction I'd ever seen, in any person, to the most everyday event.

"Yes," Daphne said again, quite cheerfully really, and before I said anything else, I listened. I listened to a faint electronic buzz coming from some distant corner of the room. I listened to the soft panting of Max still sitting happily under the pansies and of Madeline, now reclined on a red fainting chair over by the tremendous windows.

"Why?" I asked.

"Why did I take it?" she asked me.

"Yes," I said. I wondered if I'd been wrong again, if maybe I shouldn't have come here alone, if maybe I should have for the first time enlisted Chaz's help and brought him with me.

"Well," Daphne began, and as she did I walked a distance into her living room. Uninvited, I sat down on her couch, a Queen Anne claw-foot couch, upholstered in a light blue and off-white stripe. Daphne followed and sat down next to me, and I took a deep breath. I don't think Daphne did; she just sat there next to me without saying anything. After a moment she placed her hand on my knee and patted it, just the way she had that first time we'd sat together in Central Park. It was all in a very "there, there" way. I felt about Daphne the way I realized only then that I had always felt about Daphne but had never quite articulated to myself. I felt she was all at once a little bit nuts, a long-lost and deeply caring great-auntie, and a little bit of a guru.

"But why? Why'd you take the painting?" I asked again, forcing myself not to get lost in fondness or sentimentalities. Daphne took a breath before speaking. As she did, Max came over and sat on my foot. He looked up intently at Daphne, as if he'd like to hear the answer for himself.

"Gil," she said.

"Gil?" I asked.

"Yes," Daphne said as she stiffened in front of me. "He promised me a museum wing."

"I'm sorry?"

"All these years, Gil has been promising me that a museum wing would be named after me. And he never gave me a museum wing, not even a small one. He had that party for me, which was lovely. But it wasn't a wing."

I felt myself soften toward Daphne, probably because I've never been all that wild about Gil. But still.

"So," I began slowly, "I want to be sure I've got this right. It was just Gil?"

Daphne shrugged. "Well, it was Gil. And of course, it was the pansies. We mustn't forget the pansies," she said. She stared dreamily across the room at them and clasped her hands in delight. "Let's not forget the pansies."

"No," I said back to her. "Let's not forget the pansies."

Daphne fiddled absentmindedly with the mother-ofpearl Van Cleef & Arpels chain that hung doubled around her neck. "I would say that there were two reasons, and I think it would be okay to call them equal," she said thoughtfully. I lingered for a moment on the word "okay." Maybe it was a subconscious final hope on my part that everything could still turn out that way. "The pansies and the museum wing," she repeated. "In that order. Or the other order. Pansies, wing. Wing, pansies." She pointed in the air in front of her as if this were all a game of eenie meenie minie mo. She stared across the room lovingly at the pansies.

"You always did say you wanted a museum wing named after you," I said, hoping to get her back on track.

"Yes, yes, I did, dear." She nodded. "Think about it. Walk through the museum one day and instead of looking at the art, look up, crane your neck back and look up high toward the ceilings and look at all the names there, engraved in the marble and stone walls and covered in gold leaf. Read those names, say them out loud to yourself. Kravis, Wallace, Petrie, Sackler, Auchincloss, Bill Blass, for goodness' sake. Everywhere you look in the Metropolitan Museum of Art, someone has a room or a wing or a hall. But do I?"

Daphne sat there across from me, waiting. She blinked at me, twice.

"No?" I offered. "You don't?"

"That's right, dear. I do not," she stated. "But it's important to remember, always, that it was so much more than that," she said next.

"What else was it?" I asked, hoping against hope that Daphne would say something next that would make it justifiable. I inched forward on the couch. Madeline ambled over. We were all there, all ears, all waiting for what Daphne would say next.

"It was the pansies, of course," Daphne said again. And then she added on, "Try to keep up, dear." If I'd had to say, I'd say the way she said it was perhaps a bit haughty. Still, I held out the hope that there'd be something else that would make it all right, all okay, all the things I wanted it to be. I persevered. I nodded with understanding at Daphne. I leaned in. I raised my eyebrows, encouraging her to continue.

"I wanted them," she said. She said it simply, in a way that could only be said by someone whose life had, mostly, offered her everything she'd ever wanted.

"Daphne," I whispered.

"Hope," she whispered back, and smiled. It was funny to her, amusing, entertaining. I knew then that it had been funny to her all along. It was funny to her still.

"How did you do it?" I asked.

"Oh, it was easy," Daphne said, once again clasping her hands together and swaying in her seat, reminding me of an actress in a movie, the kind of movie where there was quite a lot of swooning going on.

"Well, of course I never could have done it without May."

"May?" I gasped. "May Mlynowski, my old boss?"

"Yes, dear," Daphne said. "Yes. Ah, May. Such a lovely

woman with such a brilliant eye for the entirety of the nine-teenth century! Wonderful artist in her own right."

Oh my God, I thought. "May?"

"Yes. May's a good friend of mine," Daphne continued. "She was absolutely instrumental. She made the forgery. We switched the paintings a year ago and since then, I've had the real one and the fake has been hanging in its place."

"A year ago?"

"Yes," Daphne said.

"May?" I repeated.

"Yes, dear."

"What happens when May comes back from sabbatical?" I asked, and Daphne, I kid you not, and maybe it was justified, rolled her eyes at me.

"May's not on sabbatical," Daphne said with a wave of her hand.

"Where's May?" I asked, worried now, or rather, more worried now.

"Oh, May's fine. She lives overseas now."

"Where?" I asked. At this point Daphne reached down and scooped Madeline up into her arms. I wanted to do the same with Max but refrained in the service of focus. I watched as Madeline stretched herself out across Daphne's lap and looked up at me very much as if she were smiling.

"I can't tell you that," Daphne said, taking hold of Madeline's right front leg as she did and pointing it in my direction to further accentuate the word "that." "But I don't want you to worry, dear, and you do look worried, so how about this. May lives, very happily, in a place that I think is the nicest place one can live that doesn't have extradition laws with the United States. I got her a fantastic house, more of a castle really. Lovely."

"You got her a castle?" I said.

"Yes, of course I did," Daphne said. "I believe in thanking people when they help you. I believe it like it's a religion," she stated, and then she once again turned her attention away from me and down toward Madeline, rasping on her lap. She jostled the pug gently, like the bouncy horsey ride people give to little kids, and inquired in a high-pitched voice, "Don't we believe in thanking people, Miss Madeline? Don't we?"

"Daphne!" I said.

"Yes!" she answered quickly, looking up at me. "What is it, dear? Have you become hysterical?"

"Daphne," I continued, thinking as I did that, yes, I was becoming hysterical, but no more hysterical than the situation warranted. "Then how, could you please explain, did the fake wind up in the Conservation Studio?"

"Oh, right, yes," Daphne said, and the way she said it, I thought that she sounded so much like me. "Well, you see, I had the painting, and May had her new life, and it was lovely. Until it occurred to me that I hadn't gotten Gil at all, not really. And while I love the painting, because how could you not love the painting, it had never been just about the painting. I believe I mentioned that?"

"Yes, you did."

"Yes, good. That's good. So, if Gil didn't even know the real painting had been stolen and a forgery hung, I hadn't really, truly accomplished what I'd set out to do. I'd left out the most important part. But then! It all fell into place when he had that ridiculous, but lovely, party for me."

"Pug Night?"

"Yes. Pug Night! It was win-win." She turned her head then and looked right at the pansies, the real ones, and swooned once again. "Ah!" she exclaimed, unclasping her hands so that she could clap them. "Would you just look at those pansies?"

"They're beautiful," I said. I don't know, I didn't see right then how I couldn't.

"Don't you see? It was no *fun* if no one knew," Daphne said. I nodded even though I had yet to see how any of this had been fun. I tried to process. I didn't say anything else. I sat there next to her, unsure as to whether my mouth was agape or if it just felt that way. I decided that it just felt that way, because I imagine if it had been hanging wide open that Daphne, the Henry Higgins to my Eliza Doolittle, would have told me to shut it.

"See, now, follow closely. I know this is the part where

it can get confusing, because it did for me. Gil doesn't have an eye, Gil doesn't know these things."

"Right," I said, without even realizing I was saying it.

"You understand. I knew you would. We needed someone who had an eye, and we knew you would," Daphne said.

"You knew I'd have an eye?"

"Yes. May and I both. We chose you." I tilted my head at her. In the midst of everything, I paused for a moment. I lingered on those words, "chose you," and even though things would have been a lot easier for me if they hadn't chosen me, I thought there was something very nice about the fact that they had.

"You chose me?"

"Yes. We left the painting for you! See, I knew there wasn't any way that I could let Gil know the painting was a fake, without of course telling him, which would ruin everything and also cause some trouble for me. But I could let one of May's staff know, and so I took it off the wall and left it in the Conservation Studio for you. Then I sent Gil a secret e-mail to let him know it was gone."

"You took it off the wall? When you left Pug Night?"

"Sort of," she said. "After Moosie and I slipped away from the party, we went up there."

"What about the cameras?" I asked.

"Oh, the cameras were easy!" she exclaimed, so much

emphasis on "easy." "First I had someone disable the cameras in the Conservation Studio. And just so you know," she added with a wink, "they've been disabled once again."

"Yes, actually I do know that. How did you do that?" I asked.

Daphne considered this for a moment and then said, "That's not important right now. What's important is that they're disabled."

I pressed on, "What about the cameras in Nineteenth Century? They can't be broken, too?"

"No, dear, they're not. That's the brilliant part!"

"Tell me," I said.

"Okay," Daphne said, standing up and splaying her hands wide. "The Fantin-Latour is positioned in such a way that if you come at it from underneath, the cameras can't capture you."

"Really?" I asked.

"Really!" Daphne exclaimed.

"How on earth did you do that?"

Daphne moved her hands to her waist and moved her hips. "You have to shimmy, dear! You get down low and come at the painting from below. It works because of the angle of the corner," she said. And then, she shimmied. Though it looked to me like more of a limbo than a shimmy, it was still quite impressive.

"How did you get the painting from the second floor of the museum all the way down to the Conservation Studio?"

"The same way I got it out of the museum! You of all people should be able to figure that out."

I didn't get it. I waited. Daphne waited, too. Once it was clear I wasn't jumping in, she took a breath and started to speak again.

"I put it in Madeline's carrying bag, of course," she told me.

"Madeline's Sherpa bag?" I asked.

"Yes," Daphne answered, "though technically, Madeline's bag isn't Sherpa, it's Chanel."

"Oh my God," I said. I thought of all the smuggling I had done with my own Sherpa bag, even if it was only of a pug. And though I knew I'd never be a socialite, an heiress, a billionaire, or the occupant of the nicest apartment I have ever been in in my life, looking back at Daphne right then, I felt as if I were looking in a mirror.

"Yes, I had Madeline's bag with me that night. I'd told Gil I didn't want to check it, and no one seemed to mind."

"My God," I said again.

"All's well that ends well."

"What?" I said.

"You should say 'Pardon,' dear. I said, all's well that ends well."

"But don't you see, Daphne?" I implored. "Nothing has ended well. I'm not the only one who knows. Someone else is on to you. You know all those clues I was showing you? Someone sent them to me, and they led me to you. Someone else knows and helped me figure it out. Daphne," I added, with as much gravity as possible, "you're going to have to turn yourself in before someone else does."

"No one else knows," Daphne said.

"Yes they do," I said. "They sent me clues."

Daphne sighed heavily. Madeline jumped off Daphne's lap, and together, Max and Madeline scurried at our feet. And then Daphne looked at me and said, "*I* gave you the clues."

"You?" I said for the second time that morning. "It was you?"

"Yes. I wanted someone to figure it out, and so I sent a first clue to everyone. To you and Elliot and even that Sergei."

"Sergei?"

"Yes."

"Do you know where Sergei is?" I asked. I had to ask.

"No, dear, I don't. But anyway, you'd be surprised, everyone ignored my clue, but you didn't. I knew we chose you for a reason." I will admit that last part softened the blow. Daphne continued, "I found myself quite disappointed that no one had suspected me, and even more disappointed that no one even tried to figure out the clues."

"Max suspected you," I said. Daphne smiled.

"Well," she said, sitting up straighter, a hint of finality to her tone, "as I said, all's well that ends well."

"What do you mean?" I asked.

"If anyone was going to figure out the clues, I wanted it to be you. I'm very fond of you."

"Thanks," I said, in spite of myself.

"You're welcome, dear," Daphne said, and once again leaned over and patted my knee. "And like I said, all's well that ends well." I snapped myself back to attention, rallied myself forward. She had to stop saying that.

"No, Daphne," I said. "Don't you see, it doesn't end here? We can't just leave it that there's a fake Fantin-Latour in the Metropolitan Museum of Art and the real Fantin-Latour is in your living room."

"Fantin-Latour, Fantin-Latour, Fantin-Latour," Daphne said back to me. "There's such a lyrical quality to the name, only made more so if you keep saying it."

"What if I hadn't figured out the clues? What if someone else had? What if no one had?" I asked. Daphne waved her hand as if she'd long ago lost interest. I soldiered on. "Daphne, art theft is a serious offense. This, everything that's happened, is a major breaking of the law, an affront to justice! People who steal paintings from museums go to jail." I said that last part very softly. I couldn't really bear to think about that, to think of Daphne in jail.

Daphne was silent for a very long moment. Then she looked up at me, clear-eyed. "Or not," she said.

I stared back at her. "Sorry?" I said, even though I'd heard her perfectly.

She stayed there, stock-still, still looking right at me,

and repeated what she'd said only a moment before. "Or not."

"Pardon?"

"You could declare the fake painting real?" Daphne suggested.

"I can't do that," I told her. "I'm sorry, but I can't."

"Don't you see? That's the beauty of it. You don't have to be sorry. No one does! We'll put the painting back. I'll take the fake, you know as well as anyone that we can't have a fake just out there in the world. It's too dangerous. It could cause too many problems, so I'll take it. And no one will be any the wiser. I'll have gotten Gil. I had a great year with the pansies, and now I'll have the fake. Everything will be where it's supposed to be, everything will be right, and everything will be okay."

Supposed to be. Right. Okay. They were all the things I wanted, all the things I'd always wanted. I believe it was that, and my fondness for Daphne, that turned me just like a piece of furniture. This is what I tell myself. I felt that a few more things that weren't exactly legal were better than a huge scandal of which I'd obviously been a big part. In the clear serenity of her beautiful apartment, Daphne's idea, possibly illegal though it seemed, was better than a public scandal, and better, so much better, than Daphne in jail. It was an easy decision.

"But I'll need you to help me," Daphne said. Before I asked her how she thought I could help her, I had one more question. I knew that it was probably not the best question I could ask, knew that it probably didn't fall under the heading of "right questions," but I had to ask it anyway.

"Daphne?"

"Yes, dear?"

"Why didn't you take a picture of a pug?" I asked.

"Too obvious, dear," she said, completely sanguine. I would help her. I knew I would help her. I imagine I'd known that all along.

"Right," I said, and I crossed my arms in front of me. "So how do you suggest we go about this?"

chapter eighteen

This Is How It Happened: In Three Steps

Step One:

Daphne looked back at me and said, "Well, of course we'll do it the same way we took the painting out in the first place."

"We're just going to bring it back?" I asked.

"Yes," Daphne told me.

"Don't you worry that we'll get caught?" I asked her. Daphne took a breath before answering me.

"No," she said. "I don't. First of all, it's easy. You'll just walk in and out of the museum with your Sherpa bag, only instead of carrying a pug in it, you'll be carrying a painting."

I stared back at her. "And second, I believe karma is on our side."

"Karma?" I asked.

"Yes, karma. I believe in karma. I believe in it like it's a religion, just like thanking people properly." She smiled.

"But what if you don't believe in karma anymore?" I asked.

Daphne looked back at me, paused, and seemed to contemplate the question for a moment before answering. "How can you not believe in karma?" she asked me. At this point, I didn't know.

"So!" Daphne continued, clapping her hands together as if to physically change the subject. "In order to protect and safely conceal the painting for transport in the bag, we're going to have to wrap it."

I nodded. I knew that.

Daphne turned and walked briskly to the elevator. There on a table beside it was her giant Chanel bag. On the floor beside it was Max's Sherpa bag, right where I'd left it when I walked in. She picked it up and carried it back to me and placed it on the floor between us. "We'll use yours," she said with authority. She bent down and pulled the fleece lining from the bottom of the bag and held it up to me. "We remove the fleece lining, like so. We put the painting in and then put the fleece over it. And then we carry it right out."

I looked first at the empty bag between us and then at the fleece lining still in Daphne's hand.

"In," I corrected her. "We carry it *into* the museum."

"Yes. Well. Alas," Daphne said, with an exaggerated sigh.

"Oh my God," I said, not so much to Daphne as out loud to myself. *Oh my God*, I thought, because really I couldn't think of anything else.

Daphne got up then and walked to the painting. She bent down and from underneath the skirted table, the one that was just to the side of the painting, she took out a roll of bubble wrap, a pair of scissors, and professional packing tape. I watched as she took the painting off the wall, laid it down carefully on the table, and with the skill of an expert and the efficiency of someone who'd done this a million times before, she began to wrap Henri Fantin-Latour's *Pansies* and prepare it precisely for transport. She stood back, the roll of packing tape still in hand, and paused for a moment, smiling, admiring her handiwork. I watched her there, an expert art handler on top of everything else, and I wondered, how well can you ever really know another person?

"Okay then," Daphne said, bending down and picking up the bag. Out of the corner of my eye I saw Max run under an ottoman. "Like so," she said softly as she placed the painting on the bottom of the bag, and then lovingly put the fleece back over it. She brought her hands together as if to clap, but didn't. "All set."

I stared at her.

"You'll just bring this in, bring it to your studio, and then call whoever it is you call, that would be Elliot, yes?"

"Yes," I answered numbly.

"Yes, call Elliot, and tell him you found this, lying out on the examination table. It'll all be terribly confusing, many things in life are. But once you have Elliot examine it, he'll see it's real and that's what matters, isn't it?"

"Won't he think I did it? Won't everyone?"

"No, they won't. If you took it, went to all that trouble to steal it, why would you bring it back?" she asked. I just stared back at her.

"It's not like they're going to turn you in. All anyone wants is the painting back. All of you. That's been obvious all along."

I couldn't think of any other way. Or I couldn't think of any other way I could live with, and apparently I could live with a lot. As if in a dream, or rather a trance, I took Max's bag as prepared by Daphne and placed it as gently as I could over my shoulder.

"Now," Daphne said. "I don't want you to think I'm sending you off like a lamb to slaughter. If anything, anything at all goes wrong, you just call Clifford and he'll come help you. It'll all be fine but if it's not, the first thing you do is call Clifford, and he'll be there in a flash."

"Clifford?" I asked. I didn't know a Clifford. The only Clifford I'd ever known was Clifford the Big Red Dog. I hoped to God that wasn't who she was referring to. "Who is Clifford?"

"My butler," Daphne told me, as if it were the most obvious answer in the world. She turned and walked a few steps over to an antique rolltop desk that I hadn't noticed before. I was surprised I hadn't, because it really was, as far as rolltop desks go, as far as pieces of furniture go, outstanding. I watched as she rolled up the top and leaned over the surface of the desk to write on a pad. She tore the page off and handed it to me. I looked at it: "Clifford" was written out in a scrawling script, the same scrawling script in which all of my clues had been written. Underneath it, a cell phone number. I folded it in half, reached carefully into the side pocket of Max's bag, and placed the paper in the back of my notebook. Goddamn hippopotamus notebook.

Max had emerged from underneath the safety of the ottoman. I looked at him there, staring at his usually loathed bag, now packed with the proper, right, original, real, not-fake Fantin-Latour inside it. He wagged his tail, signaling—I was sure of it—his approval.

"I'm going to leave Max here, okay?" I said. "I'll go do what needs to be done and then I'll come back later. I don't want to complicate things any more than they already are."

Daphne nodded. "I think that's best. I'm sure Madeline would love that," she said to me, and then turning to

Madeline, she said, "Wouldn't you like that, Moosie?" Moosie, I mean Madeline, wagged the entire rear portion of her body.

I braced myself. I mapped it out in my head. I would go to the museum. I would set everything right. And then I would come back and get Max. It would all be set right, and it would all be over.

Step Two:

It was a long and terrifying walk from the Carlyle, up Madison Avenue, over to Fifth, and up to the museum. I had to walk carefully, because of my precious cargo, yet I had to move as fast as I could. There was so much to do. As I made my equal-parts-prudent-and-frenzied way, I tried to be happy for the little things: happy it was still early enough in the morning that there was a minuscule chance I could get to the studio before Elliot. I couldn't even begin to wrap my head around how I would bluff if he was there. I walked past Alan. He didn't look in my bag; he just thought I had a pug in there.

When I at last walked into the studio, Elliot thankfully wasn't there. I went directly to the central examination table and placed the bag in the middle of it. I prayed, for so many things. I unwrapped the real Fantin-Latour *Pansies*. I stood back for just a moment and admired it. I flashed back to the image of Daphne deftly wrapping the painting in her living room, and thought again, *How well can you really know someone?* Only this time I wasn't thinking of Daphne, but of myself.

To be doubly certain, I black-lit the painting and put it under a microscope. It was right. And then I called Elliot. Elliot was almost at the studio when I reached him. He must have called Gil because moments after Elliot walked in, Gil charged in, too.

"That's it?!" Gil shouted. "That's it?!" I was dazed, nervous, and so I didn't answer him right away. Right then he looked so much like Gollum in *The Lord of the Rings* that I waited for a moment longer, a brief, distracted, confused moment for him to reach out and demand, "Give us the precious!"

"Yes," I said, "that's it."

"Where did it come from?" he asked. Elliot stopped his examination of the painting to look up at me, too.

"It was here when I walked in," I said, and hoped for the best. Sometimes, I thought, it's all you can do.

Elliot hunched back over the painting with a black light and a magnifying loupe. Gil didn't look at the painting, but he looked so relieved that there was, for the first time in all the years I'd known him and disliked him, something sympathetic about him.

Elliot stood up and brushed his hair away from his forehead. "It's right," he said. *Right,* I thought. I looked from Elliot to Gil and back again. I can't be sure, but I think Elliot might have, just barely, teared up. I know I did. It was over. It was relief, but not relief. It was victory, but not. It was closure that didn't feel quite as good as I'd hoped.

We stood in different sections of the studio, forming an almost perfect triangle, and looked at each other, zonked, dazed, exhausted, some of us confused, but more than anything, relieved. For a long time we just stood there and didn't say anything. It was Elliot who spoke first.

"I think we should wait," Elliot said, looking at his watch. "We should hang it up on Monday when the museum is closed. Just to be safe." It was, like so many other things, as good a plan as any. I took a much-needed moment to settle myself and offer thanks to some higher power—maybe it was karma after all, maybe luck, maybe something else—that no further accusations had been lobbed at me by my coworker/colluders.

"Okay," I said.

"Okay," Gil said, and then he turned to me. "Where's your pig?" he said, and any feelings of sympathy I'd had for him went the way of my sense of right and wrong.

"Pug, not pig, and he's with a . . . he's with someone."

We all stayed silent for a moment.

"Also," Elliot began again. "We have to get rid of the fake." I thought of how Daphne had declared I'd bring the fake back to her, and how I had agreed to it. In spite of everything, and though it was most likely insane, there was a tremendous part of me that wanted her to have it, so that in some small way, even if it wasn't real, she could have the painting she so loved. I wanted that, but I knew I couldn't push my luck any more. "It has to be destroyed. Someone has to destroy it," Elliot declared.

We all looked around at each other. Our trust in each other was gone. Though I'm not sure it had ever been there. I took a deep breath.

"One step ahead of you, actually," Gil said, and I spun around to face him. "I texted Chaz right after you called me," he said to Elliot, "and he actually suggested the same thing, to make sure the forgery didn't get out in the world. He'll take care of it for us. No additional charge." I wondered what exactly it was Chaz was charging us for, and right after that, I wondered if Chaz was really the man for the job. Maybe he wasn't quite, well, with it enough to be trusted with such an important job as disposing of the forgery.

Elliot spoke up again. "Yes," he said, and then paused. "I think that's a good idea. I think we should have Chaz do it. He's the most impartial," he added, and I tried not to think he looked right at me as he said that last part. "I'll do the paperwork for the Fantin-Latour to be brought in and out of conservation and additional paperwork for Chaz to get a package out of the museum on Monday once we've made the switch."

"Chaz to destroy the forgery," Gil summarized. "It's clearly the best way to go." Elliot nodded.

"Fair enough," I said. I wanted to believe that it was.

"Good," Elliot said, and he went to his computer, ostensibly to get the paperwork started.

After another moment, Gil spoke. "I think the best thing is that after Monday, we never speak of this again."

"I agree," Elliot said from behind his desk.

"I do, too," I said. I did.

"All right then," Gil said. "Monday." And he put his hands in his pockets, turned on the heel of his pointy shoe, and strode purposefully out of the room.

That was it, I thought. That was it. I inhaled, exhaled, told myself I'd done the right thing even though maybe technically I hadn't.

Elliot and I watched Gil go. I stood there and listened as Elliot inhaled and exhaled heavily. He turned to me. I noticed that his shoulders seemed relaxed, that the tension that had been etched on his face for the last week was gone. I had half a mind to say to him, "I'm sorry for thinking you might have been behind this." I wondered if he'd say the same thing to me, even though now in a way, it turns out that I am. Instead I said, "Elliot?"

"Uh-huh," he said.

"Where's Sergei?"

"I sent him up to the Cloisters for two weeks. I thought it was better to keep him out of the investigation," he said.

"You never suspected him?" I asked.

Elliot raised his eyebrows, briefly pursed his lips, and looked right at me. "He's the only person I didn't suspect."

I inhaled, I exhaled. "Yeah," I said.

*　　*　　*

That evening, I left the museum. I went back to Daphne's to get Max. As I stepped out of the elevator and into Daphne's apartment, the three of them—Daphne, Madeline, and Max—were all on the landing waiting for me. Daphne's eyes went right to my empty Sherpa bag.

"I'm sorry," I said, and even after everything, I was. "But I didn't bring you the fake. I can't bring you the fake. Elliot thinks it best that we destroy the fake." Daphne looked momentarily crestfallen.

"I have to say that I agree with Elliot," I continued. "We're going to have our private investigator get rid of it. It's for the best," I said.

"It is," Daphne said, and then she smiled. "It's for the best."

"Okay," I said to Daphne.

"Okay, dear," she said to me. "Thank you."

We didn't say anything for a minute, and then Daphne smiled again and said, "Yes, yes. We'll walk you out."

When we got to the elevator, I didn't press the call button right away, and I noticed that neither did Daphne. I stood there with Max on one side of me, Daphne on the other, and Madeline skittering on the polished wood floors just behind us. There was something between Daphne and me that I wanted to be different. I just didn't know in which direction I wanted that different to be.

"Okay then," I said. "Ahoy?" I added, remembering how, sitting on a bench with Daphne and Madeline and Max what felt like a hundred years ago, Daphne had told me that "ahoy" could be used for either hello or good-bye. I smiled. Maybe it was a normal smile. Maybe it was a lame smile. I don't know. When you're smiling through so many complicated emotions, it can be hard to tell how it comes out.

Daphne turned toward me and smiled back. It was an uncomplicated, happy, open smile, and then after that she seemed to be deep in thought for a moment. "I'm thinking we should retire 'ahoy.'" I nodded. I thought that "ahoy" was probably something I'd want to forget. I thought there were likely a number of things I'd want to forget. I didn't want to think that Daphne would turn out to be one of them.

"Yes," I agreed. "I think so, too."

"We'll change it to something else," she told me then. "I'll let you know when I think of something."

"Sounds like a plan," I said, and right as I did, the elevator arrived. I hadn't realized she'd ever pushed the call button.

I leaned over and kissed Daphne on the cheek. I bent down and hooked Max's leash onto his collar. Madeline scurried over to us. She had a bit of a frenzied look in her eyes, as if she thought it was the last good-bye. I looked into her deep brown eyes, and I massaged her right behind her ears. I said to her in a way I hoped she would enjoy, "See you soon, gorgeous, gorgeous girl."

Step Three:

All of us—Elliot, Gil, Chaz, me, and even Max—met in the studio early on Monday morning. Elliot went up to Nineteenth Century and took the fake from the wall. We didn't worry about the cameras, I didn't have to tell him to shimmy, because there was nothing unusual about a conservator taking a painting off a wall. And we'd taken care to fill out all the proper paperwork. We handed the fake off to Chaz and said our good-byes to him, to the fake, to Gil, to all of it. Elliot and I headed back upstairs with the real Fantin-Latour.

We hung the painting up together. We stood in front of it, staring at it, for a few minutes. After a while, Elliot turned to me and said, "I'm going to head back. I'm going to call Sergei back from the Cloisters. Try and catch up on everything."

"Okay," I said. "Right."

"You coming?" he asked.

"In a minute," I said.

"Okay," he said back, "but, you know, just saying, probably not the best idea to stay here too long at the scene of the, uh . . ."

"The averted crime," I finished for him, and then added, "I know."

Elliot turned and walked away. I stood alone in the empty space, and for no reason at all I counted to ten. I took one last look at the Fantin-Latour pansies, the real ones, restored to their proper, rightful place, and I walked away, too.

I turned and walked out of the exhibition hall. I walked down the grand central staircase to the first level of the museum. I walked through the Egyptian wing and stopped by William the Hippopotamus and stayed there looking at him for a while. I walked to the American Wing, to the café there. The café was closed for the day, along with the museum, and I walked past it to the wall of windows behind it that looked out onto Central Park.

And there, outside the window, ten, twelve yards away from the museum wall, I saw Chaz. He was carrying the fake painting away. He walked slowly, handling his parcel with such care, as if it weren't a fake to be destroyed but the real thing. He looked down at the ground in front of him as he walked. I couldn't say for sure, but it looked like he was whistling. Then he stopped walking and looked first back at the museum and then off in the direction of a bank of trees in the park. A squirrel darted out from a shadow, and I watched Chaz as he watched the squirrel with intent as it ran across his path. Once the squirrel had disappeared in another direction, Chaz looked down at his feet again and continued walking. He quickened his pace, and in the time that it took me to blink, he had almost completely disappeared from my view.

chapter nineteen

Hello, Pug Hill,
My Old Friend

The following weekend, after work on my Maxfield Parrish had been miraculously completed, I went ahead with the photo shoot for the pug portrait. It seemed as good a way as any to get back to normal, to get back in touch with my life beyond the heist. And I really did want to get back in touch with life beyond the heist. I had some things to figure out about the remaining-in-Kinshasa Ben. I didn't know what was going to happen, but I did know that regardless of what did, I did love him and I wanted to do this for him.

I met a photographer named Amanda in Central Park early on Saturday morning. Max and I left our apartment and traveled south and then east across the park and we went to the place where I used to spend a lot of time, a clearing on the east side of Central Park, near Seventy-fourth Street, right behind the Alice in Wonderland sculpture, the place called Pug Hill. It was the perfect place for Max's portrait. It didn't matter in the least that Max hadn't lost an ounce of weight. It was, all of it, perfect.

Amanda arrived right on time with her camera. She also had a laptop on which I could see how the shots were coming out as they were being taken. The moment she had her camera in hand, Max all but lunged at it. I stayed to the side like a proud stage mom, watching Max as he pranced around the clearing, viewing the shots as they showed up on the laptop screen. At first I didn't know how I'd be able to choose just one. There were so many great ones. There was a wonderful back view of Max, featuring his curly tail and his wrinkled back, his nose pointed skyward. There was one of him, chest forward, curving his neck to the side, his tongue hanging out. A close-up of his face. A side view in which he looked to be howling. There was one in which, right after Amanda had adjusted him and he didn't like it, he looked charmingly miffed. There was another one of him barking, a view from the front. He was standing firm on the ground, everything about him perfect, his neck stretched up, his nose skyward, his mouth almost the shape of an O.

"That one," I said, the moment it showed up on the screen.

"Are you sure?" Amanda asked. "Because I'll send you a contact sheet and you can go through it shot by shot and pick the one you like best."

"Oh," I said. "Believe me, I want that contact sheet." (Imagine the crafts projects!) "But I'm pretty sure I know which one I want."

She took a few more shots for good measure—one of Max on his back, another on his belly, and then the photo shoot was done. It was all done. I thought about how the entire time I'd been planning the pug picture, I'd been so preoccupied with another, very different sort of picture. That was done, too, I reminded myself with no small amount of relief. I watched with gratitude and contentment as Amanda packed up her equipment, gave Max a biscuit, and headed out of the park.

Though it was well past the nine o'clock end of off-leash hours by the time we were done, I flirted with a ticket and let Max stay off leash and run around the clearing for a little while longer.

I sat on a bench and stared at the grass and, for the first time in weeks, I truly relaxed. I remembered a time when this hill used to be covered every weekend from one end to the other with pugs and how it was like that for a very long time, and then it wasn't. I thought, not for the first time, and most certainly not for the last, that maybe it was true that one of the few things that could really be counted on was change.

Then, suddenly, Max's head popped up as if he'd heard a loud noise, a shot, even though there hadn't been anything. He stood, fully alert and at attention for a split second. He took off, like a bullet, just as he had that night at the museum, that night that had started everything. I watched, holding my breath, as he ran right toward me and pounced on my handbag. I heard my phone ringing inside it.

I pulled my phone out of my bag and looked at the screen. It was Ben.

"Hello?" I said as Max jumped up onto the bench beside me.

"Hope?"

"Hey, Ben," I said. "Hold on, someone wants to say hi." I held the phone up to Max's ear.

"Hey there, buddy," I heard Ben say. Max looked up at me wild-eyed and after a few more "Hey, buddys" he jumped off the bench. I put the phone back to my ear.

"Me again," I said.

"Hey," Ben said, again.

"Hey."

"Are you at the museum?" Ben asked me.

"No," I told him. "Taking advantage of Saturday. A much-needed Saturday." We were both so tentative, or at least I was. "Thank you, by the way," I added. "That was a really nice jar of dirt you sent."

"I'm glad you liked it," Ben said, and Max leapt impressively back onto the bench and sat next to me again. I tried to focus only on Ben, on how I felt about everything, and not on anything else.

"How's Kinshasa?" I tried.

"Good," Ben said, perhaps sharing my loss for any words. I nodded even though he wasn't there to see it. "Bad, actually," he said next. "Hope?"

"Ben?"

"I miss you. I love you. And I have good news. I think I'll be home in a month."

I smiled. It wasn't a smile I wasn't sure about. It was an overjoyed, exuberant smile. "First," I said, "I love you and miss you, too. And I'm sorry if I didn't handle the news so well last week. It's not that I don't support you and believe in you. Because I do. I really do."

"I know," he said. "And I wish I'd presented it all a lot differently to you."

"Yes, I know," I said. "Are you sure this is what you want?"

"Yes," he said. "There's a job in the New York office. I've already taken it." And then there was some static. I think it was the best static I've ever heard. I listened to the bad connection that brought with it this wonderful news from Ben and all I could think was, *Good*. I closed my eyes and I imagined that Ben was there with me. If he had been, he would have been smiling his wry smile, the one I was so happy I hadn't seen the last of, the one I would be seeing again soon. If he had been there, Ben would have leaned over and kissed me. And it would have been excellent.

"So, good. I have to go now, but I'm going to be home in about a month," he said, bringing me back to the present of the call.

"I'm so happy, Ben. So, so happy. I'll see you soon," I said, and then I laughed. "See you soon," I said again. Maybe it would be my catchphrase after all.

"I love you, Hope," Ben said.

"I love you, too."

After we said good-bye (for now!), I put my phone back in my bag, and Max snuffled beside me. He looked over the edge of the bench and then looked at me, as if he wanted me to help him down. Instead I reached over and pulled him close. I wanted the moment to last a little longer. It was a really good moment, one I felt might lead to a lot. The sun was shining overhead. My pug was at my side and my boyfriend was about to live in the same country as me. The real Fantin-Latour was back in its rightful place.

Right then, once again, I believed in happy endings. I believed that although it is entirely true that the universe gives things and takes other things away, the best thing you can do is focus on the things that it gives you. I believed right then that everything was going to turn out okay.

chapter twenty

Three Weeks Later

It was a Thursday night. I'd taken Max to the park after work, and on our way back up to the apartment, we stopped at the mailboxes to collect the mail. Upstairs, I keyed in with my free hand and, after hanging Max's leash on the hook by the door, headed to the couch.

Max sat on the floor right in front of the couch and looked up at me with expectation. I reached down with my free hand and scooped him up. As I hoisted him by way of his sturdy barrel chest, he wheezed and then snorted, expressing, I was sure of it, an appreciation for the lift. I believe Max enjoys going through the mail. In so many ways, but in this way in particular, Max has life figured out. To Max, almost everything can be enjoyed. I watched as he spread himself out across the pile of bills and catalogs.

I kicked off my shoes and tucked my feet underneath me. I picked up Max to move him off the mail and placed him back down beside me. He let out one more somewhat subdued snort and proceeded to situate himself on his side, his two front legs sticking out straight in front of him. His pink tongue stuck out of the side of his mouth, and he kept one of his eyes fixed on me. "Good boy," I said. "Good, good boy."

I turned to the mail. I nudged the ottoman a few inches away and used it as my makeshift desk and started sorting into piles; bills, catalogs, actual mail. And then, right underneath a flyer for an off-Broadway show, there it was: a hand-addressed envelope, made out to me. I recognized the elegant script handwriting instantly and felt a pang as I did, like butterflies in my stomach, only different. Daphne and I hadn't been in touch at all since that last evening at her apartment; I'd never again run into her in the park. I turned the envelope over. On the back of the envelope, engraved in green, was Daphne's address. I felt another surge inside, an unacted-upon need to catch my breath. I held the envelope in my hand and thought of everything that had happened.

I got up and got a letter opener. Only moments before I had been prepared to go through every last piece of mail with nary a thought to a letter opener. Generally, I don't really care about imperfectly torn envelopes. But right then, I did. I didn't want Daphne's envelope to be ripped.

I carried the letter with me to the desk. I rummaged through the drawer until I found the opener. Standing over the desk, I sliced the envelope open cleanly and took out a thick four- or five-page letter, folded in thirds. I left the envelope on the desk and carried the contents with me back to the couch and sat back down next to Max, who snorted at me. Spend as much time with your pug as I have and you will one day be able to differentiate between all their different snorts. This last one was not appreciative like the one before it but much more along the lines of, "Um, excuse me."

I unfolded the pages. The first page was the same cream-colored heavy stock paper as all my clues had been written on. I held up the page to the light to see the watermark. It wasn't one I recognized. Then I had to take a moment to remind myself that right then I wasn't cracking any case, the task at hand was just reading a letter. Up at the top of the page, also in forest green, was Daphne's monogram. Little D, big M, little F. I had no idea what the F stood for. Ever since I'd first met Daphne, I had vacillated wildly between thinking I knew her well and not at all. After everything, I'd landed somewhere in the middle, maybe a little closer to "not at all."

Dear, the letter began, just like so many of the sentences she'd spoken to me. And then it said, *Hope*. And then on a new line: *Let's turn Ahoy into Enjoy!* A few lines below the exclamation point, Daphne had signed her letter with a big, flourishy D.

That was it: almost painfully brief, to say nothing of cryptic. Confused, I put the first page aside and turned to the pages underneath it. For what must have been at least fifteen minutes, I stared at the first of the four very official-looking, filled-with-legal-jargon pages. Then I stared at each subsequent page for a long time, read everything written on them twice. And then I read it all over again. I needed the time. I wanted to be sure of what the pages were, and then I had to let the enormity of them sink in.

It took me so long to figure out exactly what they were because I, having only ever lived in an apartment and only ever rented one at that, had never before seen a deed to a house. But that was what it was. A deed. To a house. A deed to a two-bedroom cottage in East Hampton, the ownership of which, according to the pages I held in my hand, had been signed from Mrs. Daphne Markham over to me. A monogrammed Post-it note on the last page (who knew they had monogrammed Post-it notes?) indicated where I needed to sign. Another Post-it on the final page provided the address of a law firm on Park Avenue to which I needed to send a copy of everything back.

A final page of stationery at the end held two last things from Daphne. There, she'd written the words, *Hope, dear, I can guess at what your question must be so I'll answer it. Yes, this is real. Sign where indicated and send, and do enjoy your new home.* Then a small X and another big, flourishy D.

I put the pile of papers down in my lap. My hands were shaking. I looked down at the final note from Daphne again, focused on the words "this is real," and I thought in this order: *one, imagine if it is real, imagine if for some eccentric and over-the-top reason Daphne has in fact given me a house; two, this will be incredibly hard to explain to Ben; and three, why on earth would she do it? Who gives someone a house in East Hampton, even if she is Daphne?*

I looked over at Max, about to ask him exactly that question, and as my eyes fell on his calm and peaceful demeanor, all at once a memory crashed into my mind. I was standing in Daphne's living room and she was telling me about the castle she'd bought for May. "I believe in thanking people when they help you," she'd said. "I believe it like it's a religion."

Daphne was thanking me. I had a horrible, sinking feeling that she was thanking me for more than not turning her in. Call it intuition, maybe it was, maybe it was just logic, maybe it was my inner voice. But deep in my heart I knew. People, even Daphne, did not give other people cottages in East Hampton as an expression of thanks. Unless. Unless they were thanking someone for something really, really big. Or, in the case of the pansies, jewel-like and small.

Daphne had the pansies? Oh, dear God, no. But how?

I jumped up off the couch. Max jumped up, too, and stood on the chair, alert, ready, waiting to see what would happen next. I grabbed my phone, scrolled to Daphne's number. I held my breath as I waited for her to answer. It didn't matter, the phone just rang and rang and then I got a message that the number had been disconnected. Oh no. Then I remembered Daphne telling me, "If anything happens, anything at all, you call Clifford."

I dove across the room to where Max's bag had lain abandoned ever since I'd stopped smuggling him into the museum three weeks ago. After the details of the heist had been revealed to me, I'd made the executive decision that Max would no longer come to the workplace. I took the godforsaken hippopotamus notebook out of the side pocket and went to the back, where I'd stashed the piece of paper on which Daphne had written down Clifford's number for me. I took it out and as I did, all of Daphne's clues fell out onto the floor, like giant pieces of confetti.

I read the number and dialed. But then as soon as I'd keyed in the number, Chaz's name came up on my screen. What? I hung up and dialed the number Daphne had written down for Clifford again. Again, "Calling Chaz Mobile" came up on my screen. I was about to hang up again and dial again but then I didn't because I was too busy thinking, *Dear! God! No!* The line picked up after just one ring.

"Hello," said a cheerful male voice.

"Chaz!? Clifford!?" I frantically asked. In the moments

before he, whoever he was, answered, I heard the sound of calypso music in the background.

"Either is fine," he answered.

"What?"

"Yes?" Chaz or Clifford or whoever it was said back.

I forged ahead. "Chaz?"

"Yes?"

"Oh, God," I said. "I'm not entirely sure what's going on, but I have a number for you in my phone, and I have a number written down for Daphne's butler, and I don't know what's happening but I keep trying to call the butler and I, um, keep getting you?" I heard myself talking. I heard what I was saying. Before there was any response from the other end of the line, I knew.

And then Chaz/Clifford said, "Yes."

"Chaz?" I said and paused for one last moment. "You're the butler?" I asked. Daphne had tried to tell me. Daphne had told me more than once that it was always the butler. The butler always did it.

"Yes," he said. "I am."

It all came rushing at me. Chaz, concerned about the cameras more than anything else. Chaz lurking around whenever I found a clue. Chaz always one step behind me, or was that ahead of me? Chaz offering to destroy the fake painting, and then running away from the museum that morning with what I'd thought was the fake but (oh, no!) could have been the real Fantin-Latour.

"Chaz? How?"

"It was all very simple, really. I followed you that morning. I had the fake Fantin-Latour you'd all given me to destroy in another Sherpa bag. I was right behind you. I switched them right after you left. And then since I had the paperwork Elliot made me, I just carried my parcel right out of the museum."

"What about the cameras in Nineteenth Century?"

"What about them?" he asked back.

"Did you shimmy?" I asked.

"You can't believe everything you hear," Chaz said. "There's no shimmy, Hope."

"No?" I said. I had so much to be disappointed about, but somehow, right then, I felt disappointed that there was no such thing as a camera-evading shimmy.

"I damaged those cameras as well," Chaz explained. *Oh,* I thought, *God.*

"But how did you ever even get to be our private investigator?"

"So many questions," Chaz said. "Months ago, Daphne planted the seed. She told Gil that if he ever needed a discreet PI, she knew someone. Gil is very impressionable. She knew he'd remember that."

"But then why do any of it, why not have left it all when you took the pansies the first time?"

"It was a case of conflicting desires, Hope. So many things are," he said.

"I'm not sure I follow," I said.

"Yes. See, as you know, Daphne wanted to get Gil, but she also wanted the pansies," Chaz began. "Daphne wanted Gil to think the painting was stolen from his party, but just for a little stressful while, not forever. She didn't want anything to get blown out of proportion. She certainly didn't want you all to ever wind up with the police." None of this, I thought, would have happened if we'd gone straight to the police. Chaz kept talking.

"Daphne's hope all along was that once you learned the truth you'd let her keep the real Fantin-Latour and designate the fake as real. But once it became obvious that you were going to insist Daphne return the painting, she had to amend her plan. And it all worked out."

"What?" I asked. "How?"

"Daphne tormented Gil," Chaz continued. "Even if just a bit, and she got the painting she loves. And everyone else thinks the painting in the museum is real. May assures us that as long as it's left alone, it's likely no one will ever discover otherwise. Daphne's very happy with the way it all turned out. And she hopes you're not upset with her. This was the best way."

"I don't believe it," I said.

"That," Chaz, Clifford, whoever the hell he was, said, "is probably for the best. In fact, I think Daphne would prefer it that way."

"Daphne!" I said. "Where is she? I called her number

and it was disconnected." I told Chaz this even though he surely already knew.

"Daphne's no longer in New York," Chaz said, and I listened to the way he phrased it: "no longer in New York." It wasn't "not in New York," as in "coming back soon." It was "no longer in New York," as in "never to return." I teared up a little bit at that prospect, and at the other prospect, too.

"I thought you knew she was leaving," Chaz said.

"No, I didn't know. Do you know where she went, Chaz?" I asked.

"Yes, Hope," he said, "yes, I do."

I waited, and I believe Chaz waited with me. He gave me a moment to let it all sink in, even though it was going to take so much more than a moment. I felt like my life was that game where a coin is hidden underneath one of three shells and you can never figure out which one. I listened to the calypso music tinkering softly but festively in the background of wherever Chaz was.

"Can you tell me where?" I asked again.

"That I can't tell you," Chaz said. "But I can tell you that she's living very happily in a lovely place that doesn't have extradition laws with the United States."

We were both silent again.

"Hope?" Chaz said after a while.

"Chaz?"

"I'm going to have to hang up now. And once I do, this line is going to be disconnected and you won't be able to get in touch with either of us again. That's for the best. It's all for the best."

"But—" I started to say, but I didn't know what came next. I didn't want to know what came next.

"Hope?" Chaz said, one last time. "Enjoy the house. It's lovely. It's what Daphne wants. And, after all, you earned it." And then the line went dead.

chapter twenty-one

A Pansy, a Pansy, My Kingdom for a Pansy

I leaned back on the couch with the dead phone in my hand and closed my eyes. I told myself I wouldn't believe that the pansies in the Met were fake until I saw them for myself. As I did, I remembered Max in the Conservation Studio on Pug Night, apoplectic over the fake Fantin-Latour. I saw him sitting peacefully wagging his tail at the real Fantin-Latour when we discovered it at Daphne's that morning. Yes, there were a whole slew of tests to determine whether a painting was fake or real, and yes, I knew how to administer them all. But the one most readily available was sitting next to me. The pug knew a fake when he saw it.

I turned to Max. He turned to me. "We have to go," I said.

As we sped cross-park to the museum, I repeated to myself over and over again that I wouldn't believe it, I wouldn't really freak out, until I'd seen for myself. And, yes, until Max had, too.

Alan the trusted security guard was thankfully on the night shift, as it was nearing ten o'clock by the time we arrived. He smiled at me, at us, and looked the other way as we approached. I walked past with Max nestled safely in his bag. The museum was quiet, empty, just as it had been that first night, after Pug Night. I carried Max in his bag through the back corridors to the main hall. We walked together through the almost darkness.

I stood in front of the grand central staircase and looked up it. I started to walk, very slowly, up the steps. At important moments in my life, I've often heard song lyrics being sung in some imaginary background inside my head. It's as if I'm always scoring the movie of my life. As I walked up the stairs that night, I didn't hear song lyrics, but I did hear music. It was classical music. It wasn't the light, lilting melody that had played at Pug Night. It was Beethoven's Fifth Symphony, I was sure of it. I turned left at the top of the stairway and walked through a few rooms toward the nineteenth-century paintings wing.

Once we were standing right in front of the pansies, I put Max's bag on the floor. I reached into it and took out

Max, to hell with the security cameras that I now knew had long since been compromised anyway. I held Max aloft in front of the painting. He looked at it thoughtfully, and in that moment the whole world stopped, or at least mine did.

And then, Max started to bark. It was that patented Max bark, the one that is somewhere between barking and something else. Up until that moment, I'd never known the right way to describe it. Suddenly I knew. It was as if a hundred metal cans were assembled, the kinds with the pull tab tops, and all at once, every one of them were opened at exactly the same time.

I clenched my teeth. I started sweating. I started shaking and I think I couldn't feel my knees. It didn't change anything.

Max barked, foamed at the mouth, and went altogether pug crazy. I looked at Max. I looked at the painting. I looked down at Max again. He did something I'd never seen before. He threw his head back and started baying, like a coyote at the moon. Only there wasn't any moon. Just as soon as he'd begun, he stopped, and then he looked up at me. As if to further drive the already well-driven point home, he barked at me.

I looked at the pansies again. I looked at them as if for the first time. I knew. The pansies weren't real. The painting on the wall was a fake.

"Aw," I said to myself, to Max, to the universe, "shoot."

Readers Guide for
A Pug's Tale
by Alison Pace

Discussion Questions

1) Who did you suspect was the art thief and why? Did you suspect a different person/different people as the novel progressed? What made you suspicious of each of these possible culprits? Did Max's actions throughout the novel sway your feelings toward any of these characters?

2) Discuss the art thief and her accomplices. Can you sympathize with each of their motives? Could you see yourself acting as they did? Do you think Hope became an accomplice herself in the end?

3) Do you think Hope made the right decision in not going directly to the police after the painting was first found missing? What would you have done in her shoes?

4) Discuss Hope's final deception by the art thief and the gift she receives in return. Does she have any choice but to be manipulated by the thief and to accept the gift? Would you have acted differently?

5) Throughout the novel, Hope has dreams in which Max helps her solve the clues left throughout the museum. Max also seems to bark at things that we find aren't quite right in the end. Knowing that Hope believes pugs have their own brand of superior intuition, do you think that Max was indeed trying to help her solve the mystery? Have you or anyone you know encountered this sort of sixth sense in an animal?

6) Discuss Hope's relationship with Ben. Did you begin to doubt the relationship's viability along with Hope? Why or why not?

7) Alison Pace has an Art History degree from American University, has worked at the famed Sotheby's auction house, and started writing her first novel, *If Andy Warhol had a Girlfriend*, while working at an art gallery. As you read *A Pug's Tale*, did you feel transported into the art world? Do you find that authors who write most successfully about a

subject are those who have real-life experience with that subject, or do you think that research can achieve the same effect?

8) Discuss Daphne. Do you believe that she is truly a bit crazy or is it a ruse? After Hope discovers who the real art thief is, did your feelings about Daphne change?

9) Daphne believes that everybody should have a catchphrase such as her "Ahoy!" What do you think Hope's catchphrase should be? What would yours be?

Book Group Enrichment Activities

1) Host an art-inspired book group: Hold your book group at your local art museum. Alternatively, pass around images of paintings during your discussion. Does having the artwork in front of you heighten your experience of the novel?

2) Host an animal-friendly book group: Allow members to bring pets (pugs especially welcome!) to your book group, or hold your book group at a local park or dog run where animals gather. Bring along pictures or books featuring pugs or your favorite pet. Do you appreciate Hope and Daphne's reverence for pugs? Do you feel similarly about a certain kind of animal?

3) Discuss any recent (or past) art heists in the news during your book discussion and plan to watch one of the many popular art-heist movies available (*The Thomas Crowne Affair, Entrapment, Oceans 12*, et cetera).

4) Discuss a combination (or all) of Pace's novels at your book group (*If Andy Warhol Had a Girlfriend, Pug Hill, Through Thick and Thin, City Dog*, and *A Pug's Tale*). Are there unifying themes or subjects in the novels that you have chosen? Which novel is your favorite and why?